IN THE BLOOD

BY
LESLEY WELSH

First published in 2018 by Bloodhound Books

www.bloodhoundbooks.com

Print ISBN 978-1-912175-92-5

Also By Lesley Welsh
The Serial Killer's Daughter

The author of this novel, Lesley Welsh, was my lover, partner and best friend for over thirty years. She died from a heart attack in the early hours of 17thApril 2017, so she did not know that In the Blood, *her third novel, was to find a home with Bloodhound Books. I know she would have been enormously proud to see this final work in print and I'd like to thank all those who have made it possible. On her behalf I dedicate this novel to her daughter, Estelle and her grandchildren, Maia, Kamara and Nathan, with love.*

Ian Jackson – December 2017

CHAPTER ONE

London, January 1989

Ronald Merchant-Jones glanced up at the clock at 6.45 p.m. Where was she? He'd be closing the doors shortly. She always cut it fine on the last Friday of the month but today ... Well, he mused, she may well miss today. After all, a rich and beautiful woman like her could be off anywhere. Even though the weather had been mild for the time of year, perhaps she was luxuriating in sunnier climes with a man just as wealthy as she.

He chided himself for being so enamoured of her. Maybe it was the smile she had flashed at him when she first opened the safe-deposit box account, the way her burnished brown hair glistened under the subdued lights, or the subtle fragrance that followed her like a delicate shadow. He acknowledged that it was ridiculous for a man of his years to furtively glance up from his blinking screen to catch a glimpse of her gliding down the stairway to the strong room with a casual elegance that took his breath away. But that is what he had done, every final Friday of every month for seven months; he'd watched her like a love-struck schoolboy.

His computer chimed, the indication that a client had entered the correct code into the faceless metal sentinel stationed at the entrance. Ronald flicked the intercom switch. 'Please enter,' he said in studied Received Pronunciation, and glanced at the clock once more. One minute to go. The client stepped onto the sensor hidden beneath the rubberised exterior doormat and the automatic doors opened with a swish that allowed a moment's cool outside air to infiltrate the climate-controlled cocoon.

'Hello,' she said before he looked up and he couldn't help but let down his professional guard with a broad smile in her direction, so potent was her presence.

'You know the way, of course, madam,' he said as she sent a radiant glow his way.

She paused at the other side of his desk and began to search inside her patent-leather Moschino handbag. 'My key is in here somewhere,' she said, in a voice he thought marginally less refined than her usual, almost whispered, tones. And he watched, as her elegant fingers appeared to reach for her key but pulled out something else instead. He froze as she pointed a gun at him.

'Put your hands where I can see them. So much as twitch in the direction of that alarm button under your desk and I'll blow your fucking head off.'

Shaken to the core, he glanced up at the CCTV camera that surveyed the room.

She caught his look and laughed. 'Oh, those two 'guards' over the road. First floor up, watching this place with one eye and porno videos with the other; already been taken care of, mate. So, there'll be no cavalry thundering to the rescue. You're on your own.'

From that moment, his eyes never left the barrel of the gun. He knew nothing about such things but was sure the one aimed at his head was real enough and, although small, it was no doubt lethal.

'So, you be a good boy,' she was saying, 'Open up to my three colleagues out there and you won't get hurt.' She indicated to the switch on his desk that opened the doors should the sensors fail. 'After all, sunshine, it's not *your* worldly goods in those boxes, now is it?'

Ronald Merchant-Jones did as he was told and became unwittingly embroiled in one of the biggest unsolved safe depository heists in British history.

'I was tied to my chair, gagged, and had a black, drawstring bag placed over my head,' he later told the investigating police officers. 'I heard the voices of three men. One gruff sounding, another had a Welsh accent, and the third one had a clipped vocal mannerism that reminded me of Michael Caine.'

'You say the only one you actually saw was the woman,' the police inspector had said. 'Can you describe her?'

So, Ronald did his best to convey the shimmering brown hair, then added that it could have been dyed, or even an expensive wig. He seemed to recall blue eyes but then, on the day, he had thought they were brown.

'Any distinguishing marks?'

Ronald made an attempt to picture her face, but its bland beauty sidestepped him. Perfection, he later mused, combined with all the outward trappings of wealth and class, had managed to disguise the real woman beneath as efficiently as any grotesque mask could have done.

***

On his first day in his new home on the French Riviera, some flowers arrived for Ronald, accompanied by a card marked merely with a lipstick kiss, the initial C, and the hint of a perfume that he recognised only too well.

He recalled sitting, trussed up and terrified, hooded and disorientated, before feeling the warmth of her face so close to his as she whispered in his ear, 'Be careful how you describe me, my dear. Your cut-glass accent and double-barrelled moniker don't fool me one bit. I know who you are, where you live, and where you come from.' Her laugh tinkled at his quick intake of breath and she put her hand on his shoulder as though to reassure him. 'But you're not a bad actor,' she continued, 'so if you tell a believable tale to the cops – or anyone else who makes enquiries – then I promise you will be well looked after.'

With the memory of her buzzing around in his head, Ronald picked up the card, held it to his nose and breathed in her essence. Then he stepped out onto his balcony, looked across at the sunlit Mediterranean Sea glistening close by and raised his glass of vino in silent salute.

***

Paris, December 1991

She was in the Boulevard Saint-Germain when she stopped at a news kiosk beneath a tree that still dripped with rain from a recent downpour. She loved these ornate news-stands with their plethora of colourful magazines and newspapers. It felt good to be in Paris and to maybe settle for a while. Her mood was not to be deflated, not even by the grumpy man behind the counter with the Gauloise apparently glued to his lower lip, since the cigarette smelled as quintessentially French as the Art Nouveau Metro façade that mirrored the metalwork of the kiosk itself. She was after *Paris Match,* to help improve her French, when she noticed a newspaper headline about a horrific murder in the South of France.

Although she struggled with some of the terminology she certainly got the gist. Police thought it was a burglary gone wrong. The owner of the apartment had been stripped naked, tied to a chair, gagged, burned with cigarettes, and had a finger cut off, before being killed. The perpetrators had then ransacked the victim's home.

'Are you feeling ill, Madame?' the cantankerous kiosk proprietor asked.

She leaned against the tree in that Paris street and took a deep breath. Dreadful though the story was, it was the name of the victim that had jumped off the page. Ronald Merchant-Jones. She also knew who had done the deed. She regained her composure, paid for the newspaper and walked back to her rented apartment to pack. It was time to move on, she had to stay lost.

CHAPTER TWO

Western Australia, July 2012

A single clap of thunder almost masked the sound of the first shot. Ma though, highly-strung as ever, sensed something was up. She moved towards the window and peered out from amongst the display of handmade, local goods, artisan soaps, and those Aboriginal knick-knacks that came all the way from China.

'What was that?'

Grace Dobbs sighed. The weather was turning nasty, so Ma would be sure to make that yet another argument for Grace not to go to practice. 'Driving ninety kilometres in this storm,' she'd say, 'are you mad?' And if it wasn't too hot, or too wet or there wasn't even a vague possibility of a bushfire somewhere in the vicinity, it would be, 'I don't know why you need to go all that way three times a week, you always win the competitions.' As Grace had long since abandoned any attempts to explain the concept of practice making perfect, she would ignore Ma's protests and just go.

'I'm sure I heard gunfire,' Ma continued as she craned her slender neck to peer this way and that from her position behind the window displays.

'You've made me lose count now,' Grace complained, trying to concentrate on the money beside the till. 'Not that there's a lot of it to cash up.' Monday, out of season, hardly any traffic on the road with few tourists on their way down to Margaret River to make a stop on the journey for a coffee at Kayleen's Kaffe and maybe step across the road to snap up some curios.

'Did you hear that?' Ma sounded concerned. 'There's someone shooting a gun off out there.'

The distinctive crack of single-shot rifle fire rang out. Not that unusual a sound around there. 'Yeah, I did,' Grace said. 'Someone out back maybe, killing vermin.'

'Sounds closer than that.' Ma shifted the display of bright scarves supplied by the local silk farm, and moved closer to the glass. 'I can see someone with a rifle walking out of the bush. Looks like a cocky.'

Just another farmer, then, Grace reassured herself. 'See, I told you. He's chasing vermin.'

Another roll of thunder, this time further away, a clear message that any storm was merely passing by.

'Jesus Christ!' Ma ducked down, her face registering panic. 'Get down, Grace. He's just shot a cyclist.'

Still uncertain that this wasn't simply Ma jumping to one of her panicky conclusions, Grace did as instructed. 'He shot someone? You sure?'

As Ma crawled towards her on all fours, Grace noticed that all the colour had drained from her mother's face. 'He raised the rifle, aimed and the cyclist hit the deck. What more do you need to know?'

Ma was spooked. And Grace was jolted by the thought that what had always been Ma's worst nightmare might actually be happening. When Ma reached her, Grace wrapped her arm around those slim shoulders. 'Are you sure the cyclist didn't just fall off his bike?'

'I know what I saw.' Ma sounded close to tears.

Grace held her close while attempting to listen for any other sounds emanating from the world outside their little gift shop as the thunder rumbled and retreated into the distance.

At that moment, someone tapped on the shop door.

Ma stiffened. 'Leave it.' She was panting, distraught and seemed about to faint.

Tentatively, Grace looked out from her crouched position behind the wooden counter. The glass door was four metres away; it was locked with the CLOSED sign hanging at eye-level from its kangaroo-shaped holder. The tapping continued but she couldn't see anyone standing outside, or squatting down beside the door. Then she spotted the hand, just above ground level. A hand whose knuckles were leaving bloody smudges on the glass.

'Someone's injured,' she said, unwrapping her arm from around Ma's shivering body.

'Don't go.' Ma made a grab for Grace as she slunk down on her belly, about to move towards the door commando-style.

Grace shucked Ma's hand away. 'Whoever that is, I can't just leave them out there.'

'Please, Grace,' she whispered. 'No!'

'Do something useful. Move into the office and call the emergency services.'

Grace started making her snaking move towards the door, pushing with her feet and dragging herself forward on her elbows. As she got closer, she recognised the face that belonged to the bloodied hand. It was Trey Palmer, a local lad of about fifteen. She knew him as the not very bright, eldest child of an overworked single mom. He was just a big goofy kid really, always skipping school to ride around on his bike. She could see that he was flat on his belly, eyes glazed with a mixture of pain and terror, and realised that she needed to get to him, to bring him to safety inside the shop. But to do that, she'd have to stand up to open the locked door. Easing her way towards the narrow wall between the door and the window, where hopefully she couldn't be seen from the outside, she slowly stood up and was about to reach across to the lock when a tall figure blocked out the light from the door.

Not able to move for fear of being spotted, she was horrified to hear the familiar sound of a gun being cocked. Trey let out a sobbing cry. There was just the wooden lintel between the gunman and Grace.

Bang! A shock wave vibrated the door as Trey's brains were plastered over the glass. Grace was so close to the shot that her ears were buzzing. She stood stock-still, convinced the shooter could hear the blood thundering through her veins and expecting another bullet to shatter the glass. She held her breath and waited for the bullet, but the long shadow gradually faded away.

Heart beating like the clappers, Grace forced herself to take a look outside. Trey's blood spatter reached halfway up the glass but through the spots she could see a man, baseball cap on backwards, casually walking away. Like Ma had said, he looked like a farmer and had a rifle hoisted over his shoulder. Grace wasn't sure if he was someone she knew, *but whoever he is*, she thought, *he's one well tooled-up bastard.* He had that rifle plus the handgun he'd used to slaughter Trey. She watched him as he crossed the road and with rising fear, realised he was headed towards the kindergarten.

She turned away from the door to see Ma still huddled behind the counter, teeth chattering with fear.

'Did you call the police?'

Ma stared at her blank-faced.

'Well, did you?'

'Someone else will have done,' Ma said.

'What if everyone thinks like that?' Grace pulled her mobile phone from her shirt pocket and thrust it into Ma's hand. 'Do it. Now!' She headed into the office.

'Where are you going?'

'The gunman's moving towards the kindy. There are little kids in there. I'm going after him.'

The cabinet in the office held a Walther GSP Expert target pistol and ammunition. Grace unlocked it, picked up the gun, loaded the clip with shaking hands and took a deep breath. *Keep it together*, she told herself. *A human being is a very different target to a practice bullseye but the cops are sixty kilometres away. It'll take them thirty minutes to get here. And those kids are defenceless. This guy has got to be stopped.*

She turned and walked back to the interior of the shop.

Ma was still sitting on the floor holding on to the phone. 'The police are already on their way.'

'How long?'

'Twenty minutes.'

'That's too long.'

Ma stared in horror at the gun in Grace's now steady hand. 'Wait for the police to deal with this. Don't go. I beg you.'

Grace ignored her, walked to the door and unlocked it. At that moment, Ma spotted poor young Trey's body and stifled a scream.

'Lock the door after me,' Grace instructed.

'Don't get yourself killed.'

'I'll try not to.'

***

What the fuck are you doing, Grace? she asked herself a dozen times as she made her way cautiously across the two-lane road between the shop and the kindergarten. Trey's bike had been abandoned in the middle of the bitumen and there was a trail of blood glistening in the wintry light. She felt sick, realising that the poor kid must have dragged himself to the doorway. *Forget it, stay in the zone.*

Grace went into competition mode and concentrated on what lay ahead. Next door to the kindergarten, Kayleen had pulled the inner blinds down on the Kaffe's windows and was probably hiding somewhere out back. On the other side of the kindy's open doors was Harri's hairdressing salon but as he was closed on Mondays, there'd be no help from there. Grace felt like the character in *High Noon*, confronting her fate alone.

The loud handgun shot from inside the building propelled her forward. A woman screamed. A man's voice yelled, 'Shut your fucking trap.' As Grace reached the door, Joan Latimer collapsed at her feet. Grace looked down into unseeing eyes and tried not to think about the gaping hole in Joan's chest. She quelled the revolt in her stomach, tried to breathe slowly and think logically. She knew this building well; the first room held two desks facing each other across the narrow reception area. Joan always sat at one with Nora at the other. With her spine pressed hard up against the outer wall, gun cocked, held in her right hand and pointed downwards, Grace chanced a quick look inside. Nora was hiding under her desk. The floor was wet under her knees where she'd peed herself with fright. She saw Grace and stared wide-eyed for a moment. 'He shot Joan for no reason,' she whispered.

'Where is he?'

Nora raised a trembling hand and pointed. 'In the playroom.'

Stepping over Joan's corpse, Grace walked in. Ahead of her, beyond the reception area, was an even narrower corridor, with built-in cupboards containing school supplies, plus two doors leading to the boys' and girls' toilets. Beyond there was a room she remembered well; it was some fifteen metres square, its walls covered with the tots' finger paintings and drawings, a big cardboard clock for learning to tell the time and all the other gaudy stuff that pre-schoolers find so exciting. To the right and left were floor-to-ceiling windows and an exit that led into a grassed playground with brightly painted slides and swings. Grace had been a kid there too, twenty-odd years before.

With her back to the wall, she slowly edged her way along the corridor, trying not to make any noise. In a clumsy effort to remain quiet, she nudged against a framed poster of Winnie the Pooh and Piglet. The metal frame clanked against the wall and stopped her in her tracks. She had no idea where the gunman was within the playroom but, in a hyped-up state, he might be alert to every sound. She was fearful that if he spotted her and started shooting wildly, those kids would be in even more danger. That was when she heard a man's harsh voice, a child crying, a woman begging, another shot, and the little kids beginning to wail as one.

CHAPTER THREE

Emotional tunnel vision descended as soon as Grace stepped into the playroom. Beneath her protective blanket of calm, she focused on the man with the flipped-back baseball cap. He was pointing his rifle at a blonde woman who was jabbering something inaudible while attempting to shield six or seven little kids with her body. The children were clinging to her skirt, to her legs, to each other. What seemed strange to Grace was how surprisingly quiet they had swiftly become, as though intuitively aware that their remaining silent was a matter of life or death.

She steeled her soul, stood at the exit from the narrow corridor and shouted, 'Hey, you raggedy-arsed bastard. You crazy fuck! Pick on someone your own size.' She hardly recognised her own voice as it echoed around the room and seemed to rattle the tall windows with its force.

The man's weather-beaten face registered slack-jawed amazement as he turned away from his targets. Grace expected him to express anger maybe, a mouthful of expletives perhaps but what she got was a broad grin. It was neither the manic leer of a lunatic, nor the dismissive sneer of someone with a superiority hard-on. In fact, his expression bore more resemblance to a welcoming smile, an acceptance that this was either his last moment on earth – or hers.

He spotted her weapon and sneered, 'What'ya gonna do with that, little girl?' She heard the bolt action click three times on what she recognised as a Winchester: open, pull back, bullet in chamber, which made him just a fraction too slow at aiming the rifle. Grace reacted immediately, adopted the stance she had used so often in target practice, feet well apart, arm raised and outstretched, gun held in her steady right hand. Only when she fired, did it occur to her that a practice target is the same size as a human head.

She instinctively took him down with a headshot. His legs collapsed from under him. Grace had never understood what the phrase 'went down like a sack of spuds' really meant until that moment. He keeled over backwards with his knees bent beneath him. She ran over and kicked the rifle out of his hands because he was still twitching, and she couldn't be sure if his finger was on the trigger or not. Once the firearm was safely out of reach, she stood and observed him, feeling a strangely detached sense of satisfaction until all movement had ceased, before reaching down to retrieve the handgun that was tucked in his belt.

An eerie silence lasted for maybe half a minute before the kiddies kicked off again, crying, screaming, 'I want my mommy' and Grace looked around to see the blonde shepherding the little tykes out into the playground. As she walked away, Grace finally recognised the kindergarten teacher as Chelsea Forsyth, the younger sister of an old boyfriend. As Chelsea left, she turned her head towards Grace to mouth a brief 'thank you' before closing the door to the playground as a barrier between the children and the dead man seeping blood and brain matter onto the wooden floor.

When Grace looked back on that day, the thing that really haunted her wasn't killing someone she considered to be a worthless bag of shit or the cruel death of poor Trey or even Joan's bloody gaping wounds and vacant eyes. No, what really got to her was when she turned to go back to the reception area and await the arrival of the police. She spotted what she first assumed to be a broken doll by the wall of the playroom. But as she got closer, she realised with mounting horror that while she'd been creeping down the corridor, too concerned for her own safety to approach any faster, the shot she heard had killed the tiny girl lying crumpled on the playroom floor.

Momentarily stunned by the sight, Grace heard a cry of anguish emanating from somewhere. Wondering where it was coming from, she took a proper look around the room for the first time. There were several pink balloons attached to a handmade poster on the far wall. The poster read *Happy Birthday Vikki. Three Today.*

The sound of distress continued until Grace finally realised that it was coming from her. And as she looked down at little Vikki, with her pink frilly party dress soaked in blood, something inside Grace shattered.

She wanted to pick the child up, to cuddle her broken body, to fix the pink glittery ribbon that had come loose in her dark curls, to comfort her, to say, 'I'm sorry I didn't get here sooner.'

Instead, she sat on the floor beside the child, held her still-warm, little hand, and sobbed.

***

That was how they found Grace. Or so they told her because she didn't remember much. She knew that she was arrested but it was all a bit of a blur. Though she did recall Ma going ballistic at the cops. 'My Grace just saved those children's lives. That dirty animal murders three people and *Grace* gets arrested. This is bullcrap!'

Grace didn't know where she slept that night, presumably in a prison cell as she had a vague recollection of a drive in a police car to a magistrates' court appearance in Perth the next morning. Some guy in a suit put in a plea of self-defence on her behalf. The next thing she knew she was being taken to a hospital, sedated, and treated with kid gloves. Post-traumatic stress disorder, the shrink told the police. Grace had flashbacks for a while.

'What were your feelings when you shot the man?' the psychiatrist asked.

If Grace had been being brutally honest she'd have said, *not a lot.* She could recollect standing over the gunman and thinking, *just a fraction of a millimetre higher and that would have been a perfect shot. Damn it! There would have been no twitching if*

I'd done it right. But as that sounded freaky even to her, she didn't voice it. Though she did tell the shrink that all her thoughts were always about little Vikki and the guilt she felt for not getting there before Lionel Benedetti had a chance to pull the trigger.

That was his name, Grace learned early on.

The guy in the suit at the magistrates' court turned out to be a balding, middle-aged defence lawyer by the name of John Hillside. He visited Grace in hospital. Apparently, with the possibility of her facing serious charges, the magistrates' court had 'kicked the case upstairs', as he put it. 'However, what any prosecution would have to prove, is that you took your gun into the kindergarten with the express intention of killing Benedetti.'

His dark brown eyes bored into Grace and she wondered if the prosecution argument was actually the truth of the matter. In the heat of the moment, having seen the cold-blooded killing of poor Trey, had she been out for revenge? But, as with her less-than-honest response to the psychiatrist's questions, she plumped for pragmatism.

'The man was armed with both a rifle and a handgun. A police response was at least twenty minutes away. For me to have gone unarmed to the aid of those helpless children would have been suicide. What was I supposed to do? Just think of my own safety, hide away and do nothing?'

He nodded sagely. 'Of course, we now know that before shooting the boy, Benedetti had also murdered his daughter and ex-wife.'

'I've heard,' Grace said, while thinking, *so why all the fuss? Some might say that I'd actually provided a public service.*

He appeared to have read her mind. 'Not that you were aware of that at the time.'

After that comment, she was left wondering just whose bloody side this man was on. 'No, I didn't know about that,' she said, 'but I'd seen him shoot Trey Palmer and then watched him heading over to the kindergarten.'

'Tragic though that young man's death was, it was perhaps fortuitous.'

She realised he was urging her to rationalise her actions in preparation for a future court hearing, so played along. 'Otherwise, I wouldn't have acted as I did, and Benedetti may well have murdered all of the children and teachers?'

'That would be a perfectly logical assumption on anyone's part.' He sat back in his chair. 'However, young Trey *was* killed and, under the self-defence law of Western Australia, if you believed that arming yourself before going after Benedetti was necessary to protect yourself or others …' He glanced at her for confirmation.

'That's exactly what I thought,' she said with a good deal of relief.

'And that shooting him was a reasonable response on your behalf under the circumstances you encountered once you were inside the kindergarten.' He gave a tight smile. 'Then I am hopeful that the Supreme Court will rule in our favour.'

'Only hopeful?'

'There are no cast-iron guarantees as far as the law is concerned.' He collected his notes, stood and shook her hand. 'But don't worry about anything. Leave everything to me and you concentrate on getting well.'

Grace watched him leave, sat back and stared at the ceiling for a long time, running a frame-by-frame replay of that fateful day in her mind, almost projecting it onto that white space above her head. When she shot Benedetti, did she believe he would kill the children if she didn't pull the trigger? Was it wiser to kill him straight off or could she have just incapacitated him? And was she feeling any of the guilt for shooting Benedetti that the psychiatrist appeared to be implying that she should? The answers were yes, possibly, and not at all. She sat up straight, crossed her arms and thought, *bugger it. I did what I believed to be right at the time. That is my defence and I'm sticking to it.*

It finally filtered through to Grace that there was a great deal of local media interest. Which made sense, she thought. *After all, it's not every day in WA that a man goes about killing innocent folk only to be shot dead in his tracks by a female civilian.*

Ma was keeping her up to date with the story. 'And do you know why Benedetti did it?' She was reading aloud from a report in the local newspaper. 'Why did Benedetti go on his killing spree?' She looked up, as though about to make an important announcement. 'It says here that poor little mite, Vikki, was the illegitimate child of Benedetti's daughter. The daughter he had abandoned fifteen years earlier.' She stopped and shook her head sadly. 'Can you believe this, Grace?'

It seemed that, after deserting his wife and child, Benedetti spent most of his useless life boozing and womanising. During that time, he'd been locked up for some petty crime or other and got religion while in prison.

'There was some kind of preacher on telly last night,' Ma said. 'I don't know why they give these vile people airtime. And he was saying that Benedetti had visited his ex-missus and daughter to make amends for his past bad deeds.

'However, when Benedetti discovered that his daughter had had a child out of wedlock, his newfound piety triggered so much moral outrage that he shot both his ex-wife and his daughter, and then went in search of his only grandchild to kill her too.'

Ma was appalled. 'And there was that horrible preacher, large as life and twice as ugly, trying to make that murdering scumbag out to be some kind of tragic victim. He even implied that Benedetti was in some way justified for killing his family, as they had brought shame upon him. I was saying to Len, that these people should to be deported.'

'Len?' Grace asked.

'You know Len, from my bridge club. His wife died and he took early retirement. He's helping me in the shop while you're in here.'

'I'm glad.'

Ma flushed slightly 'Anyway, he agrees with me and everyone who knows you. You did the right thing, Grace.'

After the story broke, the national newspapers, TV, and radio were all over it. Grace was dubbed a heroine. Some journalist called her a feminist icon. As in, woman takes revenge for the killing of other females. 'Obviously to her mindset, poor Trey doesn't count as a victim,' Grace remarked to Ma. 'Chelsea Forsyth was really brave too. She tried to shield the children but even she makes me out to be an avenging angel.' Grace threw the newspaper on the bed. 'I hate all of this. I'm not some kind of super-freaking-hero.'

'Just an ordinary hero,' Ma said. 'And all the more fascinating because they can't get to you.'

While Grace had still been in hospital, a reporter had disguised himself as a doctor in order to gain access to her room and take photos of her. The orderlies made short work of him, but he did get some pretty unflattering shots. Then someone at the shooting range sold a photo of her at target practice. It appeared in the media the next day and apparently freaked out John Hillside, as he had Ma hand over a recent, less controversial photo of Grace with a neighbour's dog,

'You look so pretty in that one, Grace,' Ma said. 'It brings out the blue of your eyes and just look how your hair shines in the sunlight. You look like a movie star.'

'That's not me though, is it? What was wrong with the photos taken after I'd won pistol-shooting competitions?'

Ma looked a bit sheepish. 'Mr Hillside said those pictures made you appear menacing.'

'Menacing?' *That's ridiculous*, she thought. *Okay, so I don't suffer fools gladly. I've never played the girly card to attract men and I did once floor a guy who pinched my arse but 'menacing' is a bit of a stretch.*

'He told me it's all to do with image,' Ma said.

Grace was confused. 'But Hillside said there'd be a court appearance and my plea of self-defence would probably be accepted. All over bar the shouting and I'd be able to get on with my life.'

'Yes, but there's a lot of shouting going on already. That preacher and his followers are making such a fuss that it's best to be on the safe side, not emphasise your ability with a gun.'

'They should thank God for my expertise or Benedetti might have killed more than five people.'

'That's exactly how all the children's parents feel,' Ma said soothingly. However, not being one to pull punches, she also told Grace the bad news. 'Though some other people are suggesting that rather than shooting Benedetti dead, you could have wounded him instead and taken the gun off him.'

Grace was the epitome of what Ma would have termed 'gobsmacked'. 'What the hell are you telling me, Ma?'

'There are some people who've been whipped into a frenzy by that mad preacher. And they're calling you a murderer, Grace.'

CHAPTER FOUR

Western Australia, November 2012

A date was set for a Voluntary Criminal Case Conference. John Hillside had advised Grace that this was the best route to take. 'If you volunteer to take this fast-track hearing, then under WA law, the Supreme Court will be able to consider your plea of self-defence, review all the witness statements and decide whether you should stand trial or not,' he told her.

Hillside was hoping for them to come up with a 'trial not in the public interest' response. However, since that proselytising preacher was still banging on and getting his face all over the media by trying to make Benedetti out to have been the victim, it was touch-and-go as to whether the court might take Grace to trial just to silence him and his handful of mouthy, placard-waving followers. 'All in the name of political expediency,' Hillside said with a disgusted tone in his voice. Either way, Grace had been out of hospital for three months and, although she had to report to a police station once a week, she was able to work in the shop part-time with Len helping out for two days a week. Grace refused all media interviews on the grounds of *sub judice* but that hadn't stopped people she had previously thought of as friends talking to the press.

'I'm not a freaking loner,' Grace exploded after reading an interview with someone she'd been at school with describing her that way.

'You're just not very outgoing,' Ma said tactfully. Little wonder really, as Ma had always been so overprotective of her only child, and her only family as far as Grace knew, so although Grace tried to understand her mother's anxiety, Ma's constant fussing about safety had embarrassed her no end as a kid. And the only time Grace had been on holiday without Ma, to Bali with a friend when she was twenty, Ma had phoned her every night to make sure she was okay. No bloke Grace had ever dated was good enough in Ma's eyes. But, if Grace was being honest, she had always been very picky. The high flyers from school had all pissed off to Perth or Sydney. She was aware that no bloke with brains would stay around the area for longer than necessary. So, what was left were the cockies, the small town tradesmen, her gun club mates or the very odd, as she had discovered to her cost, school teacher. 'A right bunch of no marks', as Ma put it. It hadn't been so bad when Grace was younger and had female mates but they'd since all married or left for pastures new, while she was still stuck with Ma and the gift shop that Ma refused to sell, even when she'd been offered a decent price for it.

Unfortunately, that 'loner' comment poured fuel on the protestors' flames and the store's website got a dozen or so misspelt comments about Grace being a gun-obsessed freak, plus a couple of death threats. With her gun licence suspended, Grace felt a little vulnerable until Ma bought a cricket bat.

'Heavier than one of those silly baseball things,' she said, wielding it in a very unsporting manner. These threats to their safety had brought out a side to Ma that Grace had rarely seen. 'And there's always that axe we use to chop wood,' she joked.

'You're making me and my gun sound decidedly peaceful by comparison.'

'I grew up in the backstreets of Liverpool,' Ma said. 'In those days if you were bullied by someone bigger, you didn't go running to your mam, you cornered the bastard in an alleyway and hit them with a brick.' She laughed. 'Soon stopped 'em.'

In all of Grace's twenty-six years, Ma had never spoken about her childhood, or given any insight into her life before emigrating to Australia when Grace was two.

'Tell me more.' As the door on her mysterious Ma's life was suddenly and surprisingly ajar, Grace decided to edge her way through.

Ma shrugged. 'Nothing interesting about me, Grace. Worked in a shop, got pregnant by a nasty character, saved up some money and got out of England when you were little. End of story. The rest you know 'cos that's your life too.'

'Don't we have any family in England?' Grace asked casually, not wanting to sound so interested that Ma would clam up again.

'Everyone's dead.' Ma put the bat down, threw her arms around Grace and held on tight. 'You're all I need.'

After Ma's little insight, they were back where they started. All Grace's questions over the years had been neatly sidestepped. She didn't look much like Ma, who was as slim as Grace was curvy, dark as Grace was fair. The only thing they had in common to indicate they were even related was their blue eyes, although Ma's had a piercing quality that made the young Grace believe Ma could read her mind. Fibs were always seen straight through, so Grace just stopped telling them.

'Come on, Ma, there must be more.'

'Nothing more to say.' Her body stiffened. 'Better get on,' she said as she walked away and the door to her past slammed shut once more. 'Len's in the shop on his own.'

November was upon them, one of the spring months when the tourist season kicks off and Perthites begin to pine for weekends away at Margaret River. As business picked up again, they got the odd gawpers at first, the ghouls attempting to sneak into the kindergarten to check out where Benedetti got his comeuppance. After a while, neighbours such as Kayleen from the Kaffe, and Harri the hairdresser learned to clam up when leading questions were asked, so the curious went on their way, disappointed.

Business was good and Grace learned not to rise to tasteless jokes such as, 'Got any replicas of the gun, have ya? I'd buy that.'

And she got used to the sidelong glances, happy to earn the money from customers' purchases so long as they took it no further than curious stares or the odd comment like, 'I'd like to say how much I admire you.' Or, 'I think you're very brave to have done what you did.' A polite thank you was all they got in return. She learned to handle it all.

Then came the day that Ma lost it with a customer. Grace noticed that the woman entered the shop alone and wandered about for a while. Grace eyed her casually; the woman seemed liked a bored browser, looking at this and touching that. She didn't look like a five-finger discount type, but you could never be sure, they got shoplifters from time to time. Finally, the woman picked up one of the handmade, arty greetings cards from the twirly riser in the corner of the shop and shoved it under Grace's nose.

'Sign that!'

'Don't do it,' said another casual browser with the English accent. 'She'll sell it on eBay.'

'What do Poms know?' The woman snarled at the man in the Manchester United T-shirt.

'I know what *you're* up to, love.' He smiled at Grace and winked. He was about thirty, dark-haired, and pleasant-looking with a pallor that indicated he hadn't been in the country long. So, she reckoned he was more the typical English tourist type.

Ma rolled up her sleeves, rushed around the counter and pounced on the woman. She snatched the card off her, grabbed her by the arm and pushed her out of the door.

'Fuck off! We don't want your sort in here.'

The English guy picked up a soft, toy kangaroo and took it to the till where Grace was standing.

'Very protective of you, isn't she,' he said, indicating to Ma, who was still red-faced but now fussing over the window display. 'Your mother, is she?'

Grace thought he sounded like one of the characters from Ma's favourite TV show. Aussie fans call it 'Corra' but Ma always referred to it by the full title of *Coronation Street*.

'Always has been,' she said.

'Did I hear the faint northern English twang in her voice when she saw that woman off?'

'Ma was originally from Liverpool,' Grace said.

'And you?'

'I was born in the UK, but we've been here since I was two.'

'Any other relatives in Australia?'

'No, it's just the two of us.'

'That's twenty-five dollars.' Ma appeared as if from nowhere and virtually pushed Grace out of the way. She held out her hand to the man.

He seemed momentarily taken aback.

'For the kangaroo,' she said.

He gave her a fifty, she rang up the sale, put the kangaroo into a bag for him and handed him his change. Grace was shocked. What the hell was wrong with her today? She was never rude to customers and he seemed like just a friendly bloke. And after he'd been kind enough to intervene on her behalf with that awful woman. Annoyed with her mother, Grace left Ma to stew by the till and walked around the counter to see the customer to the door.

'I'm curious,' she said, 'why would anyone want to buy my signature?'

'You're famous.'

'In Western Australia, maybe.'

'Not just here,' he said. 'I mean, I know it's a bit remote here, but you must have the Internet.'

'I don't look at it much.' Death threats notwithstanding, social media had never interested Grace. She didn't have many friends anyway. All the news she needed to know was on the TV, so the computer was used for work-related stuff and that was it.

'Well I'd heard about you in England.' He stopped as they reached the door and held out his hand to be shaken. 'It's been very nice to meet you, Grace.' And he left the shop.

Grace turned to Ma. 'How rude are you? What the hell was that all about?'

'He asked too many questions,' she said, sniffily.

Grace walked towards the back room to make some coffee. 'He was being friendly, Ma. That's all.'

'I didn't like him,' Ma called after her. 'His eyes were too close together.'

***

Tony Boyle strolled back towards his car and tossed the bagged kangaroo in the nearest waste bin. Behind where he'd left his hire car was a small scrubby park containing a swing, a seesaw, and a bench. As there was nobody in the park, he strode over to the bench, sat down and took out his mobile phone. Just before he hit the number he wanted, he remembered that Frank had told him to use Skype when he was in Australia. 'Only Skype, understand? If you forget and I get some great big fucking mobile phone bill, then I'll take it out of your face.'

Tony found the app, dialled up the one contact number on there and was surprised that even at that vast distance, it sounded as though he was phoning next door.

Come on, he thought impatiently, *answer the bloody thing*. He was exhausted. He hated long haul. He hated flying full stop. Not that he was legally supposed to leave the UK but only mugs allowed petty restrictions to stop them. Even so, travelling to Benidorm for a week once a year was about his measure, so the twelve hours to Singapore had just about knackered him. He'd tried to sleep but someone had a brat with them and the little fucker had screamed nonstop for half of the flight. If he could have stayed even overnight in a Singapore hotel, he might have felt more awake now, but Frank had insisted he get straight on the next flight to Perth. Five hours later he was in Oz, hiring a car and making the three-hour slog down the roads towards Margaret River. Still, he thought, he'd followed orders and got a result. He wasn't sure if it was exactly what Frank wanted but it was something.

***

Nine thousand miles away the phone was ringing. Frank Gilligan reached out from beneath his duvet, grabbed the phone from the bedside table and blinked myopically at the time display.

'This had better be fucking good,' he said to the caller. 'It's five in the bleedin' morning.'

'Sorry, boss,' Tony said. 'You told me to call you straight away.'

'Yeah, yeah. I suppose I did. So, what have you got?'

'It's her alright. Grace Dobbs.'

'And the other woman?'

'Grace says it's her mother.'

'But is it Celia?'

'According to some tart in the café, that's the name she goes by.'

'But is it her?'

Tony hesitated.

'Come on, sunshine.' Frank was in no mood to be pissed about. 'You've seen the photos. Is it Celia or not?'

'Let's put it this way,' Tony said. 'There is no way the woman I just saw could ever have been a glamour model.'

'Time might have been unkind,' Frank suggested.

'Dark hair, scrawny as all get out and no tits to speak of. It wasn't her, boss. I'm pretty sure of that.'

'Shit! Any chance Celia might be around some place?'

'I got chatting to Grace before the older one got all antsy and she said it was just the two of them.'

'Double fucking shit.'

'You want me to come back?'

Frank pondered for a moment. If Celia wasn't in Australia, then he'd have to smoke her out. And to do that he had to get Grace to England pronto, before all the media fuss died down. The problem being, that Grace would not be allowed out of Australia until all the legal stuff was put to bed. The last thing he needed was for the girl to be languishing in some godforsaken Aussie prison. And from what he could tell, there was just one thing standing in the way of her case being swiftly settled.

'Is that hairy-faced preacher cunt still making trouble for Grace?'

'Yeah, from what I can make out.'

'He get-at-able?'

'Everyone's get-at-able.'

'Then deal with it, will you? Permanent. No comebacks.'

Tony laughed. 'This is Australia, boss. Lots of sharks off the coast.'

'Take him up country and feed the fucker to the crocodiles for all I care. No traces, understand?'

Frank turned off his phone, lay back in his super-king-sized bed and gazed up at the mirror on the ceiling above him. He could almost see Celia's reflection beside him, under him, riding him, reverse cowgirl – yee-har! Fucking his brains out all those years ago. What did that silly squeaky-voiced tart in that film say? 'A body for sin and a brain for business.' That was Celia all over.

And with all this publicity unearthing the whereabouts of Grace, it had dawned on Frank just what an elaborate Find-the-Lady trick Celia had pulled on them all. He really had to hand it to her. He chuckled ruefully. Hand it to her, or she'd just go ahead and take it anyway. *But not this time, Celia old girl, because at long last you are going to be outsmarted. And this long, drawn-out game of hide-and-seek will be over forever.*

Frank turned on his side, closed his eyes and drifted back to sleep with a smile on his face. 'Come out, come out, wherever you are.'

CHAPTER FIVE

Tony Boyle watched the gesticulating man sitting opposite him. He saw his mouth moving but, unwilling to listen to any more of his bullshit, had mentally blocked his ears. You could do that with a little practice, he'd discovered. Why listen to screams of pain if you didn't have to? Some of his compadres got off on that sort of thing but he'd always considered those guys to be bordering on the psychopathic, whereas to his mind, he was merely doing his unpleasant duty. And what applied to victims of torture also worked with supposedly pious gobshites like this preacher.

So, he let the recorder on the coffee table between them pick up the weirdo's ramblings while Tony did what an old mate of his who now worked for the telly termed 'the odd noddy' – a nod of the head to reassure the talker that you are all ears.

In between nods of implied agreement, Tony poured more coffee for his bombastic interviewee, watched him guzzle it down, and waited. He glanced at his watch; they'd been in the hotel room for half an hour and this geezer had drunk three cups, so any minute now.

'Mr Boyle,' the guy said between loud slurps. 'When will your newspaper run this story?'

'Should be in the next day or so,' Tony said. 'Just as soon as I've transcribed it and emailed it to my editor in London.'

The preacher smiled. 'That is good news, it must appear before that woman goes before the Supreme Court. They must not be allowed to sweep the whole incident under the carpet. The deceased brother Benedetti will have his side of the story heard in open court. And that woman must suffer for her crime. Women should not be allowed to have guns.'

'No problem,' Tony said as he watched the preacher's face gradually turn a nasty shade of puce.

***

Tony hit the road in his rented campervan and tried not think about just how far he had to drive. No comebacks, Frank had said, so travelling up to the saltwater-crocodile-infested Mary River just east of Darwin had seemed like a good idea at the time. Those big bastards left no trace, eating a bellyful and then storing the rest in some underwater hidey-hole to snack on later.

Tony *had* intended to kill the preacher in the hotel room then bundle him into the lift to the underground car park where he'd left the campervan. But when he'd scrutinised a map and seen just how far he was going to have to drive, that put the kybosh on that plan. Tony recalled staring at the map in dismay and checking the distance twice. Perth to Darwin, three thousand kilometres, would take about eight fucking days to get there. Even if he turned the internal aircon to arctic, by the time he got to his destination, the body would have been stinking to high heaven and leaking all over the place. Even a croc might turn its snout up at that. So, the drug-induced, simulated heart attack was the next option. And it worked a treat.

'I am feeling unwell,' the preacher had gasped as he clawed at his chest and tried to stand.

'I'll get you some water,' Tony offered. 'What with this whirlwind roundabout of publicity you've been on, perhaps you've overdone it?'

The preacher collapsed back onto the sofa, his face a picture of pain and fright. 'Call for an ambulance.'

'Perhaps you should wait, this may well pass.'

'Ambulance!'

'Look, the hospital is just five minutes away, I'll take you there myself.'

Actually, Tony mused, Plan B had worked out much better than the original. Why carry the dead weight of your target to your vehicle if it could be persuaded to get there under its own steam? Once inside the van it had been a piece of cake to overpower the fucker and inject him with enough Valium to keep him quiet for a day or so. Top it up along the way and hey presto. Once at the Mary River campsite, he planned to bump off the pompous gasbag to provide some nice fresh meat for the wildlife.

Tony headed towards the highway and turned on a local radio station. The second tune up was Elton John's 'Crocodile Rock' and Tony almost pissed himself laughing.

***

Summer arrived and so did the tourists, rubberneckers included. Len was brought in more often to help out and Grace noticed how well he and Ma got on. He was gentle and became skilled at side-tracking the more persistent types. Generally, the little community closed ranks on outsiders and they coped well, with Grace hoping that once the legal problem was out of the way, everything would return to normal.

The good news was that the mad preacher had suddenly disappeared from the scene. Rumour had it he'd gone back whence he came, unable to cope with an obstinately decadent Australian society that refused to take heed of his rants. Though it seemed that nobody could say for sure where he was. However, with the head of the snake gone, the body of followers went very quiet.

The death threats ceased, as did the nasty messages, but there was one rather disquieting email that popped up early one morning.

Your Mother Wants To See You.

'Another nut job,' Grace told Ma and deleted the message.

'Where was it from?' Ma asked quietly.

'Not signed and it's from one of those Google addresses, so it could have been from anywhere.'

Other news was better. Grace and her lawyer attended the Supreme Court in Perth. The imposing building with its Greek-style colonnades was completed in 1903, standing next to the original court which was built in 1837. All was very much in the style of classic architecture with the exception of the statues of life-size kangaroos dotted about the verdant grounds and the odd glimpse of a kookaburra in the trees. Very Aussie touches. Even so, Grace had never been inside the courthouse before and felt dutifully overawed and frankly terrified. Here, her fate was to be decided by three judges. Stern faces surveyed her as she stood before them, knees quaking. She was thankful to have John Hillside to speak for her. The judges listened, accepted the plea of self-defence, examined all the witness statements and, after deliberation, decided that a trial would not be in the public interest. Grace was free to go.

'Justice has been served,' Hillside announced to the reporters waiting outside, which gave Grace time to slip out of the backdoor unnoticed.

Back home, Ma hugged her with joy and Kayleen threw a party.

'I always knew it would be all right,' Kayleen slurred as she downed her vodka. 'My Facebook page has had over a hundred thousand 'likes'.'

'What Facebook page?'

'I set it up when you were in hospital,' she said. 'Grace Dobbs is a Heroine.'

She led Grace into the office at the back of the Kaffe and turned on her laptop. And there it was, the photo with the neighbour's dog plus links to every newspaper and TV report on there as well.

'I don't allow anyone to post on there,' Kayleen said. 'You know, because of the crazies.' She paused for a moment to allow Grace to take in what she obviously perceived as grateful wonderment. 'And look at how many 'likes' we've got from all over the world.'

Grace had dismissed as chatty exaggeration what that English tourist had told her about his having heard of her in the UK. She'd thought of his comment as just something to say, so this evidence of wider interest on social media took her by surprise. She'd hated what was merely local interest, a thunderstorm in a jar that would swiftly pass when something else grabbed the attention of the inhabitants of WA. So, she loathed this Facebook page for having attracted global commentary.

Grace was mad as hell but Kayleen appeared ecstatic. 'Have you Googled yourself?' she asked. 'The story was even reported in the *Washington Post* in America, just think of that. Fame at last, eh? Here, let me show you.' She reached down to the laptop's track pad.

'No thanks.' Grace turned her back on the screen and walked away. 'You've already done enough. I'll look it up myself when I get home.' Not.

'You're welcome,' Kayleen called after her sarcastically.

Grace ignored her. *Do I really want to see what the world and his goddamn wombat think of me? I know what happened that day. The Supreme Court believed me, and all the evidence was on my side, so do I really need the approval or the condemnation of complete strangers? Thanks, Kayleen, but no thanks.*

Next day the second email.

Congratulations. Your Mother Wants To See You.

Grace decided not to mention it to Ma.

'Better than death threats, I suppose,' Ma had said of the first message by way of brushing it off. But Grace had known there was something troubling her. It had always amused Grace that people thought they could hide things from their offspring, unable to see that even little ones knew when something was in the wind. Grace reckoned that if a language-ignorant dog or cat knows when a person is ill or sad or stoned then why wouldn't a child guess if, say, a divorce was brewing. She had lived in close proximity with Ma for all her life, so could glean her discomfort with that email. Even though Ma insisted on maintaining the fiction that she wasn't bothered, Grace knew the reality. So, given that she didn't want to upset Ma any further, she deleted each missive as it arrived. There had been three in all.

31

However, it was the fourth message that took her aback.
This Is Your Mother. She Wants To See You.
Attached was a photograph of Grace. But it wasn't Grace. She had never stood in Trafalgar Square feeding pigeons but there she was, though the long, straight hair with a middle parting wasn't accurate. Grace wasn't one for heels either, but this photo had her in tight black jeans, a deep red slash-neck top and leopard-print, high-heeled ankle boots. The first thing she thought was, *this is a Photoshop job. Someone has snaffled pictures from that stupid Facebook page and put them on the body of another person.* But it was the second attachment that took her aback. It was a close-up shot that bore the same strong resemblance to Grace but here she was, perhaps a few years older. She was seated on a brown leather sofa, with her long blonde hair tied back. She was smiling for the camera and holding a tiny baby in her arms.
She Misses You. Your Mother Wants To See You.
Grace was sitting by the computer staring at the image when Ma entered the room and stood behind her. Ma put her left hand on Grace's shoulder and as the sun from the window beside the desk hit the signet ring she never removed from her left little finger, the reflection from it swept across the screen like a searchlight.
'That's not you,' Ma said.
'I know that,' Grace said. 'It's some kind of stupid prank. It's a fake.'
Ma sighed. And Grace was surprised just how sad that sounded. 'It's not a *fake*, Grace. That's my sister.'
Grace turned her head and noticed a look of distress cross Ma's face. 'But you told me that all your family were dead.'
'I thought she was,' Ma said. 'And maybe she is. These are both old photos. I took that one of you in her arms.' She reached across and took Grace by the hand. 'Come and sit with me.' She looked back at the screen once more, taking in the face. 'I have something to tell you.'

***

Martha stood by the door and watched Grace sleeping; the child did look cute with her thumb stuck firmly in her mouth. Martha smiled down at the little girl she thought of as her own blue-eyed, curly-haired angel. Of course, thumb-sucking was much worse for the child than the dummy Martha had recommended but Celia had refused.

It was fine for her sister because she'd never had to deal with Grace when she was teething, never once had to soothe her when she was fighting sleep. The baby would fall asleep in Martha's arms, but the minute Grace was placed in her cot, she'd be wide awake again and yelling blue murder. Even now Grace was almost two, she would be nodding off on the sofa but wide awake when put to bed. Martha had tried reading to Grace but that just got her all excited. 'More, Ma, more,' she'd say. Maybe one day it would be a good idea, perhaps when Grace was bigger and could follow the story better. If, of course, Celia still wanted her living with them after all the excitement of Eddie's release had died away and they'd settled down as a proper family. But for now, it was a round of coming-out parties, with Celia dressed up to the nines and Eddie falling about drunk when they got back as dawn broke.

Martha often had to restrain herself from going downstairs and telling them not to wake Grace at this unearthly hour. She always had to remember that she was now in their home on sufferance and they might send her packing any day.

Anyway, she reasoned, after over three years in prison, Eddie probably needed to kick up his heels a bit. Ending up behind bars for something as petty as handling stolen goods was nothing compared to what he might have gone down for. Had the police and court known the full story, Eddie's feet wouldn't have touched. But everyone else involved in that particular little caper had kept *schtum*. 'People in alternative enterprise know which side their bread is buttered,' Celia had remarked.

After such a close call, Martha hoped that maybe Eddie could be persuaded to go straight. An expert driver like him could get a job as a chauffeur, perhaps. That was good money, she'd heard.

Better than driving getaway cars, anyway. She couldn't understand why he needed to take those chances anymore; he and Celia already had this nice four-bed detached house with a lovely garden in a leafy lane. It was far better than where either of them had started out: Eddie from some neglected London council estate and Celia raised in Mum and Dad's pokey two-up two-down off Scotland Road in Liverpool. That had been one of the last properties to be demolished in the late 1980s. Of course, by that time Dad had gone to his just reward, Mum was unwell, and Celia had long since buggered off to London to pursue her modelling career. Not that it had lasted long after she met Fast Eddie.

'Martha!' Celia's voice came from downstairs. Martha looked at her watch. They were home early tonight and Celia sounded sober. Martha wondered if she was about to get her marching orders. After almost three years living in Surrey playing nursemaid, first to her just pregnant sister and then to little Grace, Martha had nothing to return to in Liverpool. She'd given up her council flat and her job in Lewis's department store. She wondered if perhaps Eddie would give her some money to set her on her feet again. She'd always assumed that he had quite a bit secretly stashed away from the many robberies he'd taken part in.

'Martha!'

'Coming,' she whisper-called, closing the nursery door behind her. 'Shhh, don't wake Grace.'

Down in what Martha always considered to be the glitzy sitting room, she was surprised to see Celia alone. She and Eddie had been joined at the hip ever since he got out of the nick.

'We need to talk.' Celia patted the seat beside her on the leather sofa and moved the silver-threaded Indian cushion out of the way for Martha to sit down.

This is it, Martha thought. *I'm about to be told, thanks for everything but now's the time to hop it*. If Celia wanted to play house with Eddie from now on, then Martha knew they'd view her as a spare wheel. So, with some apprehension Martha sat beside her sister.

Celia smiled, showing perfect white teeth courtesy of the expensive dental work Eddie had paid for way back when he was promoting her glamour-modelling career. In those days he'd had an interest in a top-shelf magazine business. He wasn't much more than a silent partner at the time since the business was being used as a cover for his more illicit income. But when he met Celia on a photo shoot he'd been dragged along to, he became determined to turn her into a soft-core porn star. Trouble was, Eddie had a jealous streak a mile wide and his naked and oiled-up girlfriend preening and pouting for some horny photographer did not sit well with him. After a while, he gave Celia an ultimatum: modelling or me. She chose him.

'Why such a sour face?' Celia frowned prettily and ran her fingers through her shoulder-length blonde hair.

'Just wondering why you're home so early.' Martha looked pointedly around the room as though searching for any trace of Celia's paramour. 'And alone.'

'Eddie's got some business to take care of.'

It wasn't so much the words Celia had used but the tone of voice that sent warning signals to Martha. *Oh yes*, she thought, *here we go. No sooner out of chokey than he's back in the game. Bloody idiot!*

'He's setting something up that could have us all in clover.'

Martha held up her hand, palm outwards. 'I don't want to know.'

'What makes you think I was going to tell *you*?' Celia snorted. 'It's just that we'll all be busy for the next few months, so we won't have much time for Grace.'

Not that Eddie had shown much interest in the child from the moment he'd set eyes on her, while Celia's mothering skills had always left a lot to be desired. Even so, Martha felt a rush of relief. So, she wasn't being packed off back to Liverpool. They still needed her. Grace needed her.

'And afterwards, we might have to make ourselves scarce for a bit,' Celia was saying.

'I'll just stay here and look after Grace, then,' Martha said.

'You can't because we're selling the house.' Celia applied that clipped tone that brooked no argument. 'There'll be an estate agent coming around tomorrow. So just let them get on with it.'

This did not sound like good news. 'But why do you need to sell the house?'

'We want the money for setting up the operation.' Celia's voice softened and she smiled gently. 'And to take care of you and Grace until the dust settles.'

The thought of any plan kicking up dust had Martha on pins. She had visions of police searching the house, grilling her as to the whereabouts of her sister and Eddie, perhaps thinking she was implicated in some way with whatever they were up to. Her mind was racing, imagining a scenario where the social services came to take Grace away from her.

'Whatever this is, Celia, please don't get involved. For Grace, if not for yourself,' Martha begged.

But Celia was not for turning. 'This is the scam of a lifetime, Ma,' she enthused, and Martha could see the excitement in her eyes. 'It'll set us all up forever. You included.' Celia seemed to catch Martha's mood because her voice took on a soothing tone. 'But don't you worry about us, we know what we're doing. You should think of yourself for now.' She nodded reassuringly. 'And what I'm about to propose could be a brand new start for you.'

Here we go. Martha narrowed her eyes. If there was one thing she knew about her younger sister, it was that she did nothing that wasn't in her own ultimate interest.

Celia reached out with an immaculately manicured hand, gripped Martha's and gave her one of those smiles that emphasised the dimple in her cheek. Just like Grace did when she laughed. They really were two peas in a pod.

'You know I'd trust you with my life, don't you?' Celia said.

'I suppose so.' Uh-oh, Martha didn't like the sound of that one little bit.

'Then I'm trusting you'll do what's best for Grace.'

Martha took a breath and tried to calm her fluttering heart. 'So, if you sell up, where will Grace and I go?'

'How does Australia sound?'

***

Grace stared at Ma across the dining table, making an attempt to take in what she'd been told. 'But *you* are Celia Dobbs,' she said. 'Your name is on my birth certificate.' No father's name but that wasn't that unusual in those days.

Ma gave a deep sigh. 'Celia made all the arrangements for us, got me all the forms to sign. We used her birth certificate, driving licence and National Insurance number, I even dyed my hair blonde for a time to look just a little bit like her on her passport photo.'

'So, are you *really* Martha Dobbs?'

She nodded her head. 'Why do you think you've always called me Ma?'

'I thought it was short for Mother.' Other kids in school had called their mothers Mom or Mum, but for Grace, it had always been Ma. She'd never questioned it. It just was.

'You called me Ma from when you first learned to talk.' Her eyes began to fill with tears and she dabbed at them. 'You couldn't manage to say Martha.'

Too numb and not sure how she was supposed to react, Grace wondered, *should I be angry? Should I feel lied to and betrayed?* But she looked across the table to the woman who had always taken care of her, the only mother she had ever known and hated to see her in such pain. 'Don't cry, Ma,' she said. 'Nothing's changed. The real Celia gave me away so why should I care if she wants to see me or not? It's all a bit late for that, isn't it? Twenty-four years too late.'

Ma was shocked by the outburst. 'You don't understand, Grace. The plan was just for me to bring you here out of harm's way.'

'So, we've both been dumped on.' Grace had been half expecting this; for Ma to spring to the defence of the sister who had literally left her holding the baby.

'She was coming for you, Grace. After everything had been sorted out, she was coming. And I believed her, though I had no way to contact her. She told me it would be too dangerous for me to know where she was.'

'And how was she supposed to leave the country when you had her passport?'

'Getting fake identity papers would be no problem for Celia,' Ma said with a throwaway certainty that took Grace by surprise. Ma was the most scrupulously honest person she had ever known. When Grace was eight she'd nicked a plastic bracelet from a shop. Ma had found it and made her take it back to apologise. She always came across to Grace as the epitome of an upstanding, morally righteous citizen. Yet here she was talking about her sister, Grace's real mother, having taken part in God knows what illegality and able to get hold of phoney passports almost as though it was nothing at all.

'So, how would she have been able to find us?' Grace asked distractedly, because she was now wondering if Ma had been so tough on her because she was afraid that the apple doesn't fall far from the tree.

'She knew where we were all right. The money to buy this place in my name was transferred from Switzerland. The money came from the sale of the house we lived in when you were a baby.' At least that was what Martha had been told way back then. And if she had learned one thing in her life it was that with some folk, it was wise never to question the source of money.

Ma bit her bottom lip tearfully. 'I never knew what she got involved with and I never wanted to. But I'm sure that Celia would have come for you if she could. I kept waiting and waiting. But she never came.'

Grace looked across the room to Celia's photo on the computer screen.

'Until now,' she said.

'I don't know, Grace.' Ma sounded doubtful. 'Why send you such old photos? Why nothing more up to date? It feels wrong to me.'

***

The ticket arrived in the post the next morning. First-class on Emirates, Perth-Dubai-Dublin-Liverpool. There was a note with it.

This is an open ticket. Please use it if and when you wish. I will be notified when you fly, and a car will be waiting for you at John Lennon airport.

It was an offer that someone, somewhere, was sure Grace wouldn't refuse.

CHAPTER SIX

The baleful sound of a medieval call to prayer bounced around the interior of the glass-and-chrome cathedral to glittering consumerism and twenty-first century air travel that is Dubai International Airport. Veiled women glided or scurried by, heading for the women's prayer room conveniently situated by the conveniences. Considerably more casually dressed travellers proffered credit cards for eighteen-carat jewellery and expensive perfumes to heavily made-up, ever-smiling sales assistants who appeared to be mainly Filipino. Grace had never seen anything like it. Eleven hours from the modest and mundane mall-style Perth airport and she had landed in an alien universe of glistening incongruity. Every nationality on the planet appeared to have congregated in this veritable Noah's Ark of humanity. Midway between here and wherever, they wandered about shopping, eating, and drinking in bars that would probably be illegal in much of the Arab world. Yet under this cosseted dome, everything was up for grabs. If you had the money.

Having neither interest in, nor what Ma would call 'the readies' for, the gilded goods on show, Grace headed for the first-class lounge, where she hoped to be able to take a shower. But as soon as she stepped inside the ornate wooden and glass entrance, she felt overwhelmed and underdressed. The glamorous oriental lady behind the reception desk took one eyebrow-raised look at Grace's cheap jeans, shirt, and joggers. 'This area is for first-class passengers,' she announced, rather too grandly for Grace's liking.

I have only myself to blame, Grace thought. Ma had told her to dress smartly. 'You can't travel first-class looking like a bloody backpacker,' she'd warned. But had Grace listened? Nope. She'd been pissed off with Ma for trying to stop her from travelling in the first place, for putting forward such a host of objections that Grace finally tuned her out. *But you should have bloody listened to that particular piece of advice*, she thought, because the look on the receptionist's face spoke volumes.

Grace presented the boarding pass for her onward journey and those immaculately pencilled eyebrows almost flew off the woman's face. Nevertheless, she smiled warmly.

Probably reckons me to be some kind of eccentric Aussie millionaire whose one tawdry vice is shopping at Kmart, Grace thought, as she was politely informed of all the free goodies available, from a champagne and caviar bar to three-course sumptuous twenty-four-hour dining. Grace thanked her and stepped inside to look for the bathrooms where she took a long, hot shower in marbled splendour before sinking into the luxurious tan leather seats in the computer terminal room in order to email Ma.

Halfway there and everything fine. Will contact you again when I arrive in Dublin. Don't worry. If I'm not happy with the way things are going when I get to Liverpool, then I'll be back on the next available flight.

That had been the deal Grace made with Ma just to keep the peace, although even Grace had to admit that Ma had a point. The airline ticket had been sent anonymously and the promise of a car to be waiting at the final destination was hardly a reassurance. 'What if there's nobody there to meet you?' Ma asked. 'What will you do then?'

'I'll book into a hotel and have a holiday in your hometown,' Grace said nonchalantly. 'But why would anyone send me a ticket and not turn up? It makes no sense.'

'None of this makes any sense,' Ma shot back. 'Least of all you waltzing off blind.'

For the thousandth time since Grace told Ma she was going to England, Ma turned on the waterworks. 'I know I wasn't honest with you, but this is no way to react.'

Even though Grace had since gained some immunity to those tearful outbursts, she had to admit that Ma was right. However, the lure of knowledge was too strong for her to resist. Len was more than happy to help Ma out in the shop, so any guilt Grace might have otherwise felt for leaving her in the lurch, was swiftly assuaged. Len had even driven Grace to the airport. 'Don't you worry about your mom,' he'd said. 'I'll look after her.'

Grace had walked through the departures gate nervous and excited; this was one hell of an adventure for someone who had worked in the gift shop since leaving school, rarely even going into Perth city, and had been out of Australia just the once.

So here she was.

She had one more hour to kill before her next flight was due, so she sat for a while and watched the planes beyond one spectacularly panoramic window, then wandered over to the opposite side of the pamperdome from where she could see Dubai city in the distance. At this time of day, it shimmered, mirage-like, from behind a heat haze and hardly appeared to be a solid place at all. Its misty buildings competed to scrape the sky while around it the flat yet ever shifting desert seemed to be biding its time. Great cities have risen from these sands many times before, the barren landscape seemed to say, yet they are gone and I remain.

Time, Grace had told Ma, is precious. Twenty-four years is long enough to have been living in the dark. Time to let some light in.

'Then don't blame me if you don't like what you see,' Ma warned, but was characteristically unwilling to divulge any more than that.

***

Liverpool, 12 February 2013

Grace left Perth in blazing sunshine and arrived, after travelling for twenty-six hours, to overcast skies and a temperature of ten degrees. It was midday when the flight landed, so it would be nine in the evening in Perth. As she waited by the carousel for her luggage, she texted Ma once more.

Just landed, safe and sound. Will contact you again later. G

John Lennon airport was as functional as Dublin's had been with the ubiquitous coffee shops, one magazine stand and a sparse duty-free. Grace got through customs without a hitch or even a uniformed glance in her direction and, pushing a trolley loaded with her suitcase, she left the comparative silence and burst forth into the hubbub of arrivals. A crowd of expectant faces beyond the flimsy barrier looked at her for a second before fixing again on the doors that swished closed behind her.

Unlike those awaiting the appearance of loved ones, Grace walked along towards the exit point, not knowing what or who she was looking for. She'd tried to envisage what might happen all the way from Oz. Her best case scenario would have been to spot a woman who looked a lot like her, waving frantically while wiping away a joyful tear at seeing her long-lost daughter again. Perhaps she'd have a family in tow, a husband and even a bevy of blonde children itching to meet their big sister. Another possibility would be for another relative to transport her to her mother's sickbed where she would apologise for not having sought Grace out sooner. Or to be met by a lawyer, maybe, to tell her she was just in time for the reading of the will. Grace had mentally prepared for all of those possibilities and more, since long haul seemed to have had a feverish effect on her imagination. What she was not expecting was the tall man in a chauffeur's uniform holding up a small blackboard on which was chalked: Welcome Miss Grace Dobbs.

She introduced herself and was about to produce a passport by way of ID, when he lifted her case from the trolley. 'The car is outside, Miss.'

She followed in the wake of the imposing, uniformed figure as he strode out of the airport and straight to a waiting area directly outside the building. He stopped by a gold-coloured Bentley that appeared to have someone sitting in the front passenger seat. The tinted windows obscured the person, but she could tell it was a man. The chauffeur opened the boot and was about to place the suitcase inside when Grace stayed his hand.

'Who's that in the car?' she asked.

'The gentleman who sent you the ticket, Miss,' he said deadpan, as he gently moved her hand out of the way and placed her suitcase in the boot as intended.

He opened the back passenger door, and a whiff of leather assailed her nostrils. *Well I'm here now, might as well go through with it,* she thought as she climbed in.

The man in the front passenger seat turned around and smiled, showing dazzlingly white teeth. She judged him to be in his late fifties with suspiciously dark hair and even darker brown eyes. Oh-so flashy too, what with the car, the green cashmere sweater and his sporting a gold signet ring with a huge emerald that glistened on the finger of his manicured right hand.

'Hello, Grace,' he said in a voice reminiscent of Michael Caine. 'My name is Frank Gilligan and I'm your father.'

CHAPTER SEVEN

'So where is this mother who is so desperate to see me?' Grace asked the smug bloke who claimed to be her long lost sperm donor. Despite his friendly demeanour, all her alarm bells were clanging. *This man is as shonky as all get-out*, she thought.

Frank Gilligan's face split into what Grace took to be a wide grin, but may well have involved a sneer or two. 'Bloody hell, girl,' he said. 'You're the spit of her; looks, voice ... and that attitude ...' He let forth a horsey snort that made his lips flap. 'You really are Celia all over again.'

Taking an instant dislike to his manner, Grace reached for the handle of the car door. 'Which is as it may well be,' she said. 'But I'm not impressed by your fancy car and your claims to be my father, Frank. I was brought here under the impression that I would be meeting my mother. Now, if she is unwell and unable to meet me here, I will apologise to her personally. But let's cut the crap, shall we?'

'Gracie,' he said, holding out his hand to her, his face expressing concern. 'I'm sorry. This must be a shock to you and you're probably tired after such a long journey. But let me take you to my house where we can talk properly.'

That did it. Grace pushed the car door open. 'I'm going nowhere with you, until you tell me what's going on here.'

'Okay, okay.' He put up his hands in surrender and turned to his driver. 'Take us to the Premier Inn, John.'

Grace pushed the door wider.

'Don't panic.' Frank turned back to her. 'The hotel is close to the airport. It'll take two minutes. We go there, sit in the bar and I explain. And if you're not fully satisfied, you get on the next plane back home.' His watchful eyes surveyed her face. 'How's that sound, Grace?'

The idea of being driven away from this spot held not one iota of appeal. Ma's lessons in self-preservation kicked in big time. 'If it's only two minutes then why don't we walk there?'

Frank sighed theatrically. 'If only I could, babe. But I've got this gammy leg, you see. A work accident.'

Grace considered his words and wondered what sort of manual work had ever soiled the manicured hands of the man who owned this Bentley.

He appeared to have read her mind. 'I'm in the building trade. I was out surveying an old property my firm was about to renovate, and some rotten floorboards collapsed from under me. I fell through to the basement below and fractured my femur. Never been the same since.'

She wasn't buying that either. 'Then point me in the direction of the Premier Inn and I'll walk there myself,' Grace said as she exited the car. 'See you in the bar.'

****

Two minutes, my arse, she thought. She could see what looked like a hotel at the end of a road that stretched into the distance. If that was it, then it was a ten-minute journey at a swift trot. She turned up the collar of her denim jacket against the cold and trudged along the footpath beside a straight highway. The dual carriageway, conveying a sparse number of cars to their destination, was lined with winter-bare trees and had fields on either side that gave no sense of which city or even country this was; when she spotted a signpost for the hotel she was looking for, it was adjacent to another sign that had obviously been erected by the local tourist board and was trumpeting somewhere called Speke Hall, which was apparently a genuine Tudor pile and local attraction. Hailing from a country where the first European settlers landed in the eighteenth century, Grace would normally have been rapt by a building from the sixteenth – but not today. Right now, she had only one thing in mind, so she ignored the buffeting wind and tramped on, overcome by a sudden and unexpected sense of freedom, laced with determination to see this thing through, no matter the outcome.

When she reached the hotel, Frank Gilligan was seated by a window close to the bar and the sight of the walking stick propped up by his chair gave her just a moment's pause for not having believed his story about having a crook leg.

'Sorry about not standing to greet you,' he said as she pulled up a chair opposite him. The head of the stick was in the shape of a silver elephant with gold tusks. He fondled it. 'Nice, eh?' he asked, and she nodded her agreement. 'Handmade rosewood, this. There's no reason to be shy about a disability. A real man is never afraid to admit his weaknesses,' he added. He put the walking stick down beside him, rested his elbows on the table and made eye contact. 'And my weakness was your mother, Celia.'

Grace held his gaze. 'And the past tense means …?'

His eyes darkened. 'Oh,' he said. 'Smart like her, too.' He emitted that snorty laugh again. 'I would have expected …'

His attitude was starting to piss her right off. 'What? Some ocker from the outback?'

He grinned. 'Beautiful, clever, heroic.' He counted the points off on raised fingers. 'What are you, Grace? Some kind of superwoman?'

'I'm your daughter.' She leaned forward in her seat until they were almost nose to nose. 'Or so you tell me.'

He appeared taken off guard and back-peddled a bit. 'Look, we've got off on the wrong foot here, sweetheart, and I don't blame you for being suspicious.' He smiled but the sentiment never reached as far as his eyes. 'Let me tell you what happened and then you can judge for yourself.'

'Go ahead. I've got plenty of time. The next flight out of here doesn't leave for another five hours.'

According to Frank, he had been in love with Celia from the first time he set eyes on her at a party in London. 'I was doing okay there; after all it is my home turf. I had a firm renovating period properties, restoring old fixtures and the like that previous owners had ripped out. It was a pretty lucrative game for a while. Then the foreigners started muscling in with their big promises and cheap labour. It was only the beginning of the end for British tradesmen, but I was wise enough to see the writing on the wall at that early stage.'

That's not what I want to know about, Grace thought, and tried to pull him back on track. 'And Celia?'

'She was modelling for top-shelf mags and doing okay but the boyfriend, Eddie, put a stop to that.'

So far, so in line with what Ma said, so Grace sat back and listened.

'Anyway, I'd already bought my place in Cheshire. Apart from business in the south being on the slide, I hated seeing Celia throw herself away on a chancer like Eddie. So, I transferred my business interests up here. And I tried to forget her, you know, to move on. Then Eddie gets banged up for handling stolen goods and out of the blue Celia lands on my doorstep asking me for a favour.'

'What kind of favour?'

'Her sister was in a bit of bother and Celia asked me to sort it for her.'

Grace couldn't imagine Ma ever getting into any 'bother'. *But what do I know?* she thought. Ma had reinvented herself, so anything was possible. 'You knew Martha?'

'Never met her. But I did the good deed, got the sister off the hook and Celia stayed with me for a month or so.'

'During which time?'

'We got close.' When he smiled he reminded Grace of a reptile. 'If you come to my house, I can show you the room where you were conceived.'

Creepy, or what? Grace didn't know whether to laugh or take to her heels and leg it back to the airport, so she didn't respond at all.

'The plan was for Celia to go back to London, pack her stuff and move in with me. So off she trots but she doesn't come back.

I go to the sister's house to see if she knows what's happened but it's just a pile of rubble. Demolished to make way for new flats. Next thing I hear, Eddie's out of the nick and playing house with Celia, her sister, and a baby. That's you, that is.'

'So how can you be so sure that Eddie's not my father?'

'When were you born?

'1986.'

'What month?'

'May.'

'So you were conceived in?'

Grace worked it back in her head. 'Probably August 1985.'

'Eddie was banged up in early May of that year. Now, he'd either had the slowest-moving tadpoles known to mankind or he was no pater of yours, Gracie.'

Past tense again. 'Of course, a DNA test would sort out the men from the boys.'

'I'd be happy to oblige,' Frank said. 'But I heard that Eddie passed away in the early nineties. Which was when Celia also went missing.'

This little revelation explained why the photos of Celia emailed to Grace were so old. Ma's suspicions about them were proven to be on the nail. Frank had no idea where Celia was.

'When I heard the story about the lovely young woman who'd rescued all those kiddies from that nutcase gunman, I was intrigued. Then when I saw your picture, I was poleaxed, I can tell you. You were far too like Celia not to be her child. I naturally assumed that she was in Australia with you. I sent a colleague of mine to investigate and he reported back that the woman living under the name of Celia Dobbs was not her at all.'

'And you decided to deceive me into coming here?' Grace held him in her stare. 'That's not on, you know. A simple email telling me all this would have done the trick, instead of all that 'your mother wants to see you' bullcrap.'

He reached across the table and took her hand in his. 'But would you have come?'

'I might.' On the other hand, Mother trumps Father any day of the week.

'Look, I'm sorry, Gracie, I fucked this all up. But let me tell you, I'm a single man. I never married; I have no offspring but you. This leg injury restricts me too much to be able to travel to Australia and I didn't want to risk never getting to know you.'

He sounded sincere, he acted sincere. 'Please tell me you believe me,' he said in an emotion-choked voice.

Grace did.

But she didn't mean it.

CHAPTER EIGHT

The journey from the airport to Frank's home in Cheshire took just over two hours, with him wittering away about how happy he was to meet Grace at long last and how he'd like to try to make up for all the lost time. Then, every now and again he'd look out of the window to point out some place of interest. 'It's fourteenth-century, that church. Bet you've got nothing like that in Oz, eh?' Or 'This is Runcorn, nothing much of interest here, but we're about to cross the River Mersey. Here we go.' Grace looked out at the scenery as the Bentley swept over a suspension bridge above a lacklustre stretch of water while Frank chattered on. 'And that's the Manchester Ship Canal. It was the main artery of that city back when the north of England manufactured all the wealth in Britain. Fortunes were made around here. Wouldn't think it to look at it now, though.'

Outside the leathery comfort of the car, clouds glowered their warning of rain to come while Grace conjured up the coastline around Margaret River with its powder-white sands fringing the azure blue of the Pacific. She could almost hear the surf breaking, the birdcalls, recalled watching for migratory whales from June to November, and she found herself almost drowning in a giant wave of homesickness. *What the hell am I doing in this cold, grey country?* she wondered.

'Don't say much, do you?' Frank stated.

'I'm just enjoying the ride,' she lied. 'And I'm a bit tired. I'll be better company after I've had a good night's sleep.'

She must have nodded off for a bit because she awoke to Frank saying, 'We're almost there.' He began pointing out the houses his company had renovated, and Grace had to admit they were impressive. 'That one used to be a sixteenth-century farmhouse. You should see it inside. We did a beautiful job on that. Kept all the wooden beams.'

They passed through a small village that he described as part of 'his' town. 'The local mayor and me are like that,' he said, lifting his hand with crossed fingers in the universal code for conjoined. 'He looks after me and I look after him.'

Could she detect a hint of bribery and corruption there? Not unusual anywhere these days and standard business practice for some. Ma was always railing against those tawdry deals whenever they came to public attention and got reported in the news. 'As if those sleazeballs don't make enough money already without resorting to graft,' she'd storm.

'Stupid of them to get caught out,' Grace had once ventured.

Ma glared at her. 'I don't know where you learned that kind of thinking, Grace, because it wasn't from me.'

Glancing at Frank, Grace wondered too. Could you inherit 'that' kind of thought process? And, if so, what else?

They passed what looked like a newish estate of identical Little Boxes-type houses. 'That's another one of mine. Not bad money in new builds. And they keep my team of lads on their toes, seeing as there are only so many older properties.'

'But renovation is your real passion.'

Frank turned in his seat and beamed at her. 'See how well you know me already.' Then he shrugged. 'But you don't make real money out of passion, Gracie. You have to adapt to the times and take your opportunities where you find them.'

On the outskirts of the village, the Bentley came to a halt outside two white gateposts. The green-painted, wrought-iron gates were open and as the car turned in along the driveway, Grace spotted a three-car garage with a pitched roof.

'That used to be the stables,' Frank pointed out as they drove past. 'I'm not one for horses.' He gave a deep and, she thought, rather exaggeratedly pointed sigh. 'But if you'd grown up here ...'

'You would have bought me a pony,' she said, while thinking, *don't lay it on thick with me, mate.*

He turned in his seat and shot her a hard look. 'Are you being sarky?'

'What makes you think that?'

The large white house ahead was side on to the road, purposely turned away from public gaze, which gave the place a rather furtive air, as though its owner could not bear to look the world in the eye. The car continued on around the corner of the building and that was when she spotted a silver car in front of sandstone steps that led to the canopied front entrance. There was a smartly dressed youngish bloke standing almost to attention beside it and, although the sky was gradually beginning to darken, and he was initially too far away for her to see him clearly, something in his stance sparked a moment of recognition.

***

Tony Boyle stood motionless by his Jag, hands held behind his back, suited up, shoes polished, ready to make an impression of power. Frank would have wanted a more casual greeting but screw that. This girl had to know where she stood in the pecking order around here. She was a nobody, the end result of some random ejaculation on Frank's part. The old guy was losing it, trying to play daddy to a total stranger. Tony put that down to the string of hot and cold running hookers Frank always had on call. In all these years Tony had never seen Frank with a non-prozzie, a business transaction that may well be satisfying on one level but perhaps not on another. Tony reckoned it was female affection that Frank currently craved. But as with all of Frank's passing fancies: the racehorse he got bored with after six months, the Formula Two racing car he'd funded for a short while, the boat he bought and went out on once before flogging it off, Tony was betting that Grace would soon be shipped back to kangaroo-land with a padded purse and a few trinkets, but little else.

Though while she was here, Tony decided to bide his time. Rivals were not to be tolerated for long in his world. He had conjured up the scenario about what would happen with Frank's new 'daughter' living in the house. There could be no more weekend-long, coke-fuelled shagathons in the hot tub with Grace around and Frank had always been an enthusiastic orgiast. Tony knew Frank well enough to recognise any signs of a growing need to scratch that other more carnal itch. And it would happen eventually, Tony assured himself. Then there were the salty longings of Frank's various acquaintances who expected stimulating perks in return for their continued cooperation. Tony always found it amusing to see a photo of one of these guys in the local rag; smart suit and hatchet-faced wife on his arm, being feted by the local branch of the Women's Institute or some such do-goodery, when two nights earlier that same bloke had been at the house doing the dirty with a lady of the night,

Tony was only too aware that if Frank wanted to retain his notoriously unfair business advantage in this burg, he'd have to keep those tacky treats coming. Not to mention the Old Bill turning a blind eye to other non-construction-based activities, just so long as they got to partake in the occasional dipping of the beak – and the wick – in the goodies. But none of that would be possible with Grace in the picture. Although Tony decided to keep those thoughts to himself until the time was right to express them candidly, to play it crafty until Frank's enamouredness with his new toy wore off.

Tony watched the curvy, jeans-clad blonde climb out of the Bentley and found it hard to suppress a smirk. *I give it three months max before you are out of here, lady. I'll lay money on it.* But as he watched Grace being graciously offered Frank's arm as they walked towards the house, Tony acknowledged that what he was feeling was not purely business. It was also deeply personal.

CHAPTER NINE

All three sat around the dinner table and Frank was full of bonhomie, not to mention bottles of Australian red purchased especially, he had declared, to help Grace 'feel at home'. She chose beer instead and Tony had water. Frank took another slug of the wine only he had been knocking back all evening, filled up again, raised his glass as a toast and held both his guests in his full-beam smile.

'To cousins,' he announced and produced a theatrical hic that old-time comics did when portraying drunks.

'Always be wary of a man who drinks too much,' Ma always told Grace. 'But,' and she'd wag a bony finger; 'never trust a man who doesn't drink at all. They have a depth of darkness inside them they are fearful to release and don't want anyone to see.'

That was one of Ma's homespun homilies that rang in Grace's head as she glanced across at Tony sipping his fizzy water. She'd recognised him immediately as the bloke Frank had sent to Oz to check her out. He had the same dark hair and the pallid skin, but the buttoned-down suit could not have been more of a contrast to the Manchester United T-shirt clad, cheeky northerner façade he'd presented at the gift shop way back in November. Had that been an act and was the real Tony the hard man persona he currently inhabited or vice versa? Either way, as with so much of this happy families charade, she decided to keep a close watch on developments and be careful not to let her guard down.

She was feeling reasonably comfortable up until the out-of-the-blue revelation that she and Tony were related.

'Cousins, you say?' she queried.

'My sister Maggie died suddenly when Tony was just nine years old,' Frank began. 'And I tried to keep an eye on him but what with me living here and them being in the East End of London, it was a bit difficult, see. Anyway, he had nobody after his dad got into an altercation with some immigrant and found himself knifed to death.'

Frank was tucking into a roast chicken leg and waving it about as he told the tale. Grace almost expected him to chuck it over his shoulder like some cliché of Henry VIII. The housekeeper – who was the neatly uniformed wife of the chauffeur and apparently referred to only as 'Mrs John' – was hovering discreetly in the background while waiting to clear the table since both Tony and Grace had finished eating ten minutes earlier, Tony having eaten only the vegetables, which would be yet another black mark in Ma's book of the 'not to be trusted'. Grace imagined Frank's imperious throw of the chicken leg followed by a skilful flying goalie catch by Mrs J. That image kept her amused as the family saga dragged on. In truth, she was too tired to even begin to weigh up the implications of what she'd let herself in for.

'How old was you then, Tone?' Frank asked.

'Eighteen,' Tony replied curtly, and Grace sensed his discomfort with his life being laid on the line in front of some stranger, supposed cousin or not.

'So, you took him in,' she suggested in order to hurry the thing along.

Frank nodded his head. 'And he's been my right-hand man ever since, eh, son?'

Tony's face was set, although his eye twitched slightly at the word 'son'.

'After we made sure that murdering towelhead got his just deserts, eh, Tony?' Frank chuckled and winked in Tony's direction.

It was quite clear to Grace what was being intimated, but she slapped on an innocent look. 'So, he's in prison? The man who killed your father?' she asked Tony directly.

He stared across at her and she noticed his lip curl slightly. 'Dead,' he said in a tone as nailed down as a coffin lid.

She left it at that.

***

Her room was at the top of the house – 'the penthouse suite' Frank called it. It had a private stairway that could be accessed from a door beside the third-floor staircase or, Frank told her, from the side entrance beside the driveway. The 'suite' took up the whole of the fourth floor and had once been servants' quarters. 'Six tiny little rooms, more like cubicles really. Disgusting the way people treated their staff in them days,' Frank said.

Which made Grace wonder about Frank's own staff, John and his Mrs, who were all uniformed up as though to denote their place in the social hierarchy of the house. Who did that anymore? Was Frank the self-made man trying to prove himself worthy of the money he'd made? Was that Frank's Achilles heel?

The man himself was busy pointing to where the en-suite bathroom and walk-in dressing room now stood. 'That was a storage area.' He glanced across at the white leather super-king-sized bed. 'I can have that changed, if it's too spacious for you.'

His manner suggested he thought her presence was to be some kind of permanent arrangement, so she simply said, 'It's fine.'

'So long as you're sure,' he said. 'I want you to be comfortable.'

Tony had carried her baggage up the four flights of stairs and he dumped it beside the walk-in wardrobe. He peered into the wardrobe with its dozens of shelves, multitude of drawers, and acres of hanging space then looked pointedly down at the small suitcase by his feet. 'Can I get you a few more hangers?'

Grace wondered just what was behind his mocking grin. Was he taking the piss out of Frank's excesses or her modest lifestyle? 'I travel light,' she said.

Frank laughed. 'I've got a lady friend who runs an independent boutique in Chester, she'll see you right if you need anything.'

They left her to survey her new domain. The bathroom was an eye-opener; apart from the usual loo and bidet, it had a spa bath that could probably have seated four people and a shower cubicle for two or more. With that and the enormous bed, she wondered if this place had once doubled as Frank's playroom. Not a thought to be savoured.

On two opposite walls of the suite were several small sash windows that gave views out of the front and rear of the house. On one side it was pitch black with no sign of lights from any neighbouring properties, but the other looked across the vast garden leading down from the front entrance towards what could have been a river or canal in the distance. A shrouded moon stuttered its sickly light, painting everything in a monochrome glaze. At the bottom of the garden she could glimpse the outline of a summerhouse or folly. A dim light escaped from within to cast a rather ghostly glow across the swathe of grass surrounding the building and emphasise a white pathway made of oddly shaped stepping-stones leading towards it, like a giant cat's paw prints across the lawn.

Overcome with traveller's fatigue, she made a mental note to explore outside in the morning, then shed her clothes and collapsed into the all-enveloping haven of the bed.

Grace awoke with a start minutes or maybe hours later – it was hard to tell. Perhaps it was the dream-disturbing distant sounds of raised voices, but whatever it was made her get up, wander over to one of the windows and peer out into the darkness. At first, in her half-awakedness she wasn't too sure what she was seeing. The door of the summerhouse must have been open because a much brighter light emanated from within and one figure emerged. She suspected it to be Frank as she thought she detected a limp. What followed was someone of a larger build who moved with an odd shuffling motion. Behind the shuffler, a third person switched off the light and the whole scene disappeared from view. Grace blinked into the blackness of night beyond the window and momentarily wondered if she was actually still asleep and dreaming. That was when a torch was switched on down there and it picked out a pathway for the slow-moving group, the limp, the shuffle, and the swagger.

Sensing this to be something she was not supposed to witness, she thought perhaps to turn away. Instead she kept watching as that weird procession made its way along the catspaw pathway, guided by just one jittery light that flitted like a firefly ahead of them.

As they drew closer, the limping man broke away from the group and began to move directly towards the house. That was when what Grace assumed to be automatic lights on the house walls illuminated the scene. She saw Frank walk out of her sightline, but her eyes remained on the shuffling man and she shivered as cold apprehension enveloped her. The bulky figure looked like some nightmare out of Guantanamo, hooded, hands cuffed in front of him with a chain attached to what she couldn't see but could only imagine to be shackles around his ankles which would explain his hobbled gait. Under the glare of the almost blinding security lights, Tony was just as visible as he held a gun on his prisoner, prodding him in the back to get him to move forward towards what Grace couldn't see but presumed to be a vehicle parked out front. As she gazed down at them, transfixed, Tony's head jerked upwards, away from the hooded man and towards the house, perhaps instinctively aware that he was being watched. He moved his head slowly from left to right as though scanning the windows of the fourth floor. Grace ducked away and when she finally dared to look out once more, the lights had turned off and there was no sign of life.

CHAPTER TEN

Breakfast was 'taken', as the posh-voiced Mrs John termed it, in a conservatory that had been built onto the far side of original house as an extension to the second lounge. The glass walls gave a partial view of the garden that led down to what Grace could now clearly see to be a canal at the far end. The summerhouse wasn't visible from that angle.

'Sleep okay?' Frank asked as she was escorted in by Mrs John and saw him tucking into his plate of bacon and eggs.

'Out like a light,' she lied, walking towards the potted palms beside which she spotted a long table containing a variety of day-beginning foodstuffs.

'It'll take you a couple of days to get over the jet lag,' Frank said. 'I can't stand long-haul flights myself.'

'First class made it easier.' Grace sat down opposite him at the refectory table.

'That all you're having?' Frank stared at her bowl of cereal and fruit with mock shock on his face.

'Travel light, eat light.'

'Well, you don't take after me or your mother there, then. Celia ate like a bird.' He chuckled. 'As in twice her body weight every day. And she still kept that spectacular figure.' He patted his slight paunch and laughed. 'Just like me, you notice.'

'Nature or nurture,' Grace said. 'Great minds have been puzzling over that conundrum for centuries.'

'Yeah,' Frank agreed. 'Your eating habits must be that skinny sister's influence.'

'I thought you said you'd never met Martha?'

He smiled at her benignly. 'Oh, you're sharp you are. Never miss a trick, do you? I like that.' He gave a snorting laugh. 'Nope, I never met your mother's sister, but Tony described her when he did his little trip to check you out.'

Just the sound of his name gave her a sinking feeling in her gut combined with a flashback to the events of the previous night. The sneer of contempt on Tony's face as he prodded the hooded man forward and the way he'd suddenly stopped in his tracks and looked up to scan the fourth-floor windows for any sign of her presence.

'Thought you might like to take a butchers at Chester today,' Frank said. 'I love history, do you?'

'Yes,' she agreed, and was reminded of an old boyfriend of hers who got all full of himself just before he escaped bush life for uni in Sydney. She recalled proudly telling him that history had been her favourite subject in school and his chortle of derision as he dismissed her with: yeah, that's what all losers say. She'd kicked him out on his jumped-up arse and he never dared contact her again.

'Well, Chester's the place to go,' Frank went on. 'Lots of history there, all the way back to the Romans. It's got some magnificent old buildings. We'll have lunch at the Bear and Billet Inn. Genuine Tudor that is. John Lennon's granny was born there in 1800 and something, you know.' He gave her a sideways glance. 'You do know who John Lennon was, don't you?'

'I was raised in Australia, Frank, not on the bloody moon.'

He snorted his amusement. 'Anyway, we'll go and see my lady friend with the clothes shop, pick out a nice party frock for you.' He grinned at her. 'How about it?'

Party frock? The words resurrected an image in Grace's mind, a flashback to a blood-soaked frilly pink dress, to holding little Vikki's gradually cooling hand in hers. To counter the sudden and almost crippling inner pain that memory caused her, Grace reached for anger towards the man sitting in front of her. *He wants to buy me a party frock! What the fuck does he think I am, ten or something?* 'And precisely what would I need one of those for?'

'For a party.' He beamed. 'Tomorrow night. Here, to meet my friends and colleagues. I want to show off my little girl.'

'I'd rather not.' Too far, too soon, just too bloody much all round.

'Oh, come on, Gracie. Do this one little thing for me,' Frank cajoled. 'Let me buy you some nice things. It's the least I can do. No obligation or commitment on your part whatsoever, so what's the harm in it?'

Sure though she was that the guy from the summerhouse hadn't been chained up for refusing a party frock, what she'd seen the night before made her very wary of her seemingly avuncular 'father'. She was convinced that his mood could turn on a coin. On consideration, perhaps it was best to jolly him along until she could do a flit.

'Fine,' she agreed. 'Why not?'

The mobile phone next to his now-empty plate buzzed like a demented bee and he tutted his irritation before glancing at the caller ID. His expression darkened. 'Sorry,' he said, 'I have to take this.' He stood and limped towards the glass door that opened onto an outer terrace. 'What now?' he asked the caller. He opened the door as he listened to the response and, just before he closed it behind him, Grace heard him say, 'No more fucking excuses. You get it sorted. Today. You hear me?'

Grace slowly ate her cereal and fruit while feigning disinterest and merely glancing at him as he furiously paced the outer decking, his face gradually turning a deep shade of beetroot. When he finally ended the call, he stood for a moment and took a couple of deep breaths, as though composing himself, before he came back.

'I'm sorry, Gracie, but I can't go to Chester with you,' he said as he rushed by. 'I'll get John to take you, he knows where to go. And you tell Zoe to put anything you want on my tab, okay?'

Grace sipped her coffee until she heard a car start and the splatter of gravel on the driveway as he sped off. With no sign of Mrs John and left to her own devices, she decided to take a look at the summerhouse. It was cold outside, but she reckoned a swift walk down there would warm her up and allow a quick and wholly innocent-seeming nose inside. She made her way along the cat's-paw stepping-stones, and came to the building. The door was wide open and there was John, dressed in boots, heavy overalls and wearing one of those masks that mechanics use when spray-painting cars. He was holding a hose, which came from a wheeled cart that, at first glance, Grace took to be a lawn mower but then recognised as a high-pressure washer. He looked up from his task as she approached.

'Stay away, Miss,' he warned. 'You can't go in there. I'm fumigating the place.'

'Oh, why's that?' she asked, hoping her expression conveyed the epitome of wide-eyed innocence.

'Rats,' John said with a strange vehemence. 'We've had a nest of rats.'

'Ah.' She indicated to the far end of the garden. 'Do they come up from that canal over there?'

'What?' Even behind the industrial mask, she detected puzzlement in his face.

'The rats. Do they come from the canal?'

He shrugged. 'Must do.'

'So, you have to do this quite often do you? This fumigation? What with the proximity to the canal and all.'

'No, first time, Miss.'

'Okay, I'll leave you to it.' *You bloody liar. You must take me for a fool. Fumigating, my arse. Not with water you're not. You are washing away any nasty remnants from whatever went on in there yesterday.* Grace mentally placed John's name under the not-to-be-trusted column and made her way back to the house.

'Oh, Miss,' he shouted after her. 'I'll be finished here in half an hour and I'll drive you into Chester after that.'

'Cheers!' She waved back at him without turning around.

Back in her room, Grace messaged Ma.

Nothing good happening here. Coming home as soon as I can get away.

It would be seven at night in Perth and Grace knew that Ma would still be working in the shop. She didn't expect a reply for a while, so was surprised when Ma responded straight away.

Stay put, Grace. And delete these messages. Don't ask any questions. Just trust me.

CHAPTER ELEVEN

As the car entered Chester, John drew Grace's attention to some black-and-white, timber-framed buildings. They blew her away. It was like looking into the past and she was left wondering about the many generations whose lives had begun and ended within those walls; whose realities, both personal and political, had been so different to hers.

'That's Stanley Palace,' John said. 'Built in 1591. Supposed to be haunted.' They passed by a cathedral that looked like something out of a Harry Potter movie to Grace but … 'Oh, that's Victorian. Went up around 1839, same time as the new bridge.' John's dismissive tone was that of a patrician and suggested that he thought such things to be modern upstarts in what, he informed Grace, had been the largest northern port during medieval times.

'History your thing, is it?'

'Born and raised here, I was, so it's impossible not to be interested,' he said. 'I did one of those genealogy searches. I can trace my family tree back to the early 1600s, all in and around Chester.'

'Must be nice to know exactly where you belong,' she blurted out before realising that she actually meant it. How wonderful it must be to have roots that go deep into the soil of your homeland. Even when surrounded by the beauty of her part of Australia, Grace had always felt a certain amount of detachment. She assumed that was how all first-generation émigrés felt, not quite at one with the country whose passport they carried.

'Landed gentry we was back then,' John said. 'Knighted and stuff. Come down in the world since them times.'

'The only way is up.' Grace tried to sound cheerful then instantly regretted it when she heard him exude a long sigh. *I suppose doing your boss's dirty work can do that to a man*, she thought.

Morgana's boutique took up the whole of the ground floor of what John described mockingly as mock Tudor, another imposter built during the prosperous Victorian era and therefore to be dismissed out of hand. It still appeared to be pretty old to Grace, but hey, as someone who could only trace her family back as far as Frank Gilligan, she felt in no position to contradict 'Sir' John the chauffeur.

He opened the Bentley's door for her, walked across and tapped on the shop's window. 'Zoe will see to you,' he said. 'I'll go and park the car. Let me know when to come and pick you up again.' He handed her a mobile phone. 'Just press one.'

The shop with its low-beamed ceiling had one other customer, and the young assistant, who seemed to Grace to be a bit too glammed-up for her youthful looks, was attending to her. Both assistant and customer spoke with a slightly nasal singsong accent that Grace assumed to be local. She glanced around the store and noted all the clothes had designer labels, nothing she could ever have afforded in Oz – nor have occasion to wear if truth be told. As she was idly looking for anything that could possibly pass for a party dress, a tall woman approached.

'You must be Grace,' she said in a rather affected voice. She held out her large-ish hand, replete with perfectly manicured, blood-red nails.

Grace shook it.

'I'm Zoe,' she said. 'I own this place, for my sins.'

It was hard to judge just how old she was as Grace assumed that Zoe had had a bit of work done, and also slapped a lot of tut on her face, including the longest false eyelashes Grace had ever seen. She seemed pleasant enough to Grace and appraised her with a professional manner.

'Frank *said* you were a country girl.'

'I run a gift shop outside Perth, with my ...' This was the first time she had referred to Ma since she'd known who she really was and doing so with this stranger caught her unawares. 'Aunt,' she said. 'And we dress casual.' *She thinks I look like some bogan from Woop Woop.*

'Well, let's see what we can do for you. We sell everything here, clothes and accessories.' She cast a quick glance at Grace's trainers. 'And we have a nice range of shoes, too.'

The one dress became three, plus pants, tops, and a warm coat, a pair of leather boots and three pairs of shoes. They were all Zoe's idea and she packed them up in big, shiny black bags with the name *Morgana* in red Gothic print on both sides. She handed the bags over with not a word about payment of any kind.

'Frank's tab?' Grace asked.

She'd been wondering why Frank would have an account with a women's dress shop. He didn't strike her as a trannie so maybe he had a string of ladies he'd treat from time to time.

'He's been good to me,' Zoe said, 'so this is on the house.'

Those words said without one iota of enthusiasm threw Frank's supposed generosity towards Grace into sharp relief. He wasn't paying for her new duds because this lady friend he'd done favours for was dishing them out for free. Do things for people out of kindness, Ma always said. Favours done for repayment always cause resentment. Dismissed by Grace at the time, Ma's words became underlined by Zoe's attitude. And all this made Grace wonder if Frank had any grateful contacts in the travel business too, hence her first-class flights. Maybe that was the way it worked in his world, but it made Grace feel decidedly uncomfortable.

Given her new suspicions, she couldn't face going straight back to the house. She needed time alone, to think. 'Can I leave these bags here? I'd like to take a walk around the town before I go back.'

Zoe looked momentarily alarmed but hid it super-fast. 'Isn't Frank's driver waiting for you?'

'I'm sure he won't mind a rest after all his hard work this morning.'

Zoe looked mildly intrigued.

'Yeah,' Grace said casually. 'He was fumigating the summerhouse.' She placed the bags beside the black marble-topped counter. 'Rats, he said.'

Zoe said nothing but her face paled beneath the ladled-on make-up.

'So, if I can leave these here for a bit.' Grace headed for the door and called back, 'I won't be long.'

As Grace left the store she caught a glimpse of Zoe in a mirror. She was watching Grace leave and reaching for a phone.

As she turned left out of the store, Grace could see an ornate turret clock tower standing out against the pale blue sky and positioned on what looked like a bridge. She headed towards it, passed shops selling all manner of goods and finally got to what the sign told her was East Gate. She stood wondering how to get up onto the arched bridge to take a closer look at the clock and hoping there might be a bench up there where she could sit and think for a while when a hand touched her elbow from behind.

'Hello,' Tony said. 'Not lost, are you?'

Startled, she turned around, momentarily lost her balance and almost fell into oncoming traffic. Tony caught her with a theatrical flourish. 'Careful,' he said. 'We don't want any accidents, do we?'

He took her arm in a manner that could have appeared merely protective had it not been so firm. 'Good thing I ran into you,' he said. 'Frank needs to talk to you before the party tonight. So best you head back now.'

He remained holding her arm as they walked back the way she had come. John was standing facing them up ahead. His intimidating legs-apart stance emphasised his height as he took up more than his fair share of the footpath. He was clearly waiting for Grace to be brought to him. And in that busy Chester street, surrounded by so many passers-by, she had never felt so alone and vulnerable in her life.

CHAPTER TWELVE

When the car entered the drive, Grace spotted Mrs John standing outside the side entrance to the house. As they drove up there, the woman indicated for her husband to stop the Bentley.

John pressed a button to roll down the back-passenger window. 'Mr Gilligan's got a surprise for you,' the housekeeper said flatly. 'We don't want to spoil it, now do we? So, it would probably be appropriate for you to come in this way.' She pointed at the open door to what had once been the servants' entrance. Grace had been told that it led directly to the fourth floor so in days gone by the servants would not be seen to-ing and fro-ing by the rest of the household.

'John will take your purchases to your room,' Mrs John said. 'You can change into something suitable and then come down. Shall we say ten minutes?' And she held the door to the stairway open.

Apart from the bare electric light bulb in the windowless vestibule, this section of the staircase looked as though it hadn't changed much since its original users had trudged their weary way to the top. Grace headed up. After the first three floors, the stairs were carpeted, and all overhead lights shaded. Once she reached there, she felt some small relief for getting back to an indication of modernity.

John had already placed her bags on the giant, white leather bed. As it was still too early for a party of any kind, Grace chose a pair of dark pants and a blue jumper, and reluctantly replaced her trainers with the black wedged-heel court shoes. She brushed her hair and made her way down.

Mrs John was waiting at the foot of the main stairway. 'They're in there,' she said, indicating to what she referred to as the drawing room. Grace had never been too sure where that description came from; did people once have a special room in which to draw? The thought distracted her for a moment before she got to wondering just who were these 'they' Mrs John mentioned.

What greeted her beyond the double doors was what looked like some kind of filming set-up. Two chairs side by side in front of a bookcase. No doubt to give the owner of the house the look of a well-read intellectual. Some hope of that, Grace mused, taking in the scene. There were lights on stands set up and pointing in the direction of the seats. There was a studio-type camera on legs, a guy wearing a headset, and a dark-haired woman with a microphone. And in the midst of this sat Frank, beaming like a lunatic. He looked up as Grace opened the doors. 'There she is; my long-lost daughter.'

The eyes of five people were turned on Grace and a man with a hand-held camera walked towards her. No doubt to get a reaction shot.

From beside the door, a bloke with a distinct likeness to a ferret appeared beside her. He seemed agitated. 'Grace,' he said, 'Could you do that again for me?'

'Do what?'

'Come back in and look, you know, more surprised.'

Grace stood arms folded and stared at Frank across the room. He looked back. 'Come on, Grace, play along.'

She stood her ground. 'I want to talk to you. Outside.'

He sighed and made a big show of getting out of his chair, overplaying the part of the poor crippled father being forced to stand at the behest of his newfound offspring.

Grace opened the doors and stood outside until he appeared. She was steamed.

'What the hell is this, Frank?'

'The local news wants to interview us.' He looked hurt. 'I thought you'd be pleased.'

'I had enough of this shit back home. And I never gave one interview. Not one, Frank. What makes you think I'm going to do that here?'

'It's not about what happened in Australia, Grace. This is a human-interest piece. You know.' He did the air bunnies thing with his fingers. 'Successful local businessman finds his daughter after twenty-five years.'

Bull fucking shit. 'And if I hadn't saved those kids? Would your TV mates still be interested?'

His face hardened. 'It's not always about you, Grace. I'm highly respected here.' He prodded himself in the chest with his thumb for emphasis. 'I'm the story and you ...' He stabbed his index finger in her direction. 'You are just the add-on.' He grabbed her arm and held it hard. 'So, you stop behaving like an ungrateful brat and just cooperate, you hear?' He guided her firmly towards the door. 'And if they do ask you any questions you're not happy with, then you tell them exactly what you've just said to me. I don't want to talk about it.'

He glared at her. 'Simple.' He opened the double doors with a flourish.

'I don't like surprises, Frank.'

'Last one. I promise,' he said from the toothy smile he was presenting to the camera crew.

Aisha Hussein, the young female reporter interviewing them, hardly got a word in edgeways. This was Frank's big moment and he took his time explaining about losing contact with Grace's mother, which was a reasonably plausible twist on the truth, as Grace understood it. He turned towards her, smiled and she could have sworn she saw tears in his eyes. 'I loved her mother so much,' he said. 'And Grace is the living image of her.' He dabbed his eyes with a handkerchief. 'Poor Celia, she died so young and so beautiful.'

Grace felt as though she'd been hit with a sledgehammer. What the hell was this? No more surprises, eh? The lying crock of shit.

71

The reporter nodded her feigned sympathy.

'I didn't know what had happened to Grace until I saw her photograph on the telly. And right off I realised that courageous girl was my long-lost child.'

'You were raised by your aunt, I'm told, Grace,' Aisha said.

'That's right,' Frank butted in. 'She adopted Grace and emigrated to Australia.'

Grace looked at him. What was this farce all in aid of? She didn't see what advantage this gave him but was sure he was up to something.

'So good can come from bad?' Aisha said sweetly, though Grace sensed something lurking behind the comment as the reporter looked her directly in the eye. 'And your bravery in confronting that gunman has brought you back together with your father.' Aisha raised an eyebrow. She was clearly expecting a response.

Grace wanted nothing more to do with this charade, so she just stared at the reporter and there were several moments of empty air between them.

'How does that make you feel, Grace?' Aisha prompted.

'I think she's overwhelmed,' Frank said.

'Are you, Grace?' Her shrewd, dark eyes took in the impassive face. 'Overwhelmed?'

'I am finding this turn of events quite puzzling,' Grace said.

Frank took her hand, lifted it to his face and brushed it lightly with his lips.

'She's my baby girl,' he said to camera. 'And I'll be taking good care of her from now on.'

Aisha's head nodded approvingly but her eyes signalled something else. 'There was quite a lot of controversy caused by the shooting, I believe. Have you anything to say about that, Grace?'

Grace stared her down; this reporter was young, no doubt ambitious, but green as grass. Grace suspected she'd been told not to ask questions like that, but her expression indicated that she was not to be outdone in her attempts to play the hard-nosed journo.

Stone-faced, Grace held the woman in her gaze and shook her head. 'Nothing.'

The flustered ferret-man sprang into view once more. 'That'll do fine,' he said. 'We'll work with what we've got.'

Aisha looked momentarily taken aback. Grace unclipped the microphone from her jumper, stood up and walked out without looking back.

Up in her room, she texted Ma.

This is a complete balls-up. I need to leave.

Hoping for an immediate response she waited but nothing came back. Frank had told of Celia's death in such a throwaway manner that Grace was sure he was lying. *Because if he wasn't, then why not tell me straight off the bat?* she thought. *I don't buy his story of wanting to get to know me, either. He's full of it.*

Her phone made a slight pinging sound. She grabbed it and looked for a message but there was nothing. Frustrated, she walked over to the window that looked down on the car park and garden. The camera crew were loading their stuff into the TV ident van. No wonder Mrs John had instructed her to go in the back way, if Grace had seen that van she'd have bolted. As Frank well knew. *Treacherous toad*, she thought and decided to go back down and confront him.

That was it. Next off, she'd pack her stuff, find her own way back to Liverpool airport and get on the next plane home. *Screw Ma and her cloak-and-dagger messages*, Grace fumed, *she's not stuck here with people who are such obvious wrong 'uns. She warned me not to come and suddenly she's telling me to stay put. Well, sod that, I'm out of here. But not before I tell Frank exactly what I think of him.*

Frank wasn't in the drawing room but she could hear voices in the sitting room that led to the conservatory and decided to seek him out there.

Just before she opened the door to that room, she heard Tony say,

'What a fuck-up. She came across like some fucking retard.'

Grace stopped dead in her tracks.

'Nah, she came across as someone in control,' Frank replied.

'Read it how you like.' Tony sounded petulant.

'Yeah, I will. But either way, it doesn't matter. I got that TV fairy in my pocket. He'll make sure that her face and mine is on local telly tonight, and it'll go out on YouTube, Facething and Twatter. It's all sorted.'

'Why are you doing this, Frank?' Tony sounded incredulous and Grace pricked up her ears. *Yeah, Frank what's going on?*

'Why are you drawing all this attention to yourself?' Tony asked. 'You've got a good thing going here and you're putting it in jeopardy. For what? To impress *her*? I don't fucking get it.'

'You know, the trouble with you, Tony, is you talk when you should listen.'

'I'll listen, Frank. If you'll tell me what the fuck is going on here.'

'Patience, Tony, my boy, all will be revealed.'

'Fuck you, Frank. Tell me or I walk.'

The handle turned on the door and Grace backed away looking for a way out. To her left was an entrance that led to the conservatory attached to the sitting room. She ducked inside and peeked out.

The door she had been standing beside opened a little wider then was swiftly pulled shut as the conversation continued. Grace slid closer into the conservatory and listened.

'This is between me and another person and it all goes back a long way. So, you just do as you're told, keep your eyes open and button it.'

'And Grace?'

'Keep an eye on her. She is not to leave here without either you or John with her, understand? And not so heavy-fucking-handed next time. Dragging her back from Chester was not a good move. She might be from Nowhereville but she's still her mother's daughter, so she's no fool.'

'And yours too.'

'That as well.'

'You sure of that, Frank?'

'Enough! Get out there and do your fucking job.'

Then there was silence. Grace was about to try to get out of the conservatory before they spotted her, when Tony said, 'She's not dead, is she?'

'Who?'

'Grace's mother?'

Frank chuckled. 'Not yet, Tony, my son. Not yet.'

CHAPTER THIRTEEN

Grace stood with her back hard up against the wall, arms down in front of her and hands pressed together, the stance she had adopted just as she was about to enter the kindergarten and face down Benedetti. But this time her hands were empty; she had no gun to protect her or to fight back with. She stood stock still and listened, too anxious to move in case she made a noise, and praying that neither Frank nor Tony decided to come into the conservatory.

There was a fierce argument going on in her head. *Stay calm, Grace, you need to think this through*, said one side of her brain. *Screw this*, said the other, *grab your plane tickets, money, and passport and get the fuck out of here.*

When she heard Frank and Tony leaving the sitting room, she headed towards the conservatory door that would take her to the outer terrace. Here she was able to escape into the cold February air. Not knowing quite what she intended to do, she began to walk, feeling an overwhelming need to get as far away from that house as possible. With the car park and grounds in front of her, she headed towards the summer house. She had to sit down somewhere quiet and gather her thoughts. The building looked locked up when she got there, so she kept moving onward towards the towpath that ran along the side of the canal. Having never been this far from the house before, she was tempted to look back to see if the darkness that lurked within those walls showed. It didn't. About a hundred metres to her left, she spotted a canal lock with its black gates and decided to walk in that direction. Halfway there was a rustic bench and she sat down, contemplating the water and the fields beyond, as her mind whirred.

On the other side of the canal, a man was casting a fishing rod and it struck Grace just how apt a metaphor that was. She was convinced that Frank was using her as bait to catch Celia. And no matter what she did now, whether she stayed or ran away, it was too late to stop him.

Why should you care? asked her highly tuned sense of self-preservation. *Celia dumped you with her sister and never came back. Go now before Frank pulls you in any deeper.*

But what if Celia falls for this trick and he kills her? I'd feel responsible.

Why should you care? it repeated.

Because she's my mother. I came all this way to find her, not to help this man murder her.

At which point, she saw the tall shape of John heading her way. Sent to hunt for her on Frank's orders, no doubt.

The man opposite hauled a silvery, squirming shape out of the water, untangled the hook from its mouth and placed it in his keep net. And at that moment she made her decision.

***

The red party frock, just a simple sheath dress really, went down a treat with Frank, who paraded Grace around like a prize heifer amongst the couple of dozen of his mates, some with their wives but most solo, who were all glugging champagne and gobbling down canapés.

The proud father and reluctant daughter's tour of the room halted for a moment with a group of four men, aged between thirty and sixty, one of whom – who clearly thought himself the gent of the bunch – kissed Grace's hand.

'Aye oop, Frank, you get them waiters to bring them canapés quick like or Alan's likely to eat her,' one of the others said.

They all guffawed and Grace retrieved her hand.

'Not likely,' said a man with a mop of wild curly grey hair. 'She'd more as like shoot him.'

'I surrender,' chortled the older man, holding his hands aloft.

'Such wit and charm,' Grace said. 'I bet you lot have to fight the ladies off with a big stick.'

'Come on, Grace,' Frank said, as he guided her away. 'Don't be so touchy. It's English humour, you'll get used to it.'

'I'd rather not, thanks.'

Next stop was a couple.

'How did such an ugly mug like you have this princess for a daughter?' said the man with the broken-veined face of a heavy boozer.

His wife gave a thin smile and half-whispered, 'We all think you are so-ooo brave.'

'Really?' Grace said. 'Don't know why. It's not *that* bad a party.'

Frank gripped her arm just a little too tightly while over-roaring with laughter. 'Beautiful and quick. That's my girl.'

He was steering Grace towards the man who, somewhat ostentatiously she thought, was wearing his mayoral chain of office. Who did that at a drinks party?

'Put a fucking sock in it,' Frank hissed in her ear.

Stopping dead in her tracks in the middle of the crowded room, Grace gave Frank a glorious smile strictly for public consumption and said through smiley teeth, 'Screw you, Frank, you don't own me.'

He smiled back with just as phoney a countenance. 'I bought you the clothes you are standing up in.'

'You can have 'em back right this minute if you want.' She reached for the side zip on the dress.

He draped his arm around her, then hugged her and put on what she now recognised as his wheedling voice. 'Look, babe, the mayor is about to make a presentation to me. Can we talk this out later? Just be nice. Just for tonight.'

Grace was running out of fingers to count the lies she'd been told. This sorry excuse for a party wasn't for her, it was for Frank.

The room, buzzing with loud conversation, was called to order by some bloke who looked nine months pregnant while the champagne glasses were refreshed by caterers that skittered about the place like nervy wasps. The old blowhard with the fancy chain rambled on for what, to Grace, seemed like hours about how grateful the community was to Frank Gilligan, what he'd done for the area and blah, blah. Grace stood there in uncomfortable new shoes, and felt like one of those royal guards who suddenly collapse under the strain and faint dead away. Finally, Mr Borealot came to the bit about how pleased everyone was for Frank to have finally found his lovely daughter and there were a few oohs and aahs from the ladies. Frank was presented with a scroll of some kind together with what looked like a tacky golfing trophy, everyone clapped and a snapper from the local rag took their pictures.

'One for the album,' Frank beamed. 'First of many.'

Not on your life, mate, Grace thought.

Needing to get some fresh air and not wanting to draw attention to herself what with Tony lurking in a corner with his fizzy water and taking in the scene, she slipped into the hallway and swiftly nipped through the discreet servants' door that led to the side entrance. Closing the door behind her, she switched on the overhead light, only to find that the door to the outside world was locked, with no sign of a key.

Shit! she thought. *Had I decided to take my own advice, grab my stuff and disappear in the middle of the night this would have been my preferred exit route.*

Tony was waiting for her by the door as she re-entered the hallway.

'Leaving us so soon?' he asked, with one eyebrow raised and an ill-concealed smirk.

'Running away,' she said. 'As you can see I *am* dressed for the part. I only came back for my little spotted hanky on a stick.'

'Smart arse,' he said as he turned his back and walked away.

Back inside the never-ending dreariness that included the odd snide remark disguised as wit, a woman who was almost blotto approached Grace. 'What does it feel like to kill a man?' she slurred.

'Same as fucking one,' Grace retorted. 'Only quicker and less messy.'

Grace wasn't sure if she said those words too loudly or if the drunken woman had drawn the short straw to become the designated questioner and the whole room had been waiting to hear Grace's response. Whatever the reason, silence fell with a resounding thud.

As if from nowhere, Frank appeared by her side, hooting with fake laughter. 'She's so sharp, my girl.'

Grace took a step away from him and addressed the room full people who were already well pissed. 'I don't know what you've all heard or seen but I rid the world of a piece of slime that had just shot his own three-year-old grandchild dead and was about to murder a room full of children. I'm no hero, I just did what had to be done. I have no regrets and no intention of talking about it in detail with anyone. If you don't like that, then tough titty.' She stared down the slack-jawed incomprehension. 'And now I will bid you all goodnight because I'm going to bed.'

As Grace walked back into the hallway, towards the staircase and away from the guests, she heard one of them say, 'What a cold bitch.'

To which his companion replied, 'Well, look who her father is …'

***

Back in her room, Grace checked her phone for anything from Ma. There was one text, but it wasn't from her. The number had been withheld but the message read.

Chester. Tomorrow. 11am. East Gate clock. NOW DELETE THIS.

CHAPTER FOURTEEN

Grace ate breakfast alone the next morning, Frank having left the house early. To be truthful, she was pleased, as a confrontation was not really what she wanted at that time. In fact, she needed his cooperation but it seemed as though that was not on offer.

'I'd like to go into Chester today,' Grace told Mrs John as the woman cleared away the cereal bowl.

'Not possible today,' she said, tartly. 'John's busy.'

'I'll catch a bus.'

'You've missed the first one and there are only two a day.'

'Then call me a taxi.'

'I'll have to ring Mr Gilligan before I do that. But he's in meetings all day and can't be disturbed.'

So that was why John was 'busy', he was chauffeuring his master in the Bentley to impress some bunch of no-hopers like the ones she'd met the night before. 'I have money. I'll pay.'

Mrs John tutted to herself but her tone softened. 'Not many taxis around here during the day, Miss. Why not wait until tomorrow when John's less busy. Much easier all round.'

Frank had accused Grace of being a brat, so she decided to play along with his description and lay it on thick. 'Because I want to go today. And I'll find my own way, thank you.'

She got up and stormed out of the room, complete with suitably brattish flounce.

It was nine-thirty and, back in her cheap jeans and trainers once more, mobile phone, Australian credit card, and fifty quid in notes in the pocket of her new warm coat, Grace headed for the door.

'If you wait an hour or so, I might be able to arrange for someone to take you,' the housekeeper called after Grace. 'Might is not good enough.' She was in character now and not about to back down. Not that she had a clue how she'd get to Chester under her own steam.

Grace walked past the ex-stables that were no doubt full of cars she could have put to good use but had not been offered. A puzzling situation had she not overheard the instructions from Frank that she was not to leave the house unaccompanied. *I guess that mysterious text might be part of the reason*, she decided.

By the time she got to the white gateposts, a familiar car was about to turn in. Tony. He rolled down his window.

'Off out?'

'Chester,' Grace said.

'Where's John?'

'Busy.' She walked around the back of his car to head towards the village.

'You'll be lucky to get there by tonight on foot.' He got out of his car, leaned on the boot and watched her with an air of detached nonchalance that made her want to spew.

She kept walking. 'Yeah, I've heard the spiel,' she called back over her shoulder. 'No buses, no taxis, no cars.' Grace stopped and turned to face him, arms folded. 'Some pissy-arsed third world country you've got here, mate.' She turned on her heel and continued on her way.

'Okay. Stop! If you're that determined, I'll take you.'

Yeah, she thought, *like that's not what you've been sent over here to do*. She could almost hear the panicked phone call from Mrs John to Tony and his instant Pavlovian response. Frank says go, Tony says how far?

Once in the car and heading in the direction of Chester, Tony took his eyes off the road for a moment to scrutinise her. 'So, what's all the rush, then?' As she didn't want him shadowing her when she got to Chester, she had to make this sound good.

Step one. 'I just want to get out of the house.'

'Fair enough,' he said. 'But what's so urgent that couldn't wait till tomorrow?'

Step two. 'I only brought so much underwear with me and I need more.'

'Even so,' he said with his typical sneer. 'There's a washer dryer in the utility room, Mrs John would have washed your panties for you.' Although his tone was meant to be mocking, Grace noticed that he said the word 'panties' with an element of distaste. A slight clue to his nature that she packed away for future reference.

Step three. Always the sucker punch when talking to men. 'Oh, for fuck's sake, Tony,' she said in a manner full of exasperation yet tinged with embarrassment. 'I need to buy some tampons, alright? Want to come with me to do that?'

'No need to go all the way to Chester, there's a chemist shop in the village.'

Oh shit! Think quickly, Grace. 'Oh right. Sell knickers as well, do they?' She had to take back the advantage and brat attack was the best solution. 'Look if you're not going to make good on your offer to take me to Chester, then just let me out me in the village and I'll find my own way.'

'All right,' he said. 'I'll take you.'

You bet your arse you will, mate.

When they got to Chester, Tony dropped her outside Boots the chemist in Eastgate Street. She could see the clock tower from there. Problem was, it was only quarter to eleven and she needed more time. The main car park was just five minutes away, so he'd be back here before she needed to meet up with her mysterious texter.

She leaned into the open driver's window. 'Why don't you come back for me in an hour?' From where she was standing, she could see an M&S store further along the road and indicated towards it. 'I'll be in there. Buying knickers and bras and stuff. Come in and find me.' She guessed that he wouldn't.

'I'll wait outside for you.'

Tampons, knickers, and bras: gets 'em every time.

Grace nosed around inside the chemist until she was sure Tony had gone to park the car, then walked out again with a group of women who were chatting together. They were headed in the direction she wanted to go, so Grace stayed quite close to them for camouflage until they stopped to look in a shop window and she was forced to head off on her own.

When she got to the clock tower perched on the bridge over the road, where Tony had previously intercepted her, she gave a quick look over her shoulder but saw no sign of him.

She was hoping that he was now waiting for her outside M&S, tapping his feet and shivering in the cold or rooting through the lingerie department to find her.

There was a shoe shop by the bridge and Grace pretended to look in there for the few minutes she had left before eleven. The bridge had a small pedestrian access tunnel that traversed the footpath on her side of the road. Sitting on the floor beside it was a homeless person with a woollen watch cap pulled down around the ears and a body encased in a filthy oversized coat. Sticking out from beneath the coat were what looked like basketball boots with holes in the soles. Directly opposite, on the other side of the road stood a Tudor building. Grace thought that it was almost as though this ragged creature had been transported across five centuries with no improvement in their lot. Sympathetic to this person's plight though she was in theory, the stench that arose from that direction was almost enough to make her heave. But she consoled herself by thinking that as soon as whoever she was supposed to be meeting arrived, they could get away from there. In the meantime, she had no choice but to stay put.

A woman walked towards Grace. She was talking on her mobile. If it was Celia she was supposed to be meeting, then this woman looked about the right age. Grace glanced at her hopefully, but the woman just coughed as she walked by the tattered presence that held out a filthy beckoning hand to her. She shook her head at it and hurried on by.

The clock struck eleven, a charmed chiming that roused the bundle of rags who, like a character from a medieval mystery play activated by the sound, half stood and half shuffled towards Grace dragging the smell of piss, shit, and alcohol along with it.

The hand extended towards Grace and a hoarse female voice insisted. 'Give me some money.'

Shaken and trying not to gag, Grace dug in her pocket and came out with a five-pound note.

'Thank you, luvvy,' she croaked loudly as a man in a suit skirted by her and shook his head disapprovingly at Grace.

'She'll only spend it on booze,' he remarked as he hurried by.

'Fuck off, yer cunt!' the bag of rags screeched after him.

A middle-aged man emerged from the shoe shop. 'Get away from here before I call the police,' he shouted at the woman.

'Giz a pair of shoes, mister,' she beseeched as she half-staggered towards him. 'Mine's all fucked up.'

'Don't say I didn't warn you!' He disappeared back inside the safety of his shop, closing the door behind him.

The woman cackled, turned back and grinned at Grace. And at that moment Grace found herself looking into blue eyes that were the mirror of her own staring out from a disgustingly filthy face.

Celia!

CHAPTER FIFTEEN

Gobsmacked, Grace was rooted to the spot. Celia flapped her hands impatiently. 'Come on, Grace, get your arse in gear. That old bastard will have someone following you for sure.'

Was this why Frank couldn't find Celia, Grace wondered, because she'd been living rough? Grace found it hard to imagine just how hard a life that might be.

'Come with me.' Celia turned and hobbled off down the road. 'But not too close,' she instructed. 'Just follow your nose.' And she let out a loud cackle that gave a woman walking by with a dog quite a start. The creature barked, Celia hissed at it like a demented moggy and the woman dragged the pooch away.

'These people shouldn't be allowed to roam the streets,' the dog walker remarked to nobody in particular. A younger woman pushing a baby buggy stopped, stood beside the offended woman and agreed. 'Goodness knows what diseases they carry,' she said. 'They could pass on all manner of horrible things to a small child.'

'There but for fortune,' Grace said as she passed them by.

'Dirty drunks and junkies, the lot of them,' the dog walker shouted after her. Celia had increased her speed and, distracted by the kerfuffle she'd created, Grace almost missed seeing her duck out of sight. She followed after. Where Celia had disappeared to was essentially a narrow alleyway between two buildings, with not enough room for two people to walk by each other. On this overcast February morning, the alley was cast into darkness and when Grace stepped in something slimy and slippery, she shuddered at the thought of what it might be – vomit, dog mess, or worse. As if Celia's stink wasn't enough. Grace had no idea where Celia might be leading her and imagined some sort of cardboard city inhabited by the toothless and inebriated or a Fagin's den hidden deep in the bowels of this otherwise respectable tourist-centric town.

Cutting off even more light from this malodorous alley was a dumpster that had been placed half-hidden at the other end. As Grace approached, it looked as though Celia had opened up the lid. Grace's first thought was, *bloody hell, I hope she hasn't gone diving for her lunch*. But when Grace got to where Celia was standing, it was obvious that she was shoving her coat inside the bin. Underneath the now discarded, oversized covering she was wearing a dark jumper and blue jeans. They both looked remarkably clean and Grace could see Celia bending down to take off the wrecked baseball boots.

'Fucking hell,' Celia said. 'This stench permeates everything.' She chucked the boots in after the coat and closed the bin lid. 'Sorry, Grace, I'll have to open the windows until it dissipates.' She laughed. 'If it ever does.'

'What windows? What's going on?'

'I'll tell you on the way.' She indicated towards a Land Rover parked at the back of the shops they had just walked between.

Grace followed her. 'Where are we going?'

'Anglesey,' Celia said brightly, as she opened the car door, reached for a box of baby wipes and began scrubbing at her face and hands. 'I run a holiday cottages business and a dog rescue centre. You'll love it.'

'But those clothes?'

'Master of disguise, me.' She laughed, and the chortling sound reminded Grace of Ma. 'Though I'm a bit out of practice.'

'You had me fooled.'

'Too true.' Celia held her nose momentarily and snorted her disgust. 'Right now, my dear, there's a homeless woman waltzing around Chester in a black Burberry jacket and pair of green Hunter wellies. She was well chuffed.'

Celia retrieved a pair of casual leather slip-on shoes from behind the driver's seat. Then, almost as though she'd forgotten she was wearing it, she pulled the watch cap off revealing her medium-length blonde hair. 'Jesus,' she said scratching her head. 'I hope that bitch hasn't given me nits.'

'Well, I hope you gave *her* some money.'

Celia raised her eyebrows. 'You're kidding me, right? She'll be straight down the pawnshop with the jacket and boots and will be back wearing some cast-off from Sally Army donations. Did you get a whiff of that coat? It smelt like a brewery and I bet you she drank far more than she spilled.'

'Bit cynical, that,' Grace said.

'Christ, Grace, where the fuck have you been living? In a bloody convent by the sound of it. I've been to Australia and those Aboriginals in the cities are no strangers to the demon drink. Demanding money with menaces, as I recall.'

'Gee, Mom,' Grace said, all mock Yank, 'You've been to Australia and never once came to see me.' She made it sound jokey and throwaway but really meant it. When circumstances forced the issue, Ma had finally confessed that Celia had always known where they lived. At the time, Grace told herself that something must have prevented her mother from travelling. But now Celia was telling Grace that she'd been to Oz, as though it was of no importance.

'Sleeping dogs, Grace.' Her voice took on a far more serious tone. 'You'll understand in the end.'

Grace was more angry than hurt and getting mighty sick of these games. First Frank and now Celia. 'Look,' she said. 'Why don't you go back to Anglesey without me and I'll high tail it back home to Ma and the life I had before. I don't even like this country and I've had enough of this shit.'

Celia's blue eyes darkened and she brushed a stray strand of greying blonde hair out of her face with a newly cleaned hand. 'And you really think that Frank will let that happen, do you? He'll just allow you to go on your merry way, will he?' She stood upright, hands on hips. 'He's using you to get to me and he'll do whatever it takes.' She bent down to slip on some shoes. 'And even if by some miracle you did manage to run away home, I'll tell you straight, you do that and Martha's life won't be worth a light.'

'What reason has Frank got to harm Martha?'

'To punish you, of course. And just because he can.' She climbed into the driver's seat. 'Frank Gilligan is one vicious, evil bastard.' She held Grace in her gaze. 'Please believe me. Your little act of antipodean heroism has fucked it up for all of us and there is no going back. Not now. Not ever.' She patted the seat beside her. 'So just get in the car, like a good girl, and I will attempt to save all our arses.'

***

From Grace's perspective, this bizarre mother-and-child reunion took an even stranger turn as Celia hit the road and they turned onto what the signs indicated was the A55. Grace thought it was just like any highway back home except for the weather and odd place names, although she seemed to recall there was a town called Llandudno somewhere on the East Coast of Australia too and it seemed odd to have never been to the namesake in her own country, yet be passing by the original.

'Who drove you to Chester?' Celia asked. 'Was it John?'

'The chauffeur. You know him?'

Celia let out a cynical chuckle that reminded Grace so much of Ma. 'Chauffeur, gofer and random slaughterer. So the bastard's not dead yet. And what about Annie Bell? She still around?'

'Apart from the woman in the dress shop and wives of Frank's friends, the only woman I've met is the housekeeper they call Mrs John.'

Celia threw back her head and emitted a full-throated laugh. 'Oh, that's fucking priceless. Mrs John!' She turned her head from the road momentarily and Grace was glad it was quick because Celia was driving like a demon on speed. 'What's she look like?'

'Dark hair, slimmish for her age, haughty manner, very proper.'

'Posh?'

'Speaks like an upper-class character out of *Downton Abbey*.'

'Annie.' She laughed again but there was something darker behind it this time. 'Real name Annabel something triple-barrelled. The daughter of a lord. Got kicked out of all the best schools. Daddy cut her loose when he got sick of cleaning up her shit. I met her during my modelling days. Ex-junkie, ex-prostitute, ex bloody anything you can imagine and then some. Bad news, she is.'

'Well, if it is her, she's a housekeeper now.'

'Like hell she is. She'll have something going.' There was silence for a moment as the Land Rover overtook a lumbering Ute. 'Everyone and everything connected to Frank Gilligan is a front for something else.'

'He seems to be just a builder these days,' Grace said, deciding to keep her nightmare vision of the hooded man to herself for now. She had no more reason to trust Celia than to trust Frank. *We may well be related*, she thought, *but right now that means nothing*.

Celia snorted again. 'You've got a lot to learn, girl, so let's start with this piece of advice. Trust no one until they prove to you that they have your back.' She glanced over again. 'Okay?'

'Anyway,' Grace said, 'Tony drove me into Chester because John was busy.'

Celia shook her head. 'Don't know any Tony.'

'Apparently he's my cousin. Frank's sister's son.'

Celia's face paled. 'The kid who burnt the house down with his mother inside? Is that little psychopath out of prison? How old is he now, maybe thirty?'

Grace was stunned. *Blimey. Just when you think things can't get any worse.* 'That's not the story Frank told.'

'Well, he wouldn't, would he? Hello, Grace, meet your loony-tunes relative who roasted his mother and baby sister alive? Some intro that would have been.'

Every instinct had warned Grace that Tony was a bad 'un but had given no indication as to just how bad.

She was still trying to process the information when her phone pinged in her pocket. She took it out and checked it. Nothing. 'It keeps doing that.'

Celia held out her hand. 'Let me see.' Grace handed it over but Celia didn't so much as glance at it; instead she chucked the phone out of her window onto the hard shoulder. 'With any luck some kind truck driver will come along and squash that.'

'What did you do that for?'

'Not saying they *have* hacked your phone to track it,' she said. 'But just in case they did, best be rid, right?'

Grace felt like Alice, stepping through the looking glass into an alien world. And one without anything that might save Grace. Arson, phone hacking, that shackled prisoner, and whatever the reason was for Frank using her to hunt Celia down. 'This isn't my life.' The words were said as much to herself as to Celia. 'This is some kind of nightmare.'

'And if they find us, it will get much, much worse. Shall I put it this way? We don't want cousin Tony turning up in the middle of the night with his little box of matches, now do we?' That laugh again. 'Welcome to the family, Grace.'

CHAPTER SIXTEEN

Tony Boyle switched off the sound on his satnav and listened to the other refined female voice coming through his hands-free phone.

'She's heading west on the A55. Whoever's driving is really gunning it. Probably suspect they're being followed.'

'Could it be Celia?'

'Yes,' she said with her usual crisp superiority. 'From a blip on this map, not only can I tell you the make of car it is, but I can also see inside.' He could almost hear her sneer. 'You stick to being the muscle and leave the technology to me, Tony.'

'No need to get sarky, Annie. But you know Celia and I don't.'

'I can hazard a guess, maybe. Her dearly departed was a getaway driver back in the mists of time, he may have taught her a few tricks. But I can't see jolly old party-girl Celia ensconced in rural Wales, to be honest.'

'Maybe just passing through?'

'Perhaps. Either way, whoever this is may well lead you to your prey. Unless, of course, Grace stole a car and is merely on the run.'

'What? Carjacking or hot wiring? Doesn't seem the type to have those skills.'

'She exterminated that Australian gunman rather efficiently. Who knows what tricks she has up her pretty sleeve. Let's not forget her parentage.'

'You think she is Frank's kid?'

'He believes she is and that's all that should matter to you right now. Find Celia and report back to Frank. That's the job in hand. And Grace is to remain unharmed.'

'I know the order.'

'I'm just reminding you, Tony. It has been known for you to become over-enthusiastic, shall we say.' The conversation was halted abruptly. 'Here we go, they've stopped. Just by the Caernarfon turn-off. Broken down perhaps because I can't see any services sign or anything … Oh, shit. The signal's disappeared.'

'Dead battery maybe?'

'Maybe. In that case we'll be back on when it's recharged. In the meantime, I suggest you head up there and see if you can spot anything.'

Driving along the A55 Tony considered his options. One way or another he had to break Frank's attachment to Grace but straight off killing her wasn't the way. No, he had to come up with another plan. If the bitch had stayed around she'd probably have pissed Frank off all on her own. Frank never put up with lippy women for long. But her doing a disappearing act would not only make Frank want her back all the more, but would also land Tony in a world of pain if he didn't play it right.

His satnav beeped for the turn-off he was looking for and he hit his hazards, slowed right down, and crept towards the hard shoulder. Annie had been right, there was no place to park here and no sign of whatever car was transporting Grace. So it was either a flat battery or … he spotted several bits of what looked like the remains of a mobile phone scattered along the slow lane. Fuck!

***

The suspension bridge over what Celia said was the Menai Straits, shone white as the sun appeared momentarily through glowering clouds while they sped away from the Snowdonia mountain range. Everywhere was lush and green and, for the first time since she'd been away from home, although it was as different as possible from where she'd been raised, Grace was overcome by a sense of belonging.

'How long have you lived around here?' she asked Celia.

'Fifteen years. An old friend used to run the café by the lighthouse. I came here to visit him, fell in love with the place and stayed.'

'Another lover?'

Celia chuckled. 'If you saw Mickey, you'd know just how unlikely that was.' Then her demeanour changed and her tone hardened. 'But you can't see him because he's dead. The cops said it was suicide. Swore blind he'd chucked himself off the cliffs at South Stack.'

Celia recalled going with Mickey's son, Gwynn, to identify the body that had been so smashed up on the rocks it was barely recognisable. She'd had her suspicions about his death back then but, as Gwynn knew little about his father's past, she'd kept her counsel and gone along with the overall decision that Michael Hughes had killed himself. Either way, she'd reckoned at the time, Mickey was dead and kicking up a fuss might have blown her cover and brought a whole world of shit down on her. In her experience, self-preservation was head and shoulders above any skewed concept of justice. Finding closure was for straights; her kind just had to swallow it and move on.

'I knew Mickey from the old days and he was a tough bastard. He'd been in the Welsh Guards when he was young. And soldiers, I tell you, they don't know the meaning of the word pain.'

The way she spoke of him, it was clear to Grace that this Mickey had been a close friend, so she said nothing and just listened.

'He did some hard time once and came back bouncing. And five years ago, when it happened, he was well out of the game by then. He owned a business and was settled nearby his only kid.' She shook her head. 'Suicide. No way.'

'You think he was murdered?'

'Someone got to him. Someone from the past. And it would come as no surprise to find Frank Gilligan's paw prints all over it.'

Bloody hell, Mother, Grace thought, *some father figure you chose for me.*

***

'I'm in a meeting,' Frank said on the other end of the line.

'This won't keep.'

Tony could hear Frank speaking to someone else. 'Gentlemen, I do apologise but I have to take this call.' There was the sound of a door opening and closing, and Frank huffing and puffing as he walked. 'This had better be fucking urgent.'

Five sphincter-clenching minutes later, during which time Tony could imagine Frank's blood pressure hitting volcano level as he attempted not to erupt with a torrent of expletives in what Tony guessed to be a semi-public place, Frank finally spoke.

'Get back to the house and wait for me there.'

'Don't you want me to carry on a bit? Maybe take a look around Caernarfon?'

'Do you know what make of car she went off in? No. Who she was with? No. Where they were headed? No. So don't fuck things up even more than you have already. She knows you and your motor. Which gives you a fair chance of being spotted and spooking Grace even more.'

Tony held his tongue. Grace, Grace, fucking Grace. He was getting well sick of this bollocks.

'I'll send someone from the old days. Someone who would recognise Celia anywhere.'

Tony was stumped by what seemed to him a totally stupid move on Frank's part. 'Send them where? What if they've just stopped off in the town and are heading somewhere else. I'm here, right now. Why lose the momentum?'

'It's too much of a coincidence, this,' Frank said. 'Anglesey's just across the bridge and Mickey lived on Anglesey. Remember him? Owned the caff by the lighthouse.'

'Sure do.' How could he forget? They'd tracked Mickey Hughes down five years ago. He was someone from the old days, Frank had informed Tony. *If anyone has the info I need it'll be him.* Hughes was about sixty, big build and handy. Not an easy nut to crack. Everyone eventually spills their guts under torture, Frank had said, even that hard fucker.

'She's in Ibiza,' Mickey told them just before he pegged it from a heart attack after being water-boarded for hours. Inconvenient, that. But although they ended up with one dead geezer on their hands they'd also got a lead. Not a bad couple of days' work.

Only Mickey had lied. Nine wasted months later, after trawling through every villain and dealer on Ibiza, it was finally established that Celia had never set foot in the place. With Mickey six feet under and no other clues, everything had gone back to normal. It was business as usual with Frank's obsession on the back burner once more, until Grace surfaced and it went charging into overdrive. And now Tony was in the frame for Grace going missing on his watch.

'Just get back to the house,' Frank instructed, curtly. 'I'll deal with this.' He disconnected and that was the end of that.

Tony flicked off his hazard lights, started the engine and decided to take the Caernarfon turn-off anyway.

CHAPTER SEVENTEEN

Tony didn't like Wales. Although he lived just thirty-odd miles away, even his own private sideline had no direct business ties to the country. He had intermediaries who handled the local dealers, so had no reason to visit. Someone with his past had to be careful. He was still out on lifelong licence and, despite Frank's contacts, could be recalled to prison if he was nabbed for being caught up in any naughtiness. On the surface though he was legit and PAYE'd up to the eyeballs like a good little wage slave. Though even Frank's building trade never crossed that invisible Welsh border. 'If you can't speak Welsh, you're fucked,' Frank had always said. 'Plus,' he'd hold up an index finger on each hand to indicate he was about to crack one of his lame jokes, 'the scenery's pretty but the weather's shitty.'

Pretty if you liked sheep and fucking mountains. Tony was vegetarian and he didn't care for mountains either. And as for walled towns, they triggered too many bad memories for comfort: of enclosure in locked wards, the cries in the night behind Victorian walls, the months and years that blurred into one numbly medicated whole. Chester he could just about stomach but Caernarfon with its ancient bricks and looming castle made him jumpy. Not that he'd ever admit any of that to anyone. To show any weakness was to be as good as dead in his game. Either way, he wasn't about to go wandering around within the confines of those crumbling walls searching for Grace. Turning off here was a stupid idea. He'd rather go back and face Frank.

That was when he spotted her. Blonde hair, blue jeans, black coat. And she was alone, walking along the narrow pavement with her back to the traffic. He looked in his rear-view mirror. What traffic? It was just his car and her on a dull, deserted February road. A quick glance at the satnav showed no speed cameras to trap him. *Do it*! his brain screamed. *This is your chance, get rid of her now*! His foot hovered over the accelerator as his pulse quickened. *Go for it*, the voice in his head advised – *fast and furious, mount the pavement, hit and run, dead and gone. Get the bitch*.

It started to rain as the blonde woman stopped by the roadside, apparently about to cross in front of him. Tony hit the accelerator, timing his speed to hit her as she stepped into the road. It was when the woman squinted in his direction to check if the road was clear that the red mist engulfing his mind evaporated and he realised … It wasn't Grace!

He hit the brakes and the car tyres screeched their displeasure as the woman jumped back on the kerb and gave him a vehement V-sign. 'Wanker!' she mouthed at him. Clearly the same word in both English and Welsh.

Shaken by his sudden loss of control, Tony slowed right down, took deep breaths and mentally reached for the coping mechanisms he'd been taught, the ones he'd had to master to be set free. As he was about to turn off the coast road to get back home, he spotted a petrol station. A quick glance at the gauge told him it was in dire need, so he pulled onto the forecourt. He stood filling up the car and feeling a certain relief that he had not allowed his other self full rein. There was a time when he'd have run the woman down anyway, just for the hell of it. Though he'd been sure he had those impulses under control – until today. Still not thinking clearly, just as he was paying, he took out his phone and flashed the picture of Grace he'd taken on the sly at the surly, unshaven bloke at the till. Just on the off chance, like.

'Don't suppose you've seen this girl, have you?'

The guy glanced at the digital image, shook his head and grunted.

Tony took his petrol receipt and left. *Fucking uncouth Welsh*, he thought as he headed back to Chester.

***

Once off the road that was signposted to Holyhead, Celia drove through a small hamlet of elderly but otherwise unremarkable houses. The place appeared deserted, as did the village a few kilometres beyond with its cluster of bungalows and a Methodist church with a stern, scowling façade. Further along the journey, they passed a hillside pathway on which a steepled church stood alone. It was a mournful sight with its boarded-up doors and windows, its graveyard unkempt and overgrown, the surrounding gates closed to an indifferent world and held fast by a rusty padlock on an insubstantial chain.

Where are the people? Grace wondered. She thought it'd been remote in Australia but at least she and Ma had lived close to a highway, a main artery between the city and the ocean. She was confused. After all she'd been taught about her homeland, she was amazed that in what everyone claimed to be an overcrowded British Isles, you could discover such isolation. As they travelled what appeared to be an ever more winding route in virtual but not uncomfortable silence, some of the roads traversed were just wide enough for two cars to pass each other carefully without any wing-mirror jousting, and each appeared to end at a crossroads with a confusion of signs pointing towards unpronounceable place names with a surfeit of consonants. These hamlets were all well hidden from sight down snaking roads, as on this part of the journey Grace didn't spot one building.

'Not much here, is there?' she ventured.

'Says the girl from the middle of nowhere,' Celia snapped back.

Grace was peeved by the response. Just when you started to warm to someone they fucking insulted you. What was that all about? 'I could get into Perth in two hours.'

'Sweetheart, in less than two hours I can drive to Liverpool or be in London by train.'

'What is this, Celia, a contest? I was just making an observation.'

'Sorry,' she said as though the very word might grab her by the throat and choke her. 'I've got a lot on my mind.'

Bloody hell, Grace fumed, *what about me? Dragged across the world under false pretences, lied to, tricked and now being carted off to God knows where by a so-called mother who seems to blame me for blowing her carefully constructed cover. No phone, thanks to Celia's paranoia, passport and airline tickets at Frank's house so no way of getting myself out of this mess. Added to which I have only the clothes I stand up in. On a scale of one to ten, deep shit is not the word for it.*

Steady, Grace, she told herself. *Keep your cool. Right now, you need this woman.* She glanced across at Celia, who turned and gave her a rueful smile.

'Frank has been trying to find me for a long time,' she said. 'Some friends of mine have suffered to protect me. But now he's found you and knows where he can get to Martha, he's upped the ante.'

'Are you going to tell me?'

'Tell you what?'

'Why Frank is so desperate to find you? I mean, who goes to all this trouble for unrequited love?'

'Is that the tale he spun you?' The harshness of her laugh almost rocked the car. 'Unrequited love of money, more like.'

'What?' *Should have guessed it.* 'You owe him money?'

'He reckons I do.'

And just as Grace was wondering how much of a debt would send Frank on a twenty-five-year woman hunt, Celia told her.

'Forty million quid.'

CHAPTER EIGHTEEN

The Land Rover snaked its way up to the top of a hill and Celia stopped outside a white-walled house. With its slate roof it was typical of many of the others they had passed. The building itself was hidden from direct sight but the panorama it afforded was spectacular.

'Wow,' Grace said as she took in the timeless view of the Irish Sea and the wide, empty horseshoe-shaped beach laid out below her.

She was surprised by her own reaction as, despite the cold and the fact it was starting to rain, she no longer yearned so much for the Pacific.

'My mother,' Celia paused momentarily then verbally underlined the comment, 'your grandmother, was born on Anglesey and she lived with her family in this house. Until at the age of fourteen, that is, when she ran off with a good-looking no-mark Scouse conman called Alf Dobbs.'

Having lived for years with Ma's evasions, Grace was taken aback by this honest and up-front revelation. 'Fourteen? And how old was he?'

'Twenty-eight, I think. He'd be arrested these days as some kind of paedophile of course, but back then nobody gave a shit about young poor girls. And, as she was the eldest of seven children her parents were probably glad to have one less mouth to feed.'

'Wow,' Grace said. 'Ma never talked about her family.'

Celia let forth a snorting laugh. 'I bet she didn't. Our mam gave birth to Martha when she was just fifteen years old and she had me when she was seventeen. Our bastard dad never married her, what with him being married to two other women already.'

Blimey, Grace thought, *add child abuse and bigamy to the litany of family doings. Not many more deadly sins left to cover.* So instead what she said was, 'Poor girl.'

'Oh, she did okay,' Celia said. 'Dad was into all sorts of scams but mainly cheque fraud as it was in those days. When we were little we'd have expensive presents one week and no food in the larder the next. It was tough until Mam became a fence.' Celia glanced at Grace to make sure she understood the term. 'Receiving stolen goods.'

'I know what it means.'

'She was very good at it too. That sweet innocent face of hers got her out of all kinds of bother. Any coppers who visited the house looking for Dad never suspected a young woman with two small children to have a lockup full of nicked gear.'

'She sounds very resourceful,' Grace said.

'Oh, she was that alright. As hard as nails, in fact.' Celia gave Grace a look she found hard to decipher. 'You know, I don't recall her ever saying that she loved us.' She paused, deep in thought before continuing. 'I hope that Martha did that for you.'

'Did what?'

'Told you that she loved you.'

'Many times.'

A sad smile crossed Celia's face momentarily. 'Good,' she said, 'I'm glad.'

A small silence descended, before Celia swiftly moved on. 'Our mother did what she had to do, that's all. And we learned to keep quiet about things, so it was hard to make any real friends.'

'I can understand why Martha wanted to forget all that and start afresh,' Grace said.

Celia raised an eyebrow. 'Can you now?' It was a comment heavy with the implication that 'you ain't heard nothing yet'. 'Though it's true that all Martha ever wanted was a respectable job, a good husband, and a baby. As it turned out, two out of three's not bad, I suppose.' Celia unlocked the cottage door. 'Shall we go in? The sea will still be there later on. In fact, you've got a better vantage point from your room.' She scratched at her head. 'And I am in desperate need of a shower, I think I might have picked up a flea or two off that disgusting old hag.'

Grace pulled up the white venetian blinds in the cosy, though sparsely furnished, first-floor bedroom and wondered why anyone would wish to shut out that view. Although the sea mirrored the grey clouds above and the sand on the beach was flat and featureless, it remained a sight to be savoured. She was gazing on a view that her grandmother had seen, her great-grandparents had looked out on. This place was her first concrete link to her past and she was finding it both comforting and disturbing, as Ma's warning echoed back at her; 'Go then, but don't blame me if you don't like what you see.' And Grace wondered what would have happened if Ma had been straight with her all along, told her that they came from a bad lot, would Grace have stayed put in Oz? After all, many of the old Australian families were the descendants of criminals given the option of the hangman's rope or transportation to a penal colony on the far side of the world. Fremantle Prison in WA had been built by the prisoners themselves. Ma was well aware of that too, so Grace found it hard to understand the obvious shame Ma felt. Unless there was more to it? But how much more? She both craved and dreaded that knowledge. No wimping out now though, as she suspected that Celia would let her have the truth with both barrels.

'Are you hungry?' Celia emerged from the bathroom, dressed in a white towelling robe and rubbing at her newly washed hair. 'I don't half fancy a bacon butty for lunch.'

***

They sat at the wooden table in the kitchen and although Grace had a million and one questions to ask, it was Celia who interrogated Grace, mainly about what story Frank had peddled. 'If you want to know the truth, then best start at the beginning,' she said. 'So, let's set the record straight about what you've been told.'

Grace decided to play it Celia's way. 'Frank said you'd had an affair with him while your husband was in prison but instead of going back to him you disappeared. He later heard you'd had a baby and gone back with your husband when he was released.'

Celia nodded. 'Nice story. Half true. As is everything Frank says. Eddie was in prison and I needed a favour from Frank. My end of the bargain being a weekend of sex with the man himself. It was more like a business arrangement.'

'And I'm the end result of this arrangement.' Grace intended an ironic tone, but it came out sounding more like resentful.

'Oh, grow the fuck up, Grace,' Celia scoffed. 'You're healthy, intelligent and beautiful. That's more than most people get out of being dragged screaming into this world. Be grateful for that, because everything else is just over-romanticised bullshit.'

She had a point, Grace reckoned. Life is messy and you can't go out to find the truth and then be upset when it doesn't fit in with your imaginings. 'Must have been one hell of a favour he did you.'

'That's what I mean about romanticised bullshit. Martha's 'respectable'' 'husband beat the hell out of her when she was pregnant.'

Celia recalled walking into the hospital and seeing her sister. From across the room she looked normal. The bastard had been careful not to mark her face. But her body was black and blue.

'It was an accident,' Martha insisted.

Denial. Celia recognised the signs of the victim of an abusive relationship. 'He kicked you in the stomach and threw you down the stairs, Martha.'

'He didn't mean it.'

The news that not only had Martha lost the baby she was carrying but she could not have any more, left Martha traumatised and Celia raging.

'I realised there was nothing I could do about it,' Celia told Grace. 'But I knew a man who could.'

'So, you went to see Frank,' Grace said. 'For what? Retribution? To have Martha's husband beaten up?'

Celia threw Grace a look of astonished derision. 'What? And turn him into a martyr? Have him crawl back to stupid Martha all battered and bruised? She'd have taken him back and the cycle of abuse would start all over again. No way was I allowing that.'

'So what favour did Frank do for you? Scare the life out of the bloke maybe? Give him some money to move on?'

'Let's put it this way, shall we? The foundations of some Frank-constructed houses contain more than concrete.'

It took Grace a moment to take in what was being said. Then the proverbial penny clanged into place. 'You had Martha's husband killed?'

'A life for a life,' Celia said with a shrug. 'He murdered Martha's baby. He deserved to die.'

Like Benedetti, Grace thought. Benedetti deserved to die. Didn't he? She recalled her own stone-cold response to seeing his body lying at her feet and wondered if it was all just a matter of degree. 'And Frank did that for you?'

'That's what Frank does, Grace. He has people killed. They leave the building and are never heard from again.' She gave a hollow laugh. 'In the old days Frank was known as The Magician. Now you see 'em …'

Grace had a sudden flashback to the man in chains she'd seen shuffling across the lawn at Frank's house. She wondered what he had done to displease and if he was now languishing in the foundations of a newly built house.

'Anyway,' Celia said, as she gobbled down her last morsel of bacon butty, 'I reckon Martha's old man got off lightly. He was dead when he went into those foundations. If it had been up to me, I'd have trussed the bastard up and poured the concrete on him while he was still alive.'

***

'What tracking devices?' Frank looked at Annie askance.

'You might have trusted Numbnuts to keep her on a tight leash,' Annie said. 'But not me.'

'So apart from the bug in the phone, where else?'

'There's one in the heel of her shoe.' Annie smiled broadly as she sat opposite Frank in his home office. Now that Grace had done the off, she'd put her Mrs John uniform back in mothballs and was wearing dark trousers and a long-sleeved T-shirt that hid the track-mark battle scars of her former life.

'Which is fuck all use to me since she left here in her manky old trainers,' Frank growled.

'Keep your wig on, Frank. Belt and braces, you know me.'

Tony, standing in his usual spot at the corner of the room, gave a snort of derision. Smart arse, cow. Always on the clever, clever. 'Stuck up her arse, is it?'

'Sewn into the lining of her brand-new coat.' Annie preened and grinned at Frank. 'You know, the one she was wearing when the Brain of Britain over there mislaid her in Chester.'

Frank laughed and Tony looked down at his shoes. Annie tossed what looked like a remote control with a small screen in Tony's direction, taking him unawares though he managed to catch it before it landed on the floor.

Annie laughed. 'Five thousand feet range on that little beauty.'

'Feet and inches, eh,' Tony sniped. 'How much in pounds, shillings, and pence?'

'It's American-made, Einstein, *they* don't use metric.' Annie gave him the finger. 'Where did you go to school? Oh, yes, it was Broadmoor, wasn't it?'

'Knock it off,' Frank said and he indicated to Tony. 'Give that here.'

Tony handed over the tracking device and Frank examined it. 'What's the lifespan on the bug?'

'Six months, max,' Annie said. Then she turned to Tony. 'You'd better get going, sonny boy. Big island, little bug.'

Tony put his hand out to retrieve the scanner. Frank ignored him, sat back in his leather swivel chair and stared at the device in his hand.

'This techie stuff is all a bit beyond me.' He sat up straight and squared his shoulders. 'I'm gonna give this job to someone else.'

'Why?' Tony was narked. 'I can find …'

Frank held up his hand to silence him. 'No reflection on you, Tone. But I'm gonna send someone who'd recognise Celia a mile off. Someone from the old days. Someone she and Grace might just trust. Someone who would be able to get close enough.'

Frank handed the tracking device back to Annie. 'Think you can teach Zoe how to use this?'

'Sure, piece of cake,' Annie said. 'Even with those fucking awful Vampirella fingernails.'

***

Sixty miles away, Celia was still giving Grace a family history lesson and, as far as Grace was concerned, the news wasn't getting any better. 'Frank knew all about you. He was quite happy for Eddie to play Daddy.'

Grace added lying by omission to the long list of Frank's mortal sins. 'So …?'

'When Eddie got out of the nick, I was working as a croupier and Martha was my live-in nanny. You were almost two when Frank approached us with a deal. It was to be one big job that would set us all up for life.'

This was in line with what Martha had told Grace about the reason for emigrating. 'What went wrong?'

'Nothing at first. Frank had his team and we rounded up three solid guys as muscle. That job went down in history as one of the biggest unsolved heists in Britain,' Celia said with some pride.

'So why aren't you swanning around the world with your ill-gotten gains?' *Instead of hiding out on Anglesey*, she thought, but didn't say.

'It was sweet as a nut at first. Me and Eddie handled the cash, diamonds, and jewellery while Frank was to get rid of the other stuff, antiques, dodgy bonds, drugs, and the rest through his various contacts.'

'But?'

'You're catching on, Grace,' Celia said. 'With Frank, there is always a but. The deal was that after a year, we'd divvy up the money between the seven of us. It all went tits-up when Frank got paranoid and greedy. Two of our crew ended up disappearing off the face of the earth before pay-out time. My gut instinct told me was it was Frank's doing. Eddie organised a meet to try to get the lay of the land, and attempt reasoning with him.'

Celia could remember the last day she saw her husband, even down to the clothes he was wearing, not that it was any stretch. Eddie in his usual uniform of white shirt, blue jeans, and black leather jacket, standing in the departure lounge at Heathrow. 'Say hello to Martha and kiss the baby for me,' he'd shouted to her. He'd been so sure he could make Frank see sense but not convinced enough to want Celia to reveal to him the account names and numbers of the Swiss bank where the money had been deposited. He had enough doubt about both his powers of persuasion and Frank's mental state not to want to know exactly where Celia was headed or even the name she was using on her new passport. The plan was she would stay with Martha and little Grace. Every day she was to phone a particular number in London and let it ring six times. When it was safe to return home, Eddie would pick up but only speak when Celia gave him the password: Mumbles.

'Eddie's instincts were good,' she told Grace. 'But mine are better.'

Making peace with Frank was the obvious and safest option, but Celia's motto had always been 'fuck a guy for love and get to know the man on the surface but fuck him for business and you get to see his soul.' And what she had seen of Frank's inner self while pleasing him had turned her blood to ice. So, she visited Martha and Grace but wouldn't allow any photos to be taken. 'I may have to leave again and I don't want Grace to have anything to remember me by,' she told her sister. After three weeks of allowing that London phone to ring six times with no pick-up, Celia was beginning to despair. But on the Monday of the fourth week it was answered. She was shaken when, instead of the agreed silence, she heard Eddie's voice.

'Run!' was all he said.

'Cunt!' she heard Frank shout. And even before the shot, Celia knew that Eddie had failed to cooperate. Having endured God knows what torture he'd finally promised to entice her back home. But he had warned her instead.

Reeling with shock and with the sound of the gunshot still ringing in her ears, she heard Frank speak. 'That was a warning. Cooperate or the next one goes in his head.'

Celia made an attempt to stay calm. 'Let me talk to Eddie.'

And the last time she spoke to her husband, he repeated that warning, 'Run!'

She heard the click of the gun, the final shot that ended Eddie's life and Frank's voice. 'I'll find you, Celia. If it takes me a fucking lifetime, I'll find you.'

***

Twenty-five years later another phone was ringing. Celia answered it.

'Just thought you should know,' the caller said in Welsh. 'A young dark-haired man came in for petrol today. Paid in cash he did, so I haven't got a name for you. Anyway, he showed me a picture on his phone. And I thought the young woman looked a lot like you, see.'

'What did you tell him, Dai?'

'What do you think. I just shook my head, didn't I. He was not best pleased, like. Anyway, I thought you should know.'

'*Diolch i chi, Dai.*' Celia put the phone down and turned to Grace. 'I was right about your mobile, they were tracking you.'

Grace felt foolish. *All that pinging should have warned me*, she thought. *But why should I have even suspected …? Anyway, too late now.* 'But you threw the phone away,' she said.

'Yeah, but if I know Frank – and I do know Frank – it's only a matter of time before he slots all the clues into place and realises we're on the island.'

'Can't you just give him the money?'

'And he'll just go away, will he?' A wry smile crossed Celia's face as she shook her head. 'No, it's not about money anymore, Grace. It's about the unparalleled principles of the unprincipled. Give him the money and we die anyway.' She paused momentarily. 'At least I do.' She handed her phone to Grace. 'On the other hand, you could possibly save your own sweet arse by ringing your father and telling him where I am. Then, after he makes you watch me die, he might share his booty with you. Or not.' Celia stared Grace down. 'Your choice, sweetheart.'

CHAPTER NINETEEN

Grace looked out on the view that no longer appeared quite so benign even though the sun shone intermittently. She'd cast her die with her mother, although she still had trouble seeing Celia in that light, so she thought of her maybe as an ally. Grace also felt partly responsible for the desperate situation that her own search for truth had landed everyone in, including Ma. So, she tried to set her nagging doubts to one side and concentrate on following wherever Celia chose to lead, given that Celia's instincts and experience had kept her safe for a quarter of a century.

Grace opened the window to get some fresh air and stared down at the beach below. From her vantage point, she spotted two smaller houses further down the hill towards the beach. She presumed these were two of the three holiday cottages Celia had mentioned. Celia had also talked about owning an animal sanctuary and so Grace was surprised that there was no sign of pets, a dog or even a cat, in the internally modernised yet minimally furnished house. 'I don't like clutter,' Celia had said by way of explanation, but Grace wondered if the apparent lack of anything one would call personal in the house was more to do with Celia's mindset. Grace recalled her own rebuke to Tony's sneer when he saw her small suitcase. 'I travel light.' From what she could see Celia *lived* light, as though she could pack up and move on at any time. Twenty-five years of being hunted could probably do that to a person, Grace supposed. Had the forty million pounds been worth it? She tried to imagine what that amount of money looked like; was it in cash money locked away in the vault of that Swiss bank, or in gold bars or diamonds? Whatever it was, Celia didn't come across like someone who had access to that kind of dosh. She seemed more what Ma would have called 'comfortably off'.

'Come on, girl,' Celia called from the bedroom door. 'Stop daydreaming. We've got to get ready.'

'Why don't you just run?' Grace suggested. 'With all your money, you could disappear anywhere in the world.'

Celia leaned in the doorway and shook her head, 'That might have been an option a while ago. But not now. It's not just me anymore, is it? It's you and Martha, too. Three people can't just vanish like that. Not anymore they can't,' she said. 'The world's changed since my day. It's a smaller place than it was. What with everyone being watched from all sides. Plus, there are too many restrictions on travel, too many checks on people. Technology becomes the master and everybody suffers the consequences.'

'For people doing illegal stuff maybe, but not for ordinary law-abiding folk.'

'Oh, that's the way all straights think,' Celia scoffed. 'I've got nothing to hide, me, they say. Not until the rules change, that is. Not until the day dawns when something they do and take for granted, like smoking a cigarette or drinking beer becomes illegal or restricted and they suddenly find themselves stepping outside the law. Think of all those women in the Middle East who walked around in western dress, until the rules changed and are now lumbered with burqas. Legal or illegal. It's like shifting sand and all those CCTV eyes, all those bugs you know nothing about on your mobile phone are tracking your every move.'

'Smoking a crafty Doogan or swigging some beer isn't in the same league as robbing a bank or murder though, is it?'

'No, but you get my drift. It's all a matter of degree. Not to mention geography.'

Grace asked a question but had already guessed the answer. 'So, if we can't get lost, then what can we do?'

Celia's face was set. 'We can fight back.'

***

As Zoe drove across the Menai Bridge, she pondered about the two hundred and seventy-six square miles she had to cover. What with a population of sixty-eight thousand people scattered in towns, villages, and isolated houses all over Anglesey, she was of the opinion that Frank had lost his fucking marbles. He seemed convinced that this tracker thing, with a range of just under a mile, was the way to find Celia. *Why not just give me a sodding divining rod*, Zoe thought, *it would be about as much use.*

Zoe knew that all this malarkey was that Annie's fault; she'd swopped being a hooker addicted to heroin for being a technology junkie and magically turned herself into Frank's go-to techie. Zoe had never liked Annie, what with her posh education and morals of an alley cat. But then Zoe disliked most women. She detested most men come to that but she, Frank, and John went back a long way and loyalty was important to Zoe. Plus, they seemed to accept her, on the surface at least.

Given that Frank had given her this task she reckoned she might as well get on with it, which led to her wondering just where Celia would hide out on this out-of-the-way island. In plain sight maybe, the tourist town of Beaumaris with its castle, or Holyhead – the staging post for the Irish boats – or even that place with all the gogogochs at the end. There were so many small towns on Anglesey that the problem was where to start. Would Celia risk being spotted by chance by someone passing through on holiday? Zoe recalled an IRA man of her acquaintance who hid out on the Isle of Skye and worked in a pub. Then one day, in walked a holidaymaker who also happened to be a copper attached to the anti-terrorist squad. Game over. So maybe a closer-knit community would be preferable from Celia's viewpoint? Or an isolated farmhouse even. At a bit of a loss for where to start the search, Zoe decided to begin close to that big lighthouse where they'd dumped the body of Mickey Hughes five years back.

She remembered that time well. She'd been preparing to go into hospital when Frank rang and asked for one big favour. 'Keep an eye on Tony for me,' he'd said. 'Give him a hand if need be. Tony's hard but, well, you know Mickey, he's stubborn.' Zoe was about to turn Frank down flat when he made a promise. 'Do this for me and I'll see you all right. Whatever you want, it's yours.'

So, she'd got back into the old fighting gear and gone along. *Much good my being there did,* she thought. That mad bastard Tony went too far as usual and Mickey pegged it. What a monumental fuck-up that had been. Still, Frank kept his word and she got her boutique out of the deal, so that was a result.

The tracker was switched on all the way across the main body of Anglesey, but Zoe was not too surprised that there was not so much as a flutter or a blip out of the thing. She crossed a bridge rejoicing in the name of Four Mile when it was so short a little lad could piss across it, and found herself on Holy Island. When she got to South Stack, she parked in the car park, and put the device in the pocket of the stylish green leather jacket she had chosen that morning to go with her black pants, sweater, and green leather boots. On reflection she wondered if walking shoes would have been better but they'd have spoiled the look. And looking good was the most important thing in the world to Zoe.

As she made her way towards the café, it hit home what disturbing memories lurked behind those walls. It was odd but in the past five years Zoe had had less of a stomach for the violence she had witnessed and taken part in during the old days. The unexpected revulsion she felt right at that moment was perhaps because she'd worked with Mickey Hughes a couple of times, or maybe it was the manner of his death. Anyway, she veered away from the café, telling herself that as the tracking device was mighty silent in her pocket this was not the right place to be. She made up her mind to leave rather than think about the spot on the cliffs above the lighthouse where they'd watched Mickey's body getting smashed to bits on the rocks below.

Back in the car, Zoe decided to take the coast road down the east side of the island. *Nothing to lose,* she thought, although the words 'fool's errand' weighed heavy on her mind. But, if searching for Grace and Celia was what Frank wanted her to do, then who was she to argue?

***

'There's a laptop in my office you can use though the Internet connection here is shit,' Celia told Grace. 'The TV's okay although a couple of channels are in Welsh sometimes.'

'Can't I go with you?' Grace asked and even she thought that sounded like something a needy child would say.

'Sorry, I have to see someone and it's probably best he doesn't know you're here for now. He's trustworthy but if anyone spots you in the car with me then … well, word travels faster than a dose of the pox round here.'

'Can I get in touch with Ma? She'll be worried about me.'

'Leave it,' Celia snapped. 'I've already told Martha you're with me. My phone is clean and she's bought herself a new mobile, so that's safe. But I suspect your email is being monitored. It's important you have no more contact with my sister until we're ready.' Celia, clad in wellies, jeans and a big waxed jacket, stopped at the door then turned back momentarily to emphasise her message. 'Got that? No contact.'

'Yes,' Grace replied. 'I've got it.'

***

The tracking device on the passenger seat beside Zoe made a sound like the crackle of an out-of-tune, old-fangled radio; a light flickered for a moment and then went blank once more. She hit the brakes without looking in her rear-view mirror and was hooted at by the tractor she hadn't noticed following behind. As the tractor overtook her at snail's pace, the Farmer Giles lookalike driving it gave her a mouthful of expletives that she didn't understand and then the vehicle chugged off into the distance while blowing out a big black fart of disgust.

Zoe pulled the nearside two wheels onto what passed for a grass verge and stared at the tracker. It remained silent. She got out of the car and walked over to the stone wall on the opposite side of the road. The tracker flickered. The transmitter she was searching for was somewhere over there, which meant she should go towards the sea.

Shimmying over the head-high stone wall held no attraction given the gear she was wearing but she told herself that over there might lurk a big bad bull and she was ill-prepared for that kind of confrontation. Going back wasn't an option either, as the road had been shadowing this wall for a few miles and she didn't recall passing any turn-offs. She got back into her car and looked at the map she'd picked up at a local garage, gauged where she was and noticed a right turn about a hundred yards ahead. According to the map, that road led down to the sea. When she got to the turn-off, it was signposted Porth Dafarch. As she turned right the tracker said nothing, but as this was the only road that might lead to that faint signal she kept going. Half a mile or so along the way the device let out a distinct buzz and the lights lit up like New Year's Eve.

The luck of the Irish, she thought, recalling her previous incarnation and for once it made her smile. Some things never leave you.

***

Grace didn't hear anyone approach the house and the buzz of the doorbell made her jump. Celia hadn't said how long she'd be gone but as it had been an hour or so that she left, Grace wondered if she'd forgotten her keys. But, as she'd not heard the car engine, she cautiously lifted the slat of the venetian blind to see who was at the front door.

The person ringing the bell must have seen the movement because suddenly a long vermillion fingernail was tapping on the window.

'Grace, it's me, Zoe. I've come to warn you. Let me in.'

Grace glanced around the room for something she could use to protect herself. Over by the old-fashioned metal-surround open fireplace that now held just a large vase of dried sunflowers and peacock feathers where the grate once was, she spotted a set of ornamental fire tools that included a wrought-iron poker with a decorative handle and a long, sharp log roller. Just the thing. *Not against a gun, of course, but they won't take me down without a fight,* she thought.

Zoe was ringing the bell again. 'Please, Grace,' she called through the heavy wooden front door. 'I've come all this way just to talk to you. It's important.'

Grace took a deep breath, gripped the handle of the heavy poker with the lethal-looking log roller held outwards and thought about what might happen should she open the door and have Frank or, she shuddered, Tony burst in after Zoe.

'Are you alone?' Grace called to Zoe.

'Yes. I'm on my own. Frank doesn't know I'm here.'

Grace put the bulky safety chain on the door and opened up just enough for Zoe to see that she was armed with a rather deadly implement.

Zoe spotted the poker immediately. 'Christ on a bike, Grace, there's no need for that.'

'Isn't there?'

Zoe held up her hands either in surrender or to prove that she had nothing in them. Grace didn't care which and trusted the gesture even less.

'I come in peace,' Zoe said. 'Let me in so we can talk.'

'And Frank doesn't know you're here?'

'I promise,' Zoe said.

'So how did you find me?'

There was silence for a moment until Grace heard the click of a gun being cocked.

She saw Zoe flinch and heard Celia's voice say, 'Yeah, you go right ahead and tell her. Just exactly how did you find us, Jerry?'

CHAPTER TWENTY

Celia tied Zoe's hands with a pair of old tights and told her to sit on the sofa. She instructed Grace to push the heavy, oblong coffee table hard up against Zoe's green-booted legs. 'Not easy to get up fast from that position,' she explained.

'This is no way to treat someone who's trying to help you,' Zoe said.

Celia stood behind the sofa with the gun muzzle lodged hard against the back of her prisoner's head. 'Fuck you, Jerry, I know you of old.'

'I'm Zoe now, and I've changed. I'm not that person anymore.'

Celia gave a hollow laugh. 'You can say that again. Those female hormones have certainly improved your dress sense.'

'That's a bit insensitive,' Grace blurted out without thinking.

Celia put on the voice people usually use with babies. 'Oh, little Gwacie thinks I'm insensitive.' Then her tone hardened. 'How'd you find us, Jerry?'

'In my car at the top of the lane. There's a tracker.'

'What's sending out the signal?'

'Something that's sewn into Grace's coat.'

'Fuck!'

Zoe handed over the car keys and Celia sent Grace to retrieve the device.

'Have they bugged your car?'

'No. I've told you, they didn't know I was coming, so why should they bother?'

'Who bugged Grace's coat?'

'Annie.'

'Who gave you the tracker?'

'I stole it from Annie's office.'

'And why in God's name would you do that, Jerry? How long have you worked with Frank? Thirty years! And after all this time and all the dirty rotten jobs you've done for him, you suddenly grow a conscience? You're having a giraffe, mate. And you've come to warn us, have you? Of what exactly? That Frank is after us. Well, guess what, we already know that. He's been trying to find me for twenty-five fucking years.'

'You've got to understand, Celia. I'm a different person now. I was really thrown when I first saw Grace. I couldn't believe my eyes. She looks just like you did back then. And I always had a soft spot for you. I've felt guilty for all these years, for a lot of things. But what happened to you was the worst. And I couldn't stand seeing Frank using your own daughter to trap you.'

Celia pushed the muzzle further into Zoe's neck. 'Spare me the bleeding-heart crap, Jerry. It really doesn't suit you.'

Grace returned with the tracker. 'Should I break it?'

Celia held out her hand for the device. 'Short range,' she said. 'Stick it on the table over there and come and hold this gun on him.'

'Her,' Zoe insisted.

Grace took the gun and Celia guided the muzzle to the back of Zoe's neck once more. 'And if it moves, shoot it.'

'You're still as charming as ever, I see,' Zoe sniped.

'And you, my old friend, are barely fucking human.' Celia walked around the sofa until she was the opposite side of the coffee table. She jammed the heavy wood hard against Zoe's shins. 'Remember Ronald Merchant-Jones, do you? Lived in France.' Celia's eyes scrutinised her prey. 'He was a civilian, Jerry. He was harmless and look what you did to him.'

'That wasn't me,' Zoe's voice quavered.

'Bullshit!' The burning anger in Celia's face took Grace by surprise. As she stood holding the gun she wondered if Celia had handed it over to avoid losing control and killing Zoe.

'Cigarette burns all over the poor fucker's body, Jerry. As soon as I read that report in the French newspaper, I knew who'd murdered him. You might as well have signed your name in his blood.'

'It was your fault, Celia.' There was an element of mockery in Zoe's tone. 'You involved the guy by paying him off.'

'I was covering my arse,' Celia said vehemently. 'Mine was the only face he'd set eyes on. Not Mickey's, or Frank's or yours. Mine.'

'You should have killed him.'

'He was just a working stiff, Jerry. One anonymous payoff and that was both of us sorted. I didn't know Frank was about to do us over.'

Zoe let out a very unladylike snort. 'Yeah, you were well and truly fucked by Frank … twice.'

Celia leaned in even closer, her mouth twisted with loathing. 'Even without them, you've still got a lot of balls, Jerry. Here you are, trying to play the comedian with a gun to your head.'

'But Grace is a civilian too, isn't she, Celia? And you know as well as I do that she won't shoot me in the back of the head.'

'I know you had a hand in Eddie's disappearance and probably Mickey's death as well.' Celia glared at Zoe. 'Frank set you up, you know. Like a lamb to the fucking slaughter. And I am more than happy to oblige.'

'You're making a mistake, Celia. I did come to warn you.'

Celia reached back and picked up the poker Grace had put back by the fire grate. In one swift movement, she stood up and swung it hard. The blow landed on Zoe's neck. The sharp log-roller end of the poker became embedded in the flesh. Zoe pulled it out and gush of blood shot out across the sofa. She leapt up, struggling with Celia for control of the poker handle. Grace, taken off guard, and fearful of shooting Celia by mistake, took two steps back to get a proper line on her target. Zoe, bleeding profusely, grabbed the poker and lurched forward at Celia. Making sure that Celia was out of the line of fire, Grace pulled the trigger. *Back of the neck, clean shot,* she thought, as the bullet went straight through Zoe and lodged in the whitewashed stone wall above the fireplace.

Celia jumped back as Zoe collapsed across the coffee table. 'Fuck it,' she said. 'I always liked this settee. I'll have to buy a new one now.'

***

Frank was staring at the screen of Annie's laptop. 'How long has the car been parked up?'

'Half an hour,' Annie said, looking back at the screen. 'There's not much info on the map. Could be a farmhouse. Could be a country pub. You know our Zoe, game girl that she is, she does like a good old drinkie.'

'Not on my fucking time. Get her on the phone. Now!'

'What if this is the place, though,' Annie cautioned. 'Where Celia and Grace are, I mean. You don't want to intrude on their cosy reminiscing now, do you?'

'Mark that address up,' Frank instructed. 'If that is where Celia hangs out, then Zoe will be brown bread already.'

Tony, sitting in his usual corner seat, began to pay attention. 'What do you mean, Zoe'll be dead? How do you know?'

'Because I know Celia. And Celia takes no prisoners. She won't believe that 'I've come to warn you' story for one second.' He looked back at the static blip on the screen. 'So, you get over there, Tone. Find Zoe's car. It'll be getting dark by the time you get there so just scope the place out. No stupid moves.'

'I can handle two women.'

Frank banged his fist on Annie's desk. 'I said, no stupid moves …'

'Hang on a minute,' Annie chipped in. 'False alarm, Zoe's on the move again. Must have been a pub after all.'

CHAPTER TWENTY-ONE

Grace drove Zoe's metallic blue Opel back down the hill, turned left as Celia had told her to do and glanced once more at the written instructions she had taped to the steering wheel. Left here, right there, straight across, veer left, and a jumble of other stuff, which seemed odd seeing as Celia said it would take Grace a mere ten minutes to get there. The hastily penned note was complete with little arrows in the direction she need to take along the short yet un-signposted winding roads, just in case she didn't get the message. All this was written in a scrawl so reminiscent of Ma's almost indecipherable handwriting that it pained Grace to look at it. *Jesus*, she thought, *I'm glad she can't see me now.*

Celia had been so convinced that Zoe's car was bugged, she'd insisted on getting rid of it before they dealt with the corpse that lay leaking blood and brain matter all over the floor.

'What do you suggest we do? Push the car off a cliff?'

Celia gave Grace a look that translated as, 'you're joking, right?' but said, 'We need to get that motor as far away as possible.' And she picked up her phone. 'Gwynn,' she said when it was answered at the other end. 'Can you do me a really big favour?'

Grace was both impressed and disturbed at how quickly and easily the ad-lib tale tripped off Celia's tongue. The porky was all about her needing to get her sick friend's car to a dealer in Dublin as soon as. 'I'll get Grace to bring the car and some money for your fare one-way. Dermot will give you more cash when you get there, then you catch the walk-on ferry back. No credit cards, okay?'

'Why no cards?' Grace asked.

'Credit cards would leave a traceable paper trail straight back to Gwynn. Not a good idea given your cousin's penchant for fireworks. As well as providing proof to anyone who delved deep enough that Jerry here wasn't driving the car.'

Grace bowed to more experienced wisdom and Celia instructed her to fetch a tarpaulin and heavy plastic gardening sacks from the garage.

'I've got to make another call,' Celia said. 'An old contact owns a chop shop just outside Dublin.' She laughed. 'Quite fitting really. Something else Jerry used to own being chopped up and made into something fake.'

When Grace returned with a wheelbarrow full of bags, Celia handed her the car keys and directions.

'Can't I use a satnav?' Grace asked.

'They don't work very well round here,' Celia said, 'You're just as likely to end up in a field of full of cows as where you need to be.'

It seemed that her destination was a pig farm owned by Gwynn Hughes, son of Celia's deceased ex-heist partner Mickey.

'He's an organic farmer,' Celia said, 'So you'll smell the place before you see it.' And she set about stripping Zoe's dead body. 'You stick to my story, understand?' she called after Grace. 'No idle chatter.'

'If he asks, should I tell him I'm your daughter?' Grace said.

'He won't ask any questions. Just give him the money, the directions, and the car keys. Go with him to Holyhead and get a taxi back here.'

'I don't know this address,' Grace said, realising that she'd be unlikely to find her way back again.

Celia tugged at one of Zoe's green boots. 'Tell the driver it's the Celia Williams cottages. He'll know.'

'I thought you didn't want people to see me?' Grace said.

'Oh.' Celia chucked the second green boot across the room. 'I think we've gone way beyond worrying about that, don't you?'

Following the long but accurate instructions to both the letter and the arrows, Grace made it to the farm in a little over ten minutes. By the farm gate she was met by a heavyset man wearing a winter jacket, jeans, and walking boots. He was broad-shouldered, dark-haired and Grace judged him to be around mid-thirties. He opened her car door. 'Shift over, luv,' he said. 'I'll drive.'

And those were the last words he uttered all the way to Holyhead. So Grace followed his lead, figuring it was better to say nothing rather than the wrong thing.

'Here you go,' he said as he dropped her by a taxi rank just outside the train station. Grace handed him an envelope full of money. 'Ta,' he said. 'Tell your mam, I'll call her when I get back.' And he drove away towards the ferry port.

A man of few words, she thought and wondered how Celia commanded such loyalty. If Grace had been asked to drop everything and take off for Ireland on such a flimsy premise, she'd have been brimful of questions. But this Gwynn just quietly got on with it, no questions asked. Or did he simply believe the story he'd been told? He may have been quiet, but he didn't appear to be a dullard as he'd clearly spotted that she was Celia's daughter, so Grace suspected there was more to Gwynn and Celia's relationship than met the eye.

***

Watching the blip on the screen irritated Frank. 'Where's the stupid fuck going?'

'Looks like the Irish ferry to me,' Annie said.

'Ireland? I thought you said the tracker had only a one-mile radius.'

'It has.'

'Maybe Zoe's following a car,' Tony suggested. 'That's probably where they were heading when they got off the A55. To the ferry.'

'Grace flew in via Dublin,' Frank said, 'You sure her plane tickets are still in her room?'

'No, they're not,' Annie said. She waited for Frank's sharp intake of breath and then laughed. 'They're safe in your safe along with her passport. I put them in there just in case she tried to sneak back into the house to retrieve them.'

'You think of everything,' Frank said.

'That's why you keep me, isn't it,' Annie said tartly. 'As well as my acting ability and overall technical wizardry.'

'No use keeping a dog and barking yourself,' Tony said.

Frank took umbrage to the remark and glared at him. 'What the fuck are you saying? That I can't think?'

Annie's face set into a broad grin as Tony backpedalled like mad, holding up his hands in surrender to Frank's ire. 'It was a joke, Frank.'

'Well it wasn't fucking funny, eh, Annie?'

'Tasteless,' Annie said. 'Just like that disgusting aftershave you've got on, Tony.'

'Yeah, son,' Frank laughed. 'Go and wash it off. Tone it down a bit, Tone.'

Tony stormed out of Frank's home office with the sound of their laughter ringing in his head; he felt humiliated and he seethed with anger. He'd make Annie suffer for that and all the other shit she seemed to feel entitled to chuck at him. She was one bitch who was for the fucking chop. He'd do for her good and proper when the time was right. But just for now, he stored her goading insults away to fuel his internal fires.

***

Celia was at the door with money in her hand when the taxi carrying Grace pulled up, and she opened the front door just a little when she handed to money to Grace to pay the driver. '*Diolch, Idris,*' Celia called to him and he waved to her as he drove away.

Once inside the cottage, Grace stared down at the human-shaped parcel on the floor and the pile of clothes neatly stacked beside it. 'That lot's for the incinerator, along with your nice new coat.'

'What about that?' Grace indicated towards the grizzly parcel.

'I was thinking of keeping it in my garden shed and bringing it out every bonfire night. You know, like a Guy Fawkes.'

'That's sick.'

'Help me roll it in this tarpaulin, will you?'

'And then what? Take it to the rubbish dump?'

'I have a secret weapon,' Celia said. 'But we have to get Jerry here down to Trearddur Bay. I've got a small trailer in the garage but it's too short.' Celia wasn't addressing Grace but rather thinking out loud. 'No,' she finally decided. 'We need to get back to Gwynn's farm and borrow his flatbed trailer.'

'He's not there, he's gone to Ireland,'

'Then he'll be none the wiser, will he?'

Grace followed Celia through the next two hours in a daze. While she admired her mother's steely determination and the efficiency with which she dealt with their problem, she kept wondering if Zoe's death had been necessary. Had Zoe come to warn them? Had she been transformed into a different person than the vicious Jerry character Celia had described? If that was the case, then Grace had just killed an innocent human being.

Celia was driving the Land Rover along the same winding roads that Grace had negotiated earlier. 'You look pale,' Celia said. 'If you're going to throw up, then do it out of the window.'

'I'm fine, I was just thinking about Zoe.'

'Oh, come on, Grace, it's not your first.'

'Benedetti deserved it.'

'And so did that piece of shit, believe me.'

'But what if she was telling the truth? What if she was warning us? What if she had changed?'

'What-ifs can get you killed pretty damn fast in my world. Anyway, what's done is done. Get over it. Besides, I stopped believing in redemption a long time ago. Jerry and Zoe were one and the same. It's just the packaging that changed.' The Land Rover stopped at the farm gate. 'Anyway we're here now, so you can stop brooding and get on with the job at hand.'

The farmhouse was in darkness. 'No Mrs Gwynn, then?' Grace said.

'Single,' Celia said as she opened up the barn door and dropped Grace an eyebrows-raised and mocking smile. 'You interested?'

Grace ignored her and backed the vehicle into the barn while Celia coupled up the flatbed trailer and threw on what looked and sounded like heavy-duty chains. 'Okay,' she called. 'Let's go.'

***

Back at the cottage, with darkness descending they womanhandled the tarpaulin-wrapped Zoe onto the trailer.

'Right.' Celia rubbed her hands together in what appeared to Grace to be a gesture of satisfaction. 'We leave before first light. Five should do it, so get some sleep.'

'You don't really think I'll be able to sleep after all this, do you?'

'Then do something useful instead. Try and clean up that mess in the living room. There's bleach and disinfectant in the kitchen.'

Inside the house, Celia headed up for bed.

'What if we're stopped by the police in the morning?' Grace asked.

Celia acted out the scene. 'Nothing unusual going on here, officer, we're just taking stuff down to my boat in Trearddur Bay.' She turned back to Grace. 'Anyway, they don't go patrolling these roads. No point. Nothing ever happens here.'

Just the place to get away with murder then, Grace thought, but didn't say.

***

At that moment, in the spare bedroom of the rented flat above a greengrocer's shop, Tony was lifting weights in his home gym. The phone buzzed, and he wiped the sweat off his hands and answered. It was Frank. It was always Frank.

'Get your arse over to Liverpool airport. Annie's booked you into the Hilton for tonight and you're on the six o'clock flight to Dublin in the morning.'

Yeah, he thought, *good old Tony, cleaning up your mess as usual.* 'Have you got an address for me?'

'Just outside Dublin at the moment but still moving. Hire a car when you get there, Annie'll text you with the final destination when we have it.'

Bitch, Tony fumed, typically her part of the operation was working smoothly with the satnav tracker on Zoe's car still functioning.

'See what the fuck Zoe's up to, will you?' Frank was saying. 'She's either doing this job for me or thrown another fucking wobbly. Maybe gone looking up a few of her old IRA comrades.'

'They'd be in for a bit of a shock,' Tony smirked.

'I was joking. Remind me to tell you the whole story,' Frank said. 'Either way, find out what the fuck's going on. Zoe's mobile keeps switching to voice message.'

Tony was getting a real buzz out of this. *Should have sent me in the first fucking place, shouldn't you? It would all have been done and dusted by now, but no, it's let's send in Zoe. You stupid old prick.* Tony recalled the snide remarks from Annie and the laughter that had followed him out of the room earlier that day. *Not laughing now, eh? Now that it's all gone tits-up.*

'I appreciate this,' Frank said before he rang off.

Tony felt aggrieved by what Frank had obviously thought of as soothing words. *Appreciate, my arse!* Still, he mused, a trip to Dublin would be okay and he'd be there to give Zoe backup if needed. Though deep down he relished the idea of Zoe having gone off on a drunken spree and him having to take her down a peg. He'd get a great deal of pleasure beating seven shades out of that dolled-up pervert, fake tits and all.

CHAPTER TWENTY-TWO

The five a.m., pitch-dark journey's first stop was a lock-up garage in Trearddur Bay. Celia unlocked the roll-up door, disappeared inside and poked about a bit in torchlight. She cursed as she tripped over something when its clang of complaint echoed out of the cave-like building and bounced against the wall of an adjacent house. A dog went off like an automated canine alarm and a neighbouring upstairs light turned on. Grace held her breath as the glow from above filtered down through tight-pulled curtains. She expected someone to come out of their house to find out what was going on at this unearthly hour. At which point Celia emerged dragging a two-man inflatable boat. 'Help me with this,' she hissed. 'We don't want that gabby old nosy parker gawping.'

The dog howled and a voice from the house yelled, 'Shut up, Brac!' The dog growled irritably but gradually quietened down. *Poor creature*, Grace thought, it was only doing its job. In a city its warning may well have been heeded but out here, as Celia had said, nothing ever happened. Even so, she moved slowly and quietly as she helped Celia add the boat to the trailer's cargo. Job done, they clambered back into the Land Rover and headed off to somewhere glorying in the name of Port Diana. As the headlights picked their way down the unlit roads, Grace wondered what their winding journey would look like from a satellite, something reminiscent of a computer game, perhaps.

They rounded what proved to be the final bend and a sandy cove emerged in the moonlight. Grace spotted several sailing craft bobbing at anchor and was overcome by the dreamlike quality of the scene. It seemed so peaceful and she felt a twinge of regret that the innocent tranquillity of this place was being soiled by such a gruesome deed. Though Celia's next remark knocked those romantic imaginings down a peg or two. 'Welsh pirates used to use this bay a few hundred years ago. Right bunch of cutthroats they were by all accounts.'

Ah, Grace thought, *is anything ever what it appears to be on the surface?*

'That's my boat.' Celia pointed to a small yacht with a dark hull, though the actual colour was impossible to detect in the hazy moonlight.

'I don't know anything about boats and sailing,' Grace said.

'Don't need to,' Celia said. 'Just help me get Jerry into the inflatable and I'll do the rest.'

They humped the boat off the trailer and placed it in the water by a jetty. Celia expertly tied the boat's mooring rope to a post and threw in a couple of oars.

'Now what?' Grace asked.

'I sail away, and you go back to the cottage while I make sure that Jerry gets to sleep with the fishes. Just stay put and wait for my call. With any luck I should be back soon after breakfast.'

They dragged Zoe's body off the trailer and huffed and puffed her wrapped corpse into the inflatable.

'What do I do with the trailer?' Grace asked.

Celia considered the question for a moment. 'Can you remember the way back to Gwynn's farm?' She fished a set of keys out of her jacket pocket and threw them to Grace.

Grace caught them. 'Yes, I think so.'

'The big key is for the farm building. So take the trailer back.'

'Will Gwynn be there?'

Celia shrugged. 'Don't know, he might be.'

'What if he asks why we borrowed his trailer?'

'He won't ask.'

'Somewhat lacking in the curiosity department, is he?'

'His father was a villain living under an assumed name and his God-bothering mother always pretended she was the widow of a sea-going saint. When Mickey moved here, he wasn't able to publicly acknowledge Gwynn as his son. That's what life can be like on this island. Behind every closed door lies a hoard of secrets. You grow up in an environment like that, you learn not to ask any awkward questions.'

'Or your questions get sidetracked,' Grace said, recalling Ma's deft diversions.

'Everyone has their reasons,' Celia said, picking up on the implication. 'Let's leave that for another time, shall we?'

'Don't get all defensive. All I meant was that I get what you're talking about,' Grace said. 'But what if Gwynn does ask?'

'I don't know.' Celia sounded peeved. 'Use your imagination. Tell him I needed to use his trailer to load firewood for the cottages. Tell him I had to collect new rigging for the boat. Tell him what you like. Tell him we used it to dispose of a body, for all I care.'

'You don't mean that.'

'Look, it's five-thirty in the morning, I've got to sail single-handed into the middle of the Irish Sea, which is no mean feat by the way. I've got to wrap a corpse in chains and dump it where the tidal currents won't embarrass us by delivering it straight back here tomorrow morning and *you* are hassling *me* about a bloody trailer. Give me a break, Grace.'

'I'm the one on foreign territory here,' Grace sniped back.

'Just because I know how to do this stuff doesn't mean I make a habit of it, you know.'

'How do I know that?'

Celia climbed into the inflatable next to Zoe, cast off and began to row. 'Trust me,' she shouted back to Grace. 'I'm your mother.'

***

Grace got back to the pig farm just after six and was driving towards the barn when the door to the house opened and Gwynn walked out. She stopped the Land Rover as he approached. 'I wondered where that had gone,' he said.

Heart in her mouth she began, 'Celia needed it to …'

Gwynn held up his hand to halt her explanation. 'No need,' he said, patting the side of the vehicle as though it were a horse's flank. 'Back her in and I'll uncouple the trailer.'

She did as he instructed then sat and watched him through the side mirror. He wasn't bad looking with his straight Roman nose, almost black hair that sat in unruly waves, brown eyes, and strong chin. She was torn, wanting to escape from there as fast as she could but finding his unquestioning and seemingly artless trust somehow comforting.

He came around to the open driver's window and leaned on the sill. He gave her a smile that lit up his otherwise rather dour countenance. 'Fancy a cuppa and a bacon butty?'

***

Frank was up at six as was his habit. It dated back to when he was a teenage hod carrier. Back then, he'd have been pacing up and down a draughty building site at this time of the morning, but today he was pacing his office floor. There was something iffy going on, he could feel it in his water. He'd known Jerry Silver for thirty-five years. Back then he'd been a pretty-faced, Belfast lad, going into pubs rattling a collection tin. Which, with Jerry's balls of brass and penchant for violence, almost inevitably escalated to his going into banks with a sawn-off. All in the name of The Cause, you understand. Frank never really knew what Jerry did to piss off his Provo comrades but piss 'em off he did. And what better way to hide from violent Northern Irish gangsters out for your blood than entering the fold of ultra-violent English villains who didn't need no bullshit political 'cause' as a cover. Money, money, money was their religion. No one would have guessed at Jerry's salty longings, though, Frank mused, perhaps the tasteful soft furnishings in Jerry's over-neat flat might have been a bit of a clue. Mickey had wondered on occasion if Jerry had been a bit of a bum-bandit but the truth was that nobody really cared, he was a loyal member of the team who always had your back. Nuff said.

The emergence of Jerry's Zoe persona had been a bit of a shock but, after that wore off, Frank had secretly admired the bravery of the man/woman.

Frank tentatively hit the button on Annie's laptop. He wasn't comfortable with technology. Whenever he touched these devices his fingers felt like sausages to him and he was sure he'd hit the wrong key and fuck it all up. Normally he'd have waited for Annie to arrive at seven-thirty but this morning the pull of knowledge was too strong. The previous night, after seeing that Zoe had disembarked at Dublin then stopped at what appeared to be a small garage just outside the city, Annie had texted the address to Tony then packed up for the night. But something was bugging Frank and he couldn't quite put his finger on it, so he'd been up and down the stairs, in and out of the office and watching the screen off and on all night before finally dropping off at four o'clock. Two hours later, what he was now seeing on the computer screen confirmed to Frank that he had not lost his nose for the fishy stuff. If he was reading this correctly, then right at this minute, Zoe's car was headed north towards Belfast.

Having not slept on it, Frank's alarm bells were ringing off the hook as he tried to work it out. Even if Jerry had believed he would not be recognised in his current Zoe guise, Frank just couldn't get his head around this venturing into enemy territory. Belfast may have changed over the years, but old wounds were still raw with some people. Many of the Provo old guard might well be dead, in prison or have become so-called respectable politicians by now but Belfast remained a potentially dangerous place for anyone on a wanted list. Common sense told Frank that Zoe would have called for backup rather than go there alone. Though, even if Zoe was in hot pursuit, why would someone take Grace to Belfast anyway? All this speculation had Frank convinced that whatever was going on was not kosher. He picked up his phone and it connected after the first ring.

'John?'

There was a moment's sharp intake of breath before John said, 'Yes, boss.'

'Slide Annie's gob off your cock and get your fucking arse down here. And bring the old slapper with you.'

***

Grace had finished tucking into bacon and eggs, cooked to perfection by Gwynn, and was looking across the kitchen table at him as he drank his mug of tea.

'When did you get back?' she asked by way of making some conversation with this monosyllabic character.

'Last ferry back last night.'

'Did it go okay?'

'What?'

'Delivering the car.'

'Seemed fine. Your mam's friend, Dermot, only does car sales now so he'll be passing the Opel on to Belfast.' Gwynn plonked a fat brown envelope on the table. 'Here's the money, less my ferry fare. So just a little over five thousand.'

Grace glanced at the envelope almost expecting it to ooze blood, so felt a certain reluctance in touching it. Even so, there was something strange going on here. Grace knew the real story behind why the car had to be disappeared, but why did Gwynn not appear in the least surprised at how little Dermot had paid for it? A mere five grand, for a car in immaculate condition that was probably worth three times that.

So, although she knew deep down that she should have just been grateful for Gwynn's lack of curiosity, Grace couldn't help but push her luck. 'Was that all?'

'Being sold for spare parts, I was told.'

'I see.' *Maybe*, she thought, *he's either totally unworldly or pig farming dulls the senses.*

They were silent for a while and Grace considered making her escape when Gwynn spoke. 'Must be nice,' he said, 'meeting your mam after all these years, like.'

'It's early days,' Grace said. 'I don't really know her yet.' What she knew of Celia's accomplishments may well be impressive in certain quarters but pretending to be a tramp and being a body-disposal expert wasn't actually CV material.

'Do any of us ever really know anyone?' Gwynn said.

'I'd have thought that living on this island, you'd get to know most people.'

'I think people here are different to others, though. When you live on an island, off an island, the rest of the world can appear a bit alien,' Gwynn said. 'Distance-wise we are closer to Dublin than to Liverpool, and London is like a fabled land to some people, brash and blowsy with inhabitants more concerned with house prices and money than anything that really matters to folk.'

A conversation. Now we're getting somewhere, Grace thought. 'And that is?

'Being happy in your own skin and knowing who you really are, without extra trappings. Hanging expensive, designer clothes off your body doesn't make you any more of a man or a woman. Driving a flashy car is just that; you, driving a flashy car. It's nothing in the scheme of things.'

'You're quite the philosopher, Gwynn.'

'I'm just a farmer,' he said as he stood up to clear the table. 'You can learn a lot from pigs.'

***

John leaned against the door of the office, and Annie slumped in the office chair by the computer wearing a sour look and a pair of wellies because it had been raining so the drive was muddy. She'd been summoned from the flat above the garage *post haste* so was still clad only in a black kimono that barely covered what she referred to as her happy valley. Frank leaned across her shoulder, breathing in her bedroom odour, his index finger tracing the car's slow progress on the blip on the screen in front of her. Annie slapped his hand away. 'Don't! You'll leave finger marks.'

Frank stood back, eyes still glued to the screen and put his hand on her shoulder. 'What do you think, Annie?'

'It's too early in the morning to think but I'll tell you what I know. And that is Zoe wouldn't go back to Belfast in a Sherman tank with the Eighth fucking Army backing her up. Those IRA guys have got long memories. So, whoever is driving that car, it's not Zoe.'

'Let's see what Tony has to say when he gets to Dublin,' Frank said. 'In the meantime.' He turned to John. 'Get the motorbike out and go and check out that first place on Anglesey where Zoe stopped for an hour.'

'Okay, boss,' John said.

'I'll give you the info for the satnav,' Annie said.

'And just in case it turns out not to be a local hostelry,' Frank told him. 'Take a shooter.'

CHAPTER TWENTY-THREE

Tony found the place he was looking for. It was an underwhelming site, with an elderly sign that read, 'Dermot O'Reardon Used Car Specialist' hanging on the wall next to a scruffy one-storey lock-up that had just enough room for two cars, side by side in the entrance. The building stood at the end of a row of terraced Victorian houses that had seen better days, though there was some sign of gentrification going on further along the road, with skips taking up scarce parking spaces and various members of the building trade humping stuff around or swarming up and down scaffolding. There were a couple of *For Sale* signs on the less salubrious buildings and a few shiny new cars parked outside those houses, whose windows sported blinds as opposed to the proliferation of grubby net curtains elsewhere in the street. This burg was on its way up the social ladder whether the old guard liked it or not.

Directly inside the entrance to Mr O'Reardon's place of business was a wooden-framed office with dirt-streaked windows and peeling blue paint. As there was nobody in there, Tony walked straight past. Inside he found what had once been a working garage with all the paraphernalia, from ramps to aged tyres and other bits of mechanics' detritus scattered around, though today, just one old banger stood forlornly in the middle of the grey concrete floor.

'Can I help ya there at all?' called a youthful voice.

Tony turned to see a young lad of about sixteen or so, slouching towards him. He was wearing scruffy jeans and a grubby shirt, and was carrying a broom.

'I was looking to buy a car,' Tony said.

Lesley Welsh

'Is that right?' The lad brightened. 'Then you'd really want to be goin' out to our new place on the tradin' estate.'

Tony decided to keep up his fiction of punterdom for the time being and engage the kid in chat. 'Moving out then?'

'That's right,' the kid said helpfully. 'Me grandda's here these forty years but those new posh bastards want him gone. An eyesore, so they keep sayin'. And they paid money and all for him to get out.'

Friendly enough though the kid was, it wouldn't have been his scintillating company that brought Zoe here. Tony needed to have a conversation with someone more grown-up. 'Is your granddad here? Can I speak to him?'

'He's gone off to Belfast on a bit of business, so he has. But my da's out in the new place if you're lookin' to buy anythin'.'

Tony glanced around. Why would Zoe spend any time at all in this shithole? He'd been told that she came straight here yesterday, and the car was still in situ just before he boarded the plane just two hours ago. So, she'd stayed overnight. But where? 'I'm a bit confused,' Tony told the kid. 'A friend of mine came by here yesterday and recommended this place.'

The boy eyed him suspiciously. 'Yesterday?'

'Drives a blue Opel?'

'Yer man was a Brit like yerself that was drivin' the Opel, or a Welsh guy over from Wales or whatever, sure ye all sounds the same to us.'

Tony tried to keep his calm, sure this little prick was giving him an Irish jig around. 'No. My friend is a woman.'

'Honest, I swear. I'm tellin' ya that whatever he was it was him that was definitely drivin' the Opel. Grandda bought it off him and then he just went off.'

'Cheers.' Tony walked back into the street, took out his phone and hit the speed dial to Frank.

***

Grace was at the back of the cottage in the garden that overlooked some farmland and serried rows of holiday caravans in the far

138

distance. She had the large dustbin-style metal incinerator working full pelt, its chimneyed lid belching out smoke while the sides, pock-marked with ventilation holes, roared and brought to mind the image of a sleeping dragon. She watched the smoke drifting up towards the heavy clouds and hoped it didn't raise any alarm bells amongst the locals.

The covers from the sofa had been some cotton and wool mix so had burned nicely, as had her coat, although whatever had been sewn into it had crackled and popped like a demented breakfast cereal. The blood-soaked rug was rubber-backed and made a terrible stink but that was now just ashes, and all she had left to burn were Zoe's clothes, boots, and wallet. Once it had all been reduced to nothingness, she'd shovel all the ash out of the incinerator and bag it.

Her next plan was to go back into the house and carry on with the clean-up operation. A heavy tapestry that had previously hung on the sitting room wall had been draped over the sofa to hide the bloodstains and although the wooden floors were badly marked, Celia had hidden the stain beneath a kilim rug from her bedroom for the moment, so anyone casually wandering into the cottage would be hard pressed to notice anything amiss. Though, Celia had commented dryly, the whole room would light up like a beacon under police forensics scrutiny. So, she'd warned, they'd best not be drawing any attention to themselves. 'You can end up in jail for killing even the worst of bad guys.' She'd smirked at Grace. 'And what with your reputation …'

Grace had not appreciated the joke.

With what remained of the incinerator's contents now smouldering, she lifted the lid and threw in Zoe's clothing, noting that the smell from the burning of the green leather coat and boots would not be very pleasant. She added a capful of petrol she'd found in a can in the garage to the pile, tossed in a match and swiftly replaced the lid.

A clap of thunder shook the sky and forked lightning cracked across the black clouds that glowered above. *Damn it*, she thought, as she turned around and headed for the back door of the cottage. That was when she heard a man's voice: 'Hello, Grace. So, this is where you've been hiding.'

John! Mind working overtime, Grace went into attack mode. 'What are you doing here?' she asked the tall leather-clad figure. 'Just happened to be passing, were you? Took a wrong turn perhaps to find yourself at the top of a hill with just one house on it?'

She made a dash for the back door as the heavens opened. John followed her.

'Your dad's been worrying about you. Just disappearing like that.'

Once inside, she held the door for him to enter and they stood in the kitchen facing each other with Grace feigning outrage.

'So, Frank sends you to track me down me, does he?'

'He was worried,' John said.

Grace folded her arms and stared him down. 'And exactly how did you find me?'

John shrugged. 'You know me, Grace, I'm just an employee, Frank doesn't tell me anything. He just gave me this address and told me to come here.'

Two days ago, she might well have fallen for that 'just an employee' line but as she recalled Celia's description of the man now standing in front of her, it made her blood turn icy. 'Chauffeur, gofer and random slaughterer.'

***

Tony stood over the young lad sprawled at his feet. The kid's face was a mess; a trolley tyre jack will do that to flesh and bone. In truth, Tony hadn't meant to hit the kid quite that hard but, *what the fuck*, he thought, *the bastard shouldn't have tried to run away. I was only asking him a few questions. Like what the fuck had those IRA cunts done with Zoe.*

'There's no fuckin' way me grandda would be in the IRA. Sure, our family's all Protestants, so we are,' the kid had claimed. 'And it was a Welsh guy driving the Opel, I swear.'

And Tony would have been inclined to believe him, had he not been so cagey about where the car was.

'Are you a guard?' the kid had asked.

'Do I look like a policeman?'

'Then why do you want to know about that fuckin' car?'

'Because it belongs to a friend of mine. She was driving it when she left home and now you are telling me fairy-tales about some Welsh geezer selling her car to your granddad. So, you see, Paddy, something smells bad and it ain't just this rat hole of a place.'

That was when the kid made the mistake of lashing out at Tony with the broom he was carrying. Tony ducked and parried, grabbed it off the kid and, wielding it two-handed like a samurai warrior, jabbed him in the belly with the end. As the kid doubled over in pain, Tony smacked him across the head with the handle so hard that it broke in two. The kid hit the deck, snivelling, 'I don't know fuck-all about any woman, honest, I only saw yer man.'

'Where's the fucking car?' Tony kicked the boy in the ribs. The kid yelled in pain and curled up. Tony kicked him in the head. 'Where's the fucking car?'

'Grandda took it.'

With the lad still curled up, Tony kicked him in the kidneys. 'Where did he take it?'

'I don't know.'

Tony kicked him again. 'I can keep this up all day, Paddy.'

'Belfast,' the kid said. 'Grandda drove up there in it.'

Tony straddled the boy, grabbed him by the hair and pulled his face to his. They were almost nose to nose. 'If this sale was legit, then why not sell the motor here?'

'I don't know,' the boy sobbed through the bloody snot pouring out of his nose, 'he never said nothin' about it.'

Tony punched the boy in the face, then stood up, about to give him another kicking when he spotted the tyre jack close to hand. He grabbed it and brought it down on the lad's face. He heard the crunch, felt the flesh give way and heard the sound of laughter. The little cunt was laughing at him. So he hit him once more. It was only later, when Tony stood up that he realised the boy had been in no fit state to laugh at anyone. And he never would be again.

Tony glanced about to spot the source of the laughter but there was no one around. 'Oh,' he said out loud, 'must've been me.' He chuckled, looked down at the dead boy at his feet. 'Sorry, kid,' he said. 'My mistake.'

***

Grace perched on the sofa while John, biker helmet now off, sat in the chair by what had once been a cosy fireside. He was very calm about the whole thing, laid-back even, while Grace was wondering just how much longer the heavy tapestry would be able to stop Zoe's blood from seeping through from the cushions beneath her. And if John spotted that, he'd know that whatever story Grace told him was pack of lies.

'Look at it from your dad's point of view, Grace,' John was saying. 'You insist on going to Chester, then you disappear. No phone call, nothing. He was frantic.'

'I felt trapped in that house, I needed to get away.'

John frowned. 'One day and you feel trapped?'

'What are you, a Jewish mother?' And she made her decision. She realised that being at this cottage was putting Celia at risk. Maybe going back was the only way out of this situation. 'Look, take me back and I'll explain everything to Frank.'

'Why not tell me?'

Grace stood, and casually looked back at where she'd been sitting. There was a little stain seeping through. She had to get John out of the house. 'Because, John, as you said, you're just an employee.'

'I'll ring your dad to tell him we're on our way.'

The telephone on the table in the corner of the room sounded off and John sat bolt upright. 'You'd better get that.'

Grace picked up.

'Grace,' Celia said, 'I'm back. It went well, God, I'm good. Come and get me.'

'Hello, Dai,' Grace said, sensing John's eyes boring into her back. 'Thanks for the loan of the cottage but my dad's chauffeur has come to get me and I've decided to go back.'

'Stay there, Grace,' Celia's tone was decidedly steely. 'Keep him talking. I'm on my way.'

Grace ended the call and turned back to John. 'Dai's coming to collect the keys from me. So … if we can just wait till he gets here.'

'Cup of tea would be nice,' John said. 'Unless you object to making tea for the servants.'

The door of opportunity opened and Grace walked right in. She took her time brewing tea then invited him to sit by the wooden table in the rustic-style kitchen – anywhere that was well away from the tell-tale sofa.

'I'm sorry I was so rude,' Grace said sweetly. 'You and your wife have been nice to me and you do deserve an explanation.'

And for someone who had spent most of her life telling nothing but the truth, Grace was amazed by how easily the lies fell from her lips. She'd been in Chester, she told John, when a man ran across the street to her. He'd mistakenly thought she was Celia. His name was Dai and he'd known Celia's family years ago. 'They lived in this cottage way back when,' she told John. 'These days it's used for holiday lets in the summer.' Grace continued with her story, building a picture in her mind, creating an alternative universe where this had actually happened. 'When I explained that I'd come all the way from Australia to find my mother, he said he hadn't seen her in twenty-odd years, but he thought I might like to see where the family lived.'

'And you couldn't have phoned your dad to tell him this?' The Jewish mother tone again. *But was he buying it?* she wondered.

'I've lost my phone, I have no idea where it is.' Grace knew it was lying in pieces on a motorway turn-off. But did John?

143

He pulled a sceptical face. 'It's a nice neat story, Grace but I'm sensing an element of bullshit here.' A slightly aggressive tone was followed by what he clearly imagined was the killer punch because there was a faintly visible sneer going on around his thin lips. 'Is this the tale you told Zoe?'

Shit! This was all running out of control. Clearly going back to Frank was not the answer.

Grace slapped a look of surprise on her face. 'Zoe? What's she got to do with this?'

'She came here yesterday.'

Those words were final confirmation that Celia had been right all along. Zoe had been sent by Frank. 'How could Zoe come here? I didn't know where I was going to until Dai brought me.' Grace leaned forward, confronting John across the table. 'What the fuck is going on, John? Zoe, or so you say, tracked me here somehow. And now you. Who next, Tony and the Seventh Cavalry?' Grace stood up. 'Get out, John. Whatever is going on, I don't like it one little bit. And you tell Frank that I'll come back if and when I want to. I'm a free agent. He doesn't own me.'

'I've got to call Frank. See what he wants to do.' John reached into the pocket of his biker jacket.

'Tell him from me to go fuck himself.'

Bang! A gush of cold wet air filled the room as the door that led to the garden was kicked in. Vertical rain rushed in as the wood swung on its hinges to reveal Gwynn standing there with a twelve-gauge shotgun pointed at John.

CHAPTER TWENTY-FOUR

Frank hurled his mobile phone across the room.

Annie did no more than raise an eyebrow. Having heard just Frank's side of the conversation with Tony she'd expected no less. 'What's that stupid little shit done now?'

'He's only gone and killed some little Irish twat.' Frank slumped down in his chair, elbows on desk, head in hands. 'Why do I keep that crazy bastard around?'

Annie leaned back in her chair until it was at the brink of tipping point. 'Because he's your sister's son and you're a sentimental old bugger at heart.'

Frank looked up at her. She was still unwashed and wearing the short kimono that flashed her fanny at him when she moved. 'You know me so well,' he said.

'You need to keep him on a tighter leash, Frank.'

'You've got to admit that he *can* be useful though. Zoe isn't in Ireland as far as he can tell. This kid he totalled told him that some Welsh geezer took the car over on the ferry and sold it in Dublin.'

'Ah. We're back to Wales again.' Annie looked back at her computer screen. 'John should have called you by now if there was anything at that location.'

'Let's give him another half hour.'

Zoe stood, untied the belt of her black kimono and stood facing Frank Gilligan. 'In that case, do you fancy a fuck?'

Gwynn stood in the doorway, shotgun aimed at John's midsection. 'Move away from him, Grace.'

She backed off into the corner of the room.

'Hand out of the pocket, real slow,' Gwynn instructed John.

John gave a twisted smile and withdrew his hand from his pocket. It held a phone. 'Just letting my boss know where I am.'

'Put it on the table.'

John held up his other hand. 'Look, mate, I'm just a driver.'

'That's not what I've heard,' Gwynn said. 'Enforcer for Frank Gilligan, or so they say.'

'Is that right, now? And who's been besmirching my good character?'

'My dad was Mickey Hughes. He told me all about you.'

'Poor Mickey,' John said. 'What a way to go.' He lowered one hand to the table top and pushed the phone across to Grace. She grabbed it.

'Yes, it was bad,' Gwynn said. 'You'll understand why, if you move so much as a muscle, I'll happily blow your head off.'

'Depression,' John said, sardonically. 'It's a killer.'

His attitude seemed rather too cocksure for Grace's liking. She wasn't keen on the way this was panning out.

'Frank Gilligan is the killer,' Gwynn replied.

'Prove it,' John said with a snort of derision. 'In a court of law.'

'Who needs the law when you've got one of these.' Gwynn raised the barrel of the shotgun just a fraction.

'Fucking amateur,' John sneered. 'Shooting rabbits is one thing, but a man! You haven't got the balls.'

Celia stepped out from behind Gwynn. 'Hello, John,' she greeted him.

John paled visibly.

'Anything from John yet?'

Frank looked up from the computer screen he'd been gazing at. He still felt shagged out but Annie had come back into his office, showered, dressed and in full makeup. He smiled at her admiringly; the woman was a minor miracle.

'Nothing,' he said.

She hustled him out of her seat by the computer. 'Move your arse. I'll ping him.'

Frank's face epitomised the word 'baffled'.

Annie sighed. 'That app on his phone?' She had explained this to Frank several times, but it never quite sunk in. 'I make it ping. If he can talk he calls me, if he can't but he's okay he hits the hash key twice. But, if anything iffy's going on he hits it just once.'

'Sounds daft to me,' Frank said. 'What if he's taking a piss and can't reach the phone?'

'Then he'll know I want to talk to him. And he'll call me when he can.'

'What are you, his fucking babysitter? We never had anything like that when I started out.'

'Which is maybe why so many of your old crew are either doing life … or dead,' Annie suggested. 'It's all about discretion and precaution, Frank. Not a concept you are familiar with, I know.'

Frank slumped back down on the chair behind his desk. 'Then ping away, my dear. Don't let me get in the way.'

'As if.' Annie hit the icon on her screen.

'Pointless killing me, Celia.' John was seated in the kitchen, hands on the table top where she could see them, as instructed. 'Frank already knows where you are.'

With Gwynn now inside, his back to the door and shotgun still pointed in John's direction, Grace in the corner with John's phone in her hand, Celia was standing in front of John with a pistol pointed at his head. Grace marvelled at just how unfazed John appeared to be. He may well have been shitting bricks but he sure as hell wasn't showing it.

'Don't think I don't see your logic,' Celia said. 'But I'm tempted to kill you just for old times' sake. Just for all the trouble and heartache you've caused me over the years. I'm sure you understand my dilemma here.'

'I do, Celia, I really do but just think about it for a minute. Enough blood has been shed over this money and where has it got you? Hiding out in Wales.' His face took on a sardonic grin. 'Jesus, Celia, you could have at least chosen the Caribbean.'

Celia was also playing the deadpan game. 'You sound like you have a plan, John,' she said. 'Come on, cough it up.'

'It's as straight up as can be. You give Frank the money. He's getting old, Celia. He's making a new will leaving everything to Grace here. She'll get it all anyway in the end. Don't you think it's time to put a stop to all this grief?'

Grace thought handing the money over sounded like a good idea. After all, hadn't she suggested exactly the same thing herself?

'You must think I've just come up the Mersey on a water biscuit,' Celia scoffed. 'Money or no money, I'm a dead woman. You know it and I know it, so give over.'

The phone in Grace's hand made a pinging noise and she looked down at it.

The sound set in motion events that went by so fast it took Grace's breath away. One second John was seated by the table with Celia threatening to shoot him, the next John leapt to his feet and his right fist hit Celia square in the face, flooring her. He simultaneously kicked at the wooden table and it hurtled in Grace's direction, as she jumped out of the way and spotted John bend to retrieve the gun from an ankle holster secreted beneath his leather pants. He moved fast for such a big man and fired at Gwynn from a crouched position. Gwynn dodged the bullet by diving sideways while he let blast upwards with the shotgun. It took just a split second for John's face to disintegrate, to be transfigured into a horrific mass of blood and exposed bone. Despite which, like a zombie in the making, John's body lurched upright. From his position on the floor, Gwynn fired again, and his target went straight down like a felled tree.

Gwynn lay on his back, panting but still holding the gun, his face a whiter shade of pale. Celia shakily hauled herself to her feet. 'I'm losing my touch,' she said, 'he'd never have got that punch in years ago.'

Grace felt frozen to the spot, her hand clutching at John's mobile phone.

Celia appeared unruffled. 'What a fucking mess!' She looked down at the faceless body slumped by her feet, oozing life. 'Would anyone like to tell me how the hell I get all this blood out of a porous stone floor?'

'Well, your ding-a-ling didn't work,' Frank chided.

'Ping.'

'Ring the fucker.'

'Something's not right,' Annie said.

'Maybe he's had an accident,' Frank suggested.

'What? On that motorbike? I don't think so. He rode in the Isle of Man TT races when he was young.'

'No, he didn't.' Frank chuckled. 'He was banged up in borstal with me. I bet he told you he was from around here too, related to landed gentry or some such.' Frank laughed at the look on Annie's face. 'There's a star in the *Book of Liars* by John's name, my love. All the better to get into the ladies' panties with.'

'No need to bother with all that with me.'

'Old habits die hard,' Frank said.

'Whatever,' Annie said dismissively. 'I'm going to call him.'

The phone in Grace's hand rang and she almost dropped it.

'That'll be Frank,' Celia said.

Gwynn held out his hand. 'Give it here,' he said.

Celia nodded her head and Grace handed the phone to Gwynn.

'Hello?' Gwynn exaggerated his North Walian accent. 'Who's calling?'

Grace held her breath, trying not to look down at the body of John while Celia watched Gwynn.

'Well, madam. This is Sergeant Jones, North Wales Police here. I'm sorry to tell you that there's been an accident. And the gentleman you've just called has died of his injuries.'

Celia had a broad grin on her face as she listened.

'I notice that you withheld your number, madam. Perhaps you'd like to give me your name and that of the deceased as he appears to not have any identification on him.'

There was silence for a moment before Gwynn raised an eyebrow and grinned. 'She's hung up,' he said. 'Bloody rude, these English.'

'I don't fucking believe it!' Frank stormed.

'Neither do I.' Annie was staring blankly at her screen. 'You said John might have had an accident. You must have had a premonition.'

'Premonition, my hairy arse!' Frank exploded. 'I meant, I don't believe what you've been told by this …?'

'Sergeant Jones,' Annie said. She took a deep breath and it was back down to business. 'They can't trace my call but what about the motorbike?'

'Bought in England but with French plates and never registered.'

'And the gun?'

'American, unregistered, clean.'

'If he had form, they could identify him through his fingerprints?'

'Reg Harper died fifteen years ago.'

'Who's Reg Harper?'

'John.' Frank waved his hand as though to say, *I'll fill you in later*. 'Long story.' He glanced at her sideways. 'He didn't give away much during pillow talk, did he?'

'I've never been one for talk.'

'Anyway, I'll bet you that nobody's going to be trying to trace him.'

'Why's that?'

'Because if that was a cop you were talking to, I'll eat your dirty drawers.'

CHAPTER TWENTY-FIVE

The jobs had been assigned. Grace to the clean-up while Celia dismantled the motorbike. 'I've done this before,' she told Grace. 'Eddie taught me. I'm not bad with cars, either.'

The idea was for the motorbike to be thrown away in bits. A similar fate awaited John.

Gwynn's task was disposing of the body. He didn't appear overly concerned about that. 'I worked for Owen the butcher when I first left school,' he said. 'He went bust so I've still got all the saws and knives and that. Comes in handy from time to time on the farm. Pigs'll eat anything.'

No more bacon for me, Grace thought.

'Rest in pieces,' Celia remarked as Gwynn took John away on the back of his trailer.

'Not so much a trailer as a hearse these days,' Grace said.

They walked back to the cottage together.

'How are you dealing with this?' Celia's tone was gentle, concerned even, and it took Grace by surprise.

'I'll be all right,' Grace reassured her. 'It's Gwynn that amazes me. He's taking this very calmly.'

'Yeah, as I expected. He's a practical man. The older he gets the more like his dad he's become. He'll do whatever has to be done.' Celia turned and placed her hand gently on Grace's arm. 'As will you.' She gave the arm a slight squeeze. 'It's in the blood, you know.'

'It's not normal, though, is it?'

'Normal!' Celia looked puzzled. 'What the fuck is that? So-called normal people leave their kids to die in fires while escaping themselves. Have you ever seen the aftermath of accidents, natural disasters or terrorist attacks? The people that come on the telly squawking about their survivors' guilt, expecting everyone to feel sorry for them. Well, don't you believe them for one minute. I'll tell you now that most of *them* are still breathing because they trampled over others to escape. Running like fuck to save their own skin and the devil take the hindmost.'

'What does that prove?'

'I don't know.' Celia chuckled and shrugged. 'Maybe that there's a psychopath lurking in all of us that only emerges when our own life is in danger.'

'Working on base instinct, more like,' Grace suggested. 'Anyway, some people do the most heroic things to save other people. Even sacrificing their own lives.'

Celia snorted her contempt. 'Mugs, the lot of them.'

Here we go again, Grace thought. *That moment when I almost admire her, then she shows her true nature once more and I have to back away.* 'Have you ever thought that this freakish ability to detach is just us?'

'Could be.' Celia's laughter tinkled as she walked away to dismantle John's motorbike. 'And thank God for it.'

I doubt, thought Grace, *that God has anything to do with it.*

Tony's new shoes were pinching his toes something dreadful. Buy in haste, repent at leisure, as his bitch of a mother used to say. He held up a barrier to that memory and tried to breathe slowly. Her little darling son pushed out of the nest when that puking, shitting, screaming baby girl came along. He smiled at his reflection in the airport lounge window: Death is a great leveller.

Did he regret setting the fire that killed his mum and the brat? He recalled his tears of remorse for the shrink whose face had crumpled with concern for the ten-year-old sobbing his little heart out. In truth, getting found out was what he'd been whingeing about. Tony raised his hand to acknowledge his mirror image in the large pane of rain-spattered glass. There he was again. It was the only time this other self became visible. That's how Tony had always lived his life; it was the two of them, him and the twin residing within the same body. Not that he was placing the blame for any of his actions on the inner Tony; it was just that the outer version had learned how to live in the world with other people. Well, he mused, most of the time, anyway.

That kid today was unfortunate, not least because it had meant a trip to that menswear shop for a new shirt, trousers, and shoes. The assistant had given him a funny look when he'd paid for them without trying them on. In fact, she'd given his credit card more than the once over. She'd even had the nerve to register surprise when he knew the pin number. Fuck her, the suspicious old cow.

He'd changed out of his blood-spotted clothes in a cubicle in the men's toilets at a shopping centre. He hated those bogs, was disgusted by how they always stank of stale piss and how the men who used them never washed their hands afterwards. Dirty bastards. He'd never normally set foot in one. But needs must. Once in his new togs, he stuffed his old clothes in the carrier from the other store and dropped that off in the bin outside the McDonald's on the ground floor. Fast food. He loathed that too. Why not buy it and chuck it straight down the bog? Cut out the middleman.

His phone buzzed in his pocket. Frank. Probably about to give him even more earache about the dead kid. Tony turned his phone off. Fuck it. It could wait till he got back to England.

'He's switched his fucking phone off,' Frank fumed.

'He's on a plane,' Annie said. Although reluctant to make excuses for Tony she wasn't about to pour more fuel on the flames of Frank's wrath. When he got mad he was never able to think clearly, it was far too easy for him to go off half-cocked. What was needed now was a cool head. She weighed up all the evidence. Grace insisting on going to Chester so suddenly meant one of two things: either she was the capricious bitch Annie thought she was and therefore too like Celia for her own good, or she'd received a message to meet someone there. But without Grace's phone there was no way for Annie to check on that, though it seemed to her to be the most likely scenario. So … Grace goes to Chester, loses that idiot Tony and ends up in North Wales. Again, there were two possible reasons. Either Celia had contacted her daughter or Grace had been duped into meeting someone who wanted to do damage to Frank. The more Annie thought about the second possibility, the more it appealed. What with the turf war going on between Frank and Martin Evans, Annie had warned Frank against putting the frighteners on Martin's top man. But would he listen to her sound advice? Not for one minute. And all that rough stuff that took place in the summerhouse the other night had only one inevitable result: one bloke disappeared for good and a pissed-off Martin Evans.

The problem with that theory was how would Martin Evans get Grace's phone number? Unless it had been at the party, maybe someone slipped her a note. Annie mistrusted all of those council- and local business-wallahs who passed themselves off as Frank's friends. She knew that, to a man or woman, they'd do anything for a back-hander or a shove further up the greasy pole. And Frank should have been well aware of that too when the very venality of those people was what got them on his side in the first place. She looked across the room at him and wondered if maybe, just maybe, he'd started to believe his own fairy tales and thought that these people actually were his best mates.

Her thoughts went back to Martin Evans. He'd know that Frank would send someone after Grace and what better way to pick off Frank's allies one at a time? First Zoe and, on reflection, Annie wasn't buying John's accident story either. So was it Evans's cohorts or Celia in that hidey-hole on Anglesey? Either way, Annie knew that she'd have to persuade Frank to get in some heavies from Liverpool or Manchester to go there *en masse*. That was the only way forward. Mob-handed, guns blazing and put an end to this farce once and for all.

CHAPTER TWENTY-SIX

'I t's not safe here anymore,' Gwynn was saying. 'There's plenty of room at my house. Best you both come and stay with me until we decide how to handle this.'

Grace felt relieved. She was desperate to get out of a place that felt more like a slaughterhouse than the home where her grandparents had lived out their quiet, if child-ridden and impoverished, lives. 'I agree,' she said, not sure if Celia would concur. 'But you'd better talk to Celia when she gets back.'

With the motorbike now stripped down to its component parts and Celia's plan to distribute those bits amongst several scrap metal dealers from Colwyn Bay to Rhyl now in play, Celia had gone off with the parts leaving Grace alone in the house. Trying not to think about the gravity of the situation she found herself in, she had gone upstairs to her room overlooking the bay to watch the sun go down over the sea. There was a timeless beauty to this island that she sensed held fast all the secrets of the ages, the extraordinary and the mundane. This evening, the clouds that lurked above the setting sun suddenly appeared lined with gold while a molten pathway stretched out from horizon to darkened beach, as though inviting the viewer to take its lead from today into tomorrow. Grace was watching, entranced, as the fiery globe slipped silently away like a metaphor of her own lost imaginings. Why had she come here, why had she answered the siren call of those emails? Had it been the mere curiosity that she claimed for herself or had she been searching for a mother's love? Grace had to admit that Ma had done her best but there had always been an emotional distance between them, an invisible wall that all the hugs and lessons in self-preservation could not dissolve. Grace wondered if she had always been aware that there was something missing from her life. Not just a father figure but maybe the image of a woman that her two-year-old self subconsciously recalled. And what an image, she thought. Strong to the point of being hard-bitten and as cold as a marble statue. Ma may have been somewhat emotionally stunted … but Celia! Had the life she led wounded her so deeply that she felt nothing beyond her apparent iron will to survive? But, if she felt nothing at all for her lost child, then why would she leave herself open to discovery after all these years in hiding, in order to protect her?

A noise jolted Grace from her thoughts as Gwynn's Land Rover drove up to the house. She didn't want to think about exactly what he'd been doing back at his pig farm, but she knew that meat would be off her menu for quite a while to come. Nevertheless, she was glad to have company.

Once inside, Gwynn helped himself to some of Celia's whisky and Grace noted the clink of bottle on glass as his hand shook slightly. It was the only sign of nerves he had displayed ever since he'd kicked in the door with a shotgun in his hands and stood facing down John. And she wondered if even to someone apparently so calmly sure of himself as Gwynn, chopping up a human for pig food had been more than a step too far.

'Everything go okay?' she asked in as nonchalant a tone as she could muster.

'You do what you have to, don't you,' he said. 'No choice.'

'Not an easy task, though.'

Gwynn glugged down one glass of whisky then poured himself another. 'We've got it soft these days,' he said, ambling over to a chair and sitting down. 'My granddad was in the Welsh Guards during the war. He was evacuated from Dunkirk and saw two of his cousins die there, one drowned and the other shot to pieces. Later, the Guards liberated Brussels from the Germans. Granddad saw things and did things that he'd never even talk about.'

'That was war.'

'Just because some government says it's your duty to kill or be killed, that makes it okay, does it? People put on a uniform, they fight, some die and the winning side dishes out the medals. All neat and tidy, like. Heroes on one side, villains on the other.'

'What's happening here isn't war. This is different.'

'When my dad was murdered by Frank Gilligan's crew, we had no comeback. They made it look like suicide so the police didn't bother looking any further. Those bastards who killed him walked away laughing. And now Gilligan sends that John to find and kill Celia.' Gwynn threw back the last of his drink. 'If that's not a war, then I don't know what is.'

'He is so pissed off with you,' Annie said as Tony walked into the office.

'Now what?'

'You turned your phone off.'

'Battery ran out.'

'Bullshit!'

Tony sighed. 'Look, I just didn't need the earache, alright? That kid … Well, it was just one of those things.'

'Nobody gives a flying fuck about some kid, Tony,' Annie said, then looked him right in the eyes. 'Unless you left a paper trail that will lead the *Garda* all the way back here, of course.'

'You booked the ticket and the car on the cloned card, didn't you, and I used my Paul Jones passport and driving licence, so why worry?'

'No dabs on anything, including the car?'

'What d'you think I am, a fucking amateur?'

Annie's eyes narrowed as she gave him the once over. 'New clothes?'

Fuck! he thought, *the credit card.* He'd had to use his real one. What he should have done was draw cash on it and paid for the clothes that way. That would have been the smart thing to do. But what was done was done. No need to confess to yet another mistake if he didn't have to. So what he said was, 'Nah. Took a change of clothes with me, didn't I. You know, just in case.' *Anyway*, he thought, *who's going to link me buying clothes in a shopping mall to some kid beaten to death five miles away?*

'Sure I saw yer man,' the building contractor from number four told the policeman going door to door. 'Didn't get a right look at him but he was drivin' a Shadow Blue metallic VW Polo, so he was. I bought me missus one of them once. Yer man had one with one of them hired car stickers inside the back window.'

'Thank you for your assistance,' the young uniformed *Garda* said.

'Did the lad's da not tell ya?'

'I wasn't aware that his father was here at the time,' the cop said.

'No, he wasn't but I told him about the car meself after he came around askin'.'

The young *Garda* hurried away keen to get back to the station and break the news to his superiors. Despite his being a Prod, it was common knowledge that young lad's grandda was connected to the Provos. And though all that sectarian violence was way before his time, the young copper realised that the last thing the *Garda* wanted was for some kind of revenge malarkey to kick off.

CHAPTER TWENTY-SEVEN

Mick O'Reardon drove into the car park of the car hire firm he did so much business with. Selling on ex-rentals was a good earner. Last time he'd been here he'd had Brendan with him, teaching him the tricks of the trade, like, passing on his wisdom from father to son as it were. No more of that now, or ever again. Mick had left his wife crying her heart out at home, but if there was one thing he'd learned from his own father, Dermot, it was that grief lasts a lifetime but those who cause it are fleet of foot. His dad's mantra during the Troubles had been, tears will keep, get the bastards first, then mourn your dead.

After delivering that iffy car, Dermot had stayed overnight with friends in Belfast and didn't yet know of his grandson's brutal murder. That's not the kind of news you break over the phone to an old man with a dickey ticker, the missus had said. And she was right.

Mick locked his car and walked over to the little office that stood in the middle of the serried rows of rentals like a cosy oasis in Dublin's shitty weather. Pat was inside, as was his charmless assistant, Maeve. She grunted when she saw Mick, but Pat stood up from behind his desk in hail-fellow-well-met greeting. He started off grinning but soon stopped when he saw the cast of Mick's face.

'Need a favour,' Mick said and indicated towards Maeve. 'Private.'

Once Maeve had been cast out and told to grab a fag or nine, Mick watched impassionedly as Pat's face paled at the story of poor young Brendan's death.

'You sure the guy hired the car here?' he said.

'Building contractor saw your sticker in the back window of it.'

Pat's hand trembled slightly as he activated his computer screen. Mick was okay to deal with but the old man was another kettle of poison altogether. 'Dark blue VW Polo, you say.'

'The eyewitness says,' Mick said pointedly.

'Yeah, yeah. Here we are. We rented out two of them yesterday. One's still out but the other is back in. First one to a young couple and the other one to a fella. Someone called Paul Jones. He brought it back to us here the same day.'

'You got a copy of his licence?'

'Sure.' Pat rifled through his files. 'There ya are.'

Mick looked at the face of the man who had stoved his son's head in, swallowed hard and forced himself to think straight. 'Credit card?'

'Booked online by a …' Pat stared at the screen for what appeared to Mick to be far too long as his mouth slowly dropped open. 'Feck! There's a red flag gone up on that card. It's a fecking sham, so it is. Someone called M Bhabra from Leicester booked the car in the name of Paul Jones and the payment went through yesterday morning. And now look at it. It's another of those effin' clone things. I'm never ever gin' to see me effin' money for that.'

'You'll forgive me if I'm less than sympathetic,' Mick said.

Pat blanched. 'I didn't mean …'

Mick raised a hand. 'It's fine. No sweat.' He looked down at the address on the copy of Paul Jones's driving licence. 'I'm guessing this is fake as well.'

'I'm sorry I couldn't be more of a help, Mick. I hope they get the bastard.'

As he got up to leave, Mick threw Pat a hard look. 'When the guards come to sniffing around, I haven't been here, right.'

'Right ya are, Mick.'

Mick nodded in the direction of Maeve shivering on the doorstep. 'And that goes for misery tits out there too.'

'Sure enough. Whatever ya say, say nothin'. Right? That'll be Maeve. She's sound.'

Mick got back into his car and watched as the disgruntled and shivering Maeve shuffled back into the office. He'd have this Paul Jones character checked out but reckoned they'd draw a blank on the London address on the licence. So now he had no choice but to pull in a favour from his da's cop friends. He had to keep one step ahead of the investigation if he was to take his own revenge for Brendan. A life for a life, just as it should be.

Grace awoke in a room without a view of anything but a cobbled yard, and the distinct aroma of pig shit lingering in the cold air outside. Celia was sleeping somewhere along the landing of this unmodernised farmhouse while no doubt Gwynn had been up and working since before the crack of dawn.

The house was rather large for a man alone and Gwynn was clearly not one for ornamentation or even much into housework, if the old furniture stacked in the corner of her 'guest room' was anything to go by. Ma would have raised a cynical eyebrow and remarked sourly that 'this place is in desperate need of a woman's touch'. Or even a makeover by Frank's renovation outfit, Grace mused. Though the dark irony of the unwanted redecoration of Celia's cottage with the blood, guts, and brain matter of Frank's minions suddenly made her laugh. Grace brought herself up short and felt a twinge of remorse for the callous thought. What sort of person laughs about the deaths of others? Those who are at war, Gwynn would no doubt have suggested.

A noise to her right startled Grace, and there was Celia. She had this unnerving habit of sneaking up and standing in doorways, like the dishevelled ghost of some local tart.

'Get your arse out of bed,' Celia said. 'We've got to get our heads together and come up with a plan of action.' She turned away towards the stairs. 'Can't hide out here forever like some kind of old-time outlaw gang,' she called over her shoulder. 'There'll be a fucking posse on its way.' And she was gone.

'You drive over to Brum in a mini-van,' Frank instructed Tony. 'Pick up some of Vin's guys from Handsworth Wood. They're a pretty handy bunch.'

'Bit conspicuous, don't you think?' Tony said. 'Bunch of black lads with accents like Lenny-bleeding-Henry swanning around Anglesey.'

'Nobody will be swanning anywhere,' Frank said. 'We'll go in there early hours of tomorrow. In and out, and see what's what. Grab Grace and get back here in no time.'

'What do you mean, we?' Annie said. 'Stay back here, Frank. Let the muscle do the work.'

'Oh, they can work alright,' Frank said. 'But they can't think, can they?' He tapped his finger on his temple. 'They go off half-cocked, don't they? Storm in blasting away and everyone ends up as mincemeat.' He gave that snort that made his lips flap. 'That's no good to me.'

'Leave it to me,' Tony said. 'I can deal with it.'

'You?' Frank yelled, his face colouring up fast. 'You stupid cunt. You can't even question some dumb kid without going fucking postal on his arse. Do yourself a great big favour and get out of my sight.' He threw the keys to the minivan at Tony.

Tony ducked as they whizzed over his head and bent to pick up the keys from the carpet.

'Vin promised me three lads,' Frank said. 'Go and fetch them and bring them back here. And you make sure you get all of them.' He counted out the numbers slowly and deliberately on his fingers. 'One, er two, er three.'

Tony pocketed the keys and stormed out.

'You really shouldn't push him like that, Frank,' Annie said quietly. 'He's becoming more and more unstable by the day.'

'You take the piss out of him.'

'Yes,' she said. 'But Tony and I are equals. We're just employees. You're the boss. Plus, you are his lifeline to staying out of the loony bin. That makes him powerless. A bit of an explosive combination, that, for someone like Tony.'

'Stupid bint,' Frank snarked. 'You don't know what you're on about.'

'Okay.' Annie returned to her screen. 'So are you just going along as an observing supervisor or will you be carrying?'

'Dig a nine millimetre out for me, will you.' Frank laughed, 'Worst comes to the worst, I may have to shoot fucking Tony.'

'Hmm.' Annie looked across the room at Frank and wondered, not for the first time, just what the hell she was doing there.

CHAPTER TWENTY-EIGHT

Celia reluctantly answered her phone after it had rung several times and she'd ignored it.

'Someone's keen,' Gwynn said.

She glanced at the number. 'It's Dermot from Ireland. He's probably wondering if we've got any more cars where that Opel came from.'

'Maybe next week,' Gwynn said, as a passing reference to the current ongoing conversation about how the hell the three of them would cope if Frank sent in the cavalry.

Celia tuned Gwynn out and listened to the man she had invoked for the sake of expediency, hearing this voice from the past invading her today.

'That car you sent me, with the big Welsh lad ...'

'Yes.'

'Well, as I was telling you, I'm not into any of that iffy stuff these days so I took it up over the border.'

Celia kept the smile on her face but sighed inwardly. These fucking Irish, going all round the houses to get to the point.

'Just for the *craic*,' Dermot continued, 'I stuck around in Belfast for a bit. And while they were dismantling the Opel, guess what they found, Celia?'

Celia had never before understood the phrase 'my heart sank', but that's what happened right then. 'Tell me what they found.'

'You see, I know you of old and I think you have a handle on that information already.'

It's a fair cop, guv, she thought, *but no real harm done.* 'A tracking device.'

'You've got it in one, Celia. And because of that little divil, we checked out the official owner of the car. And I have to ask the question of you now, Celia, and that is this: why would anyone be tracking a middle-aged lady by the name of Zoe Silver?' The pause again, the one filled with so much menace she could sense it right across the barrier of the Irish Sea that stood between them. 'No relation to my old comrade, Jerry, I suppose?'

'Closer than that,' Celia said with a tinge of triumphalism in her tone. 'Zoe *was* Jerry.' Like everyone else in her old circle, Celia had been aware that Jerry/Zoe was a former Provisional IRA heavy who was on the run from his previous brothers in arms.

'*Was*, you say.' Still the same old Dermot, sharp as a stiletto.

'Definitely *was*.' *You owe me, Dermot, you Paddy fuck,* she thought. *So what's with this aggressive tone?*

'Well, Celia, I'd be inclined to be thanking you for that, was it not for the fact that my grandson would be after getting himself murdered.'

Celia's sense of anxiety returned two-fold. 'What the hell are you talking about, Dermot?'

'You've brought death to my door, Celia.'

'I'm sorry for your loss, Dermot, but what has this got to do with me?'

There was a long and dark pause before Dermot continued. 'While I was away taking the Opel, complete with its little tracking device, to the chop shop in Belfast, someone paid my place of business a visit.'

'Dermot, I'm asking you again what has this to do with me?'

'Shut the fuck up and listen, Celia.'

Dermot was an old bloke now, Celia guessed him to be the wrong side of seventy, but age had not lessened his ability to intimidate. She heard a long, deep intake of breath at the other end.

'And the Englishman, driving a hire car he picked up at the airport, using a cloned credit card and a fake driving licence, found my grandson, Brendan, alone. And he went and murdered the lad.'

'Dermot ...' Celia attempted to call a halt, to enable her to take in the potential consequences of what was being not so much said as intimated.

But Dermot's juggernaut was not about to be stopped. 'I have texted you a photo from the driving licence and you tell me if you recognise this man. And don't you lie to me, Celia. That I will not forgive.'

Celia looked up at Gwynn and Grace, and their concern about her end of this conversation was writ large on their faces. She flicked on to her text and up came a photo of someone she did not recognise.

'Don't know him,' she said. She waved her phone at Grace. 'I'll ask someone else.'

Grace stood up. The tension in the room was palpable and she felt her legs turn to jelly. She took the phone from Celia, stared at the photo of Tony Boyle, then nodded and placed it back in her mother's hand.

'Yes, we know him,' Celia said to her caller. 'How can we help you, Dermot?'

Grace and Celia sat in the Land Rover at the exit to Holyhead port waiting for the final Dublin ferry of the day to unload its passengers.

'Killers, conmen, thieves, arsonists, and now terrorists. Any more of your acquaintances I should know about?' Grace asked.

'Dermot wasn't a terrorist; he was a supplier of goods and services to those who believed they were fighting for a cause. Or so he says. And with some people it's best to just take their word for it.'

'And you know someone like that, how?'

'Martha was married to his son, Aedan.'

Celia recalled meeting Aedan O'Reardon at his and Martha's engagement party and taking an instant dislike to him. Unlike love-struck Martha who thought she'd landed in a pot of jam, what with Aedan owning a car-spares business down on the Liverpool Dock Road. 'One of those old-fashioned places where the guys in the brown coats knew the car parts numbers off by heart.'

'Respectable,' Grace said. Recalling Celia's comments about Ma's craving a normal quiet life.

'The word was, Aedan had IRA connections and the previous owner had been strong-armed into selling cheap. Not that Martha wanted to hear that.'

Celia had met Dermot at the wedding and, given the absence of a father of the bride, Dermot gave a speech. 'A pure Celtic mix of Welsh and Irish will mean a gaggle of children with beautiful singing voices and a roguish twinkle in the eye.'

'He said that?' Grace laughed.

'He did. Children and family mean the world to Dermot.'

The last time Celia had set eyes on Dermot was when he flew over to visit Martha in hospital. The news that Martha had lost the baby and could have no more knocked him sideways. Grey-faced with shock, he took Celia to one side. 'Our Aedan did this?' he asked.

'Yes, he did.'

Dermot's face was set. 'Then he's no son of mine.' He went back to sit with the distraught Martha and turned back to Celia. 'He's dead to me.'

An image of a body face down in a sea of concrete filled Grace's head. 'So, he never questioned his son's disappearance.'

'I reckon he'd have understood a life for a life,' Celia said. 'Though I wouldn't want to actually test that theory.'

'You and Dermot go back a long way.'

'Yeah,' Celia said scanning the cars slowly emerging from the ferry port into the gloom of a Holyhead night in February. 'That's the one,' she said when she spotted the black Nissan Pathfinder they'd been told to look out for.

Celia flashed the lights of the Land Rover. A double-flash response came from whoever was driving the other vehicle. With darkened windows, it was impossible for Grace to see how many were in the car, but they had been told to expect two guests, the father and the uncle of the dead boy. The remaining sons of Dermot elder, as Celia had described them. 'Old Dermot's past his best, I'm told,' Celia added. 'But then aren't we all.'

They were about to house the two men in Celia's cottage.

'But what if anyone else from Frank's crew turns up looking for us?' Grace had asked.

'Who is going to suspect two nice Irishmen renting the cottage for the weekend?' Celia said.

'But what if it gets nasty?'

'They're our frontline troops.'

'But do they know that?'

'No, but these guys aren't on a fishing trip. They've come here to kill your fucking cousin, sweetheart,' Celia said. 'They're no better than they need to be. Best not to ask what's secreted in the panels of that car they're driving.'

'But the only reason that boy is dead is because we killed Zoe.'

'That's life, Grace. Do you hear me placing any blame for you having blown my perfectly rendered cover?'

'No. But I feel guilty about it.'

'Then more fool you.'

Celia turned in her seat, took her daughter by the shoulders and looked her straight in the eye. 'You need to grow up, Grace. You inadvertently stepped into my world and it's a rough one. But if you ever want to get back to the life you had before, you have to face down what is here and now and defeat it. Just like you did back home with that shit-bag, Benedetti. Do you understand?'

The Pathfinder pulled in behind the Land Rover and Celia hit the ignition.

'Let's get these guys back to the cottage. Whatever's coming down the turnpike, we're better with them on board than without.'

Annie was looking out of the window of the office as the minivan drew up outside the garage. 'Ooh,' she said. 'Looks like Vin's sent four. Big lads all of them.'

'Keep your libido under wraps, girlie,' Frank joked. 'No sneaking in there tonight and doing the lot of them. They need all of their strength for the morning. You stay here with me tonight.'

Annie turned from the window and blew him a kiss. 'Then I'll just have to do you four times, won't I.'

'Once upon a time maybe, but I'm getting too old for more than once these days.'

She sat back down by her screen and swivelled her chair to face him. 'Too old, yes,' she said. 'And with a gammy leg. Which is maybe why you shouldn't go with them tomorrow.'

Frank sighed loudly, wiped a fake tear from his eye and put his hand to his chest. 'Ah, she really does care.'

Annie flipped him the finger. 'I don't give a flying fuck about you, Frank. But with you brown bread, I'm out of a job.'

'Cupboard love,' Frank said, feigning distress. 'I knew it.'

'If Tony doesn't strangle me in my bed first.'

'Yes,' Frank said. 'There's always that possibility.'

Mick O'Reardon was standing at the door of the cottage just as Grace and Celia were about to leave them to settle in for the night. Grace had taken a liking to him with his lilting accent and black curly hair. Despite his bull-like build, he had gentle eyes that were edged with sadness. The other brother, Conor, who appeared much younger, perhaps no more than twenty, was busy removing some inner side panels from the inside of the black Pathfinder. Grace turned her head away. 'What you don't see can't hurt you,' Ma would say, and Grace was hopeful that in this case it was a truism.

'Thanks for the help,' Mick said, holding out his hand for Grace to shake. 'We'll be on our way to the address you gave us just after first light. So we won't be meeting again.'

Grace squeezed the hand. 'I'm sorry about your son.'

Mick nodded his head in acceptance of her condolences. Celia was out of earshot by now, climbing into the Land Rover ready to depart. Mick leaned in closer to Grace. 'You get back home to Australia soon as ya can. There's nothing round here for a good girl like you.'

'I'm not *that* good,' Grace said.

'Sure, we all know what happened with that child killer. My da said when he saw your photo that you looked like someone he knew. It was a good day's work and that's for sure.'

'Thank you,' was all Grace could think of to say.

'You go home, Grace,' Mick said just before he strode over to help his brother unload what looked like canvas gun storage bags. 'You don't belong in this world. It'll drag you down, so it will.'

CHAPTER TWENTY-NINE

Frank's phone buzzed. Time to get up. Annie was snoring gently beside him, which was just about the only thing the old tart ever did gently in his experience. He sat up and tried not to disturb her. If she woke, then she'd give him even more earache about his going on this little jaunt.

His leg was giving him gyp as it did every morning until he got moving properly. He limped to the window and looked through the blinds in the hope that it wasn't raining. Wet roads were not recommended for quick getaways. That was what Celia's old man Fast Eddie used to say. There were times when Frank thought he'd been a wee bit hasty doing away with Eddie. Perhaps there could have been a compromise to be made back then. But what the hell, he was younger, impetuous and, if he was being truthful, a bit strung-out on the old Peruvian. Anyway, it was far too late now, the course had been set and whatever happened was in the hands of the gods. *Fuck me*, he chuckled to himself, *must be getting philosophical in my old age.*

He stood looking out at the cars parked two floors down in front of the house. Something was missing. It took a moment to register what was wrong with the scene set out before him. The minivan! Frank's pulse bumped up as he left the bedroom and went into the upper corridor, crossed the landing and stood by the window that gave a clear view onto the drive with the stables/garage on the left-hand side. The gates stood open at the end of the drive and there was no sign of the minivan.

Jesus!

He rushed back into his bedroom, pulled the covers off Annie and slapped her naked arse. 'Get up! That crazy fucker's gone without me.'

Tony had no time for Vin's guys. They all looked about eighteen years old to him and they never fucking shut up. They'd talked that black shit all the way from Birmingham. Their weird linguistic concoctions of fake Jamaican, cod-American gangsta, and that bunged-up Brummie drawl had stopped being amusing beyond the first two minutes in their company. After two hours of it, Tony had been ready to dump the lot of them at the motorway services and drive off alone. And the music they insisted he played. What the hell was that crap?

They'd been well pissed off that he got them all to dress in dark clothes. 'What the fuck is that?' he asked when he spotted one lad wearing a white Adidas baseball cap. 'We're going to rural Wales, mate, not selling baggies on corners in Balsall Heath.'

They'd all told him their street names, but he wasn't interested and after a while he just tuned them out altogether.

They didn't know that Frank was supposed to be coming along, so there was not even one oddly passive eyebrow raised between them when, having fed them on pizza and fried chicken takeaways, Tony turfed them out of the stables flats earlier than expected and drove away. As the minivan reached the gate, Tony had glanced back at the house, but all was quiet. He'd show Frank that he didn't need any supervision. He'd prove he was made of stronger stuff than Zoe and John.

As they crossed the bridge to Anglesey, he made them shut off the booming music. 'This is a sneak up not a three-ring fucking circus.' Then he had to get them to quieten down on the chat. 'Peaceful place this,' he told them.

'Like the grave,' said the one Tony thought was called Burger, or something like that, after which they all stared morosely into the darkness beyond the car windows. 'People live here?' There was an incredulous sound to the voice that made Tony smile despite himself.

'They certainly do.'

'What do they do here?'

'I have no fucking idea,' Tony replied.

The cottage was in darkness when they got there. Two of Vin's guys, Shred and Gameboy he thought they were called but couldn't be sure, were posted at the front. 'Any shots fired, kick the door in,' Tony instructed.

He, Burger and the other one whose name Tony couldn't be arsed remembering, went around the back way. The lock on the back door was easy to open. The Brummies all carried Glocks, the weapon of choice for gangsta boys the world over. Tony preferred a knife.

All was quiet in there with nobody in either the kitchen or the sitting room. Burger briefly checked the little room off the side of the entrance, nodded it was clear, and he and the other lad went upstairs. Tony waited in the kitchen. The distinct pop-pop from a silenced gun, followed by the sound of two bodies tumbling backwards down the stairs, had Tony flattening his body against the kitchen wall by the doorway where he could get a look at what was happening beyond. The front door came off its hinges as two size fourteens kicked it down. From the doorway, three swift-fire bullets from one Glock hit a guy coming downstairs and sent his body sprawling across the two black lads that he'd just taken down. From the side room that Burger had indicated was clear emerged a burly man with a shock of curly black hair. He was carrying a sawn-off. He shot one of the Brummies as he ran into the cottage. The blast almost cut him in half. The look of surprise on the kid's face made Tony chuckle. The other kid, Gameboy maybe, took out the sawn-off with three shots, one, two, three then stood staring slack-jawed at the carnage that surrounded him as Tony strode into the room. 'Fuck it, man, that was awesome,' he said just before Tony knifed him through the heart.

Tony watched impassively as Gameboy, or was it Shred? dropped to his knees in front of him. He reminded Tony of a startled rabbit up until the moment that the light departed his eyes. Tony put his boot to the kid's chest and pulled out the bloody knife. 'I fucking hate rap music,' he said and he kicked the dead kid out of his way.

Annie was driving the Bentley along the A55 road that links Anglesey with the mainland and runs from the bridge all the way to Holyhead and the Irish Sea. 'Ever get that sinking feeling?' she said to Frank when two fire engines tore past the car at speed, lights flashing and sirens screaming like banshees.

'Let's see which way they're going?'

'Only one way on this road.'

'They might turn off,' Frank said.

'Anything is possible.'

'Jesus, let's hope so.'

The Bentley kept a discreet distance behind the red vehicles on an otherwise deserted road. Frank had his eyes on the satnav all the way. 'Come on,' he kept saying in the direction of the fast-moving emergency vehicles ahead. 'Turn off, turn off.'

'Wishing it won't make it so,' Annie commented.

She turned her head and glanced at Frank. He looked like death warmed up.

The fire engine turned off the main drag. The satnav told Annie to do the same.

'Fuck me,' Frank said, 'what have you done, Tony?'

'Stay calm,' Annie soothed. 'It might not be what you think.'

Two police cars were stationed at the bottom of a side road that the satnav was also indicating was their final destination. It confirmed both of their worst fears. Annie slowed down, opened the window on the driver's side and gave the young policeman an example of her most refined accent. 'Oh dear, officer,' she said. 'Is something wrong here?'

'Where are you going, madam?'

'Holyhead,' she said, glancing up at the unnatural glow that filled the sky.

'You've come the wrong way, then,' the young cop replied. 'Go back to the crossroads, turn left and left again, then follow the signs.'

'Thank you so much,' Annie said. 'I do hope no one is hurt up there.'

'We've got four engines on the job, madam. I'm sure they'll do their best.'

'Is it an isolated property?' she asked, just before an explosion from above sent sparks hurtling into the night sky.

'Yes, it is, madam,' the young cop said calmly. 'Now you'd best be on your way.'

***

From the window of his bijou hotel room in Trearddur Bay, Tony could see the blood-red sky glow in the distance. He'd been offered a room with a sea view but turned it down for one that looked back inland, much to the hotel receptionist's consternation.

'Most visitors want the rooms that look out to sea,' she'd said.

'No thanks,' was all Tony said as he headed to the top floor. He needed to see the results of his handiwork from afar. He'd left it until the last minute to get away from there in the black Pathfinder, just to make sure that the cottage was blazing to the max.

All the better, he reckoned, to roast the already dead inhabitants to nice crispy critters and make the process of identification even harder. He'd rigged the petrol tank of that piece of shit minivan to explode well after the house fire took hold. It was an extra bit of theatricality that gave him a deep sense of satisfaction. Might even take a fire fighter or two with it. It was to be a nicely timed distraction to delay the inferno from being quelled. As it happened, it had been a while before anyone noticed that the isolated building was alight in the first place, judging by the fire brigade's response. That being the case, Tony was hoping all that might be left of the building come daylight would be scorched stone walls and fragments of human remains. Six dead bodies yet not a weapon in sight. A conundrum for Sherlock to ponder, my dear Watson. Tony chuckled as he thought about the tarpaulin-wrapped guns safely secured in the back of his newly acquired vehicle. A Pathfinder, as aptly named as the missile and now equipped with an arsenal that was set to wreak havoc on all those who stood in his way.

Tony was feeling a sense of almost delirious elation. This cock-up of immense proportions was like manna from heaven. It was fate taking a hand. It meant he was now free to do as he pleased. This was his chance to leave his past behind. No more visits to that smarmy supervising officer whenever the bastard decided to summon him. Tony loathed the man and his 'just to check up on you, son' condescending manner. Enough. No more. And no more taking orders from that over-the-hill fuck and his bitch on heat. Tony smiled to himself as his hastily conceived plan began to take shape in his mind. He'd go back to the house and do for both of them. Slit Frank's throat and hear him squeal like the fat pig he resembled. Slash the bitch to pieces and slice off her hyperactive clit for her. Then he'd find Celia and take from her whatever it was Frank had been after for all these years. It had to be money. Tony was betting his new life on that. Then he'd do away with her, too. He thought of Grace, with that blonde hair and blue eyes like some kind of plaster saint. He looked forward to killing her, nice and slow.

Tony's eyes were drawn back to the fiery light in the distance as he contemplated a new future for himself. And he smiled.

CHAPTER THIRTY

Grace and Celia stood outside the Police Do Not Cross tape that guarded the smouldering remains of the cottage. Several ambulances had taken away what Grace had overheard one fireman say were as many as six bodies. There was just one appliance remaining, with weary men dampening down what remained of the building that had stood on that spot for over a hundred years. The occupants of one police car waited patiently for Celia to accompany them to the station. They were from the local force and had addressed Celia by her first name from the time they had arrived at Gwynn's farm bearing the news that the cottage was ablaze. They had been polite and empathetic, careful to give her plenty of time to take in the destruction of her home and her livelihood. The two smaller cottages further down the hill, towards the horseshoe bay, were still standing but had also been set alight with windows broken and petrol poured through. An additional act of vandalism that implied a very personal grudge. At least that was Grace's perception.

She thought about the curly-haired Irishman with the soft voice and gentle eyes who had told her to get away, to go home. 'You don't belong in this world,' he'd said, 'It'll drag you down, so it will.'

Drag you down and kill you, she thought. *Or turn you into a vengeful automaton like Celia, standing dry-eyed outside the ruins of her home and dabbing away a theatrical tear, shed purely for public consumption. Does nothing move her?* Grace wondered. *Or is this some protective carapace she's developed over the years? One that has stuck so fast it can no longer be cast aside.*

After taking in the scene with dazed senses, Grace finally looked about to see if the black car the Irish brothers had been driving was anywhere around. The only vehicle she had set eyes on had been a burnt-out minivan that the police had hauled away earlier. She hoped that they had gone from this place before the fire had started. Maybe the other bodies were Frank's heavies. There were so many unanswered questions and Grace was itching to ask the police about the black car but had been warned off.

'You were never here today. Got it?' Celia told her. 'You're only here to give me moral support. Let me handle this.'

A large, understanding hand was gently placed on Celia's shoulder by an older police officer wearing a uniform that boasted the words Heddlu Police over his left breast pocket and a red dragon on the top of the sleeve. 'Come on, Celia, luv,' he said. 'Time to go, eh?'

'You go back to Gwynn's place,' Celia told Grace.

'We'll make sure your mam gets back home again,' said the policeman.

Grace watched Celia step into the police car then took one more look at the blackened walls of what remained of the cottage and felt stricken with guilt. *This is all my fault,* she thought. She felt truly cursed as she recalled one of the emails she'd received after having shot Benedetti. 'Whore of the Devil. Hell will be your home and you shall be consumed by fire.'

'Nutjobs,' Ma had said. 'Anyone over the age of six who truly believes in angels and devils deserves to be locked away for their own good. If we don't stamp it out, pronto, superstition peddled to idiots will kill off the human race. My sky fairy's bigger than your sky fairy ... religion reduced to a pissing contest.' And Grace thought just how much she missed Ma and her no-nonsense view of the world. 'Curses only work if you believe they will. It's a form of autosuggestion.' And Ma had reached across Grace, kissed her on the forehead and hit the computer's Delete button. 'And that's how you deal with them.'

Which was all well and good, but Grace was only too aware that the publicity from the Benedetti killing had set in motion a succession of events that had already resulted in the deaths of nine people. She fought back her remorse and stood tall. This had to stop. And it had to stop now.

***

Tony scoped the scene in one. At the end of the turn-off that led uphill to the burnt-out cottage was a local police car, and behind that, a blue Megane was also parked up. Tony stopped the black Pathfinder a few yards behind and watched for a moment. There was a conversation going on between the uniformed cop and what Tony assumed to be a civilian, as even plain-clothes cops were never quite that casually dressed. Tony got out of the car, his cover story already forming in his mind. Putting on his best concerned face, he rushed up to the two men.

'What's happened?' he said breathlessly.

The young cop stopped talking to the other man, his smile faded, and his face set back into professional mode.

'How can I help you, sir?'

'I'm asking you why you are stationed at the bottom of the turn-off to my aunt's house.'

That got the attention of both men.

'There's been a fire,' the young constable said. 'But Mrs Williams is safe. She's at the station in Holyhead now giving a statement.'

'And Grace? Is Grace there too?' Tony asked.

'The young woman with Mrs Williams has gone back to Gwynn Hughes's farm.'

'I need to see Grace,' Tony said. 'Where is this farm?' He knew the minute the words had passed his lips that they'd come out all wrong. The policeman's ears picked up on it too.

'I'm afraid I'll have to ask you for some identification, sir.'

Tony fished his phoney driving licence out of his wallet.

'Okay, Mr Jones,' the young cop said after he'd glanced at the licence. 'I can only reassure you that both ladies are unharmed. For further information I think it best if you go to the station in Holyhead where someone will be able to be of more assistance.'

With two pairs of watchful eyes on him, Tony decided not to push his luck.

'Thank you, officer,' he said, 'I'll do that.'

Damn, he thought, *there's no way I'm setting foot in any cop shop. Now I'll have to go asking questions of the locals.* He reckoned the islanders would be a suspicious bunch at the best of times, so expected to be given the run-around before he got any real info.

What he didn't expect was to be followed to his car by the unshaven man who'd been chatting with the cop.

'I'm local press,' the guy said, and he held out his hand. 'Rob Douglas.'

'Jones,' Tony said, 'Paul Jones.'

'You'll have to wait hours at the station to see anyone. Not a big force round here, nothing much happens really so this is a big deal for them. It'll be all hands to the pumps until some big brass gets here.'

'Thanks for the heads-up.' Tony opened his car door.

Rob Douglas placed his hand on the door as though to halt Tony's departure. 'So I was thinking, like. Maybe we can help each other out. I know the Hughes farm. One of his pigs won a competition a couple of years back and I covered the story. I can show you where it is.'

'That's very kind of you,' Tony said, grateful but suspicious of this stranger's motivation.

'Do I detect a southern accent there?'

'Long time ago,' Tony said. 'But I'm not sure how I can be of any help to you at all.'

'Tit for tat.' Rob Douglas grinned. 'You fill me in on the family background while I show you to the farm, then you drop me back at my car after. How's that?'

'Deal,' Tony said. 'Get in.'

'Nice motor this,' Rob said. 'Irish number plates, I notice.'

Yeah, Tony thought. *You notice far too much for your own good.*

***

'You can't do this, Grace,' Gwynn said.

'I can and I will,' Grace countered. 'This has got to stop and the way I see it, only I can do that.'

'Who'd you think you are then, Joan-of-bloody-Arc? Boudicca?'

'I was thinking of someone more peaceful.'

'We are both caught in the middle of something we don't fully understand here, Grace. There's a long history we're not part of. Best not to meddle and to leave it to the main players.'

'Which is exactly what's landed us in this bloody mess we're in. Celia can't be reasoned with but maybe Frank can.'

'And you think you're the one to do that? Get real, Grace.'

'This is all my fault, Gwynn. Since I came here nine people have been killed, including that young lad over in Ireland. And why? Because Frank used me to flush Celia out.'

'You weren't to know that though, were you?'

'That doesn't absolve me so don't argue with me.'

'She'll never forgive me if you get hurt.'

'Please listen to me. I've made up my mind. And here's the plan. When Celia gets back, you make her get on a plane, I don't care where to, just put her on a plane. She's got nothing to stay here for now. Best if you go with her.'

'I can't leave the farm.'

'Haven't you got a farm manager?'

'Yes, but …'

'Then take a fucking holiday.'

'I can't let you do this.'

'And how do you intend to stop me? I'm going to see Frank, to talk to him. He is my father. Or so he claims.'

'You'll get yourself killed.'

'No, I won't. I'll be fine. I'm famous, remember.'

***

Half a mile along the long, winding, and unlit road that housed the Hugheses' pig farm, local reporter Rob Douglas was discovering just how roomy was the boot of a Nissan Pathfinder SUV. Not that he knew anything about it, having been stabbed in the throat and unceremoniously dumped by the side of the road to bleed out. Meanwhile, the man he knew as Paul Jones muttered, cursed and arranged plastic bin sacks on the ground beside him. Through the shock, total body paralysis and fast fading of the inner light, Rob Douglas had wondered momentarily what the headline would be when his body was eventually found. Then it was lights out.

For his part, Tony was a bit stunned, too. He hadn't meant to do for the bloke, it's just that, well, he'd got on his tits. All Tony wanted to do was find out where Grace was living because find Grace, find Celia, find the pot of gold at the end of his greedily visualised rainbow. Trouble was, this Rob Douglas bloke wanted chapter and verse about the notoriously publicity-shy Celia Williams. 'Virtually a recluse,' he told Tony. 'Lived on the island for years and no one seems to know much about her. She puts money into a local animal sanctuary, you know. I was doing a report on the place a couple of years back and tried to get a photo of her for the papers, but she used some very unladylike language and hid her face. Any insight would be much appreciated.' Tony gave him some garbage about his aunt Celia being painfully shy and the guy ate it all up with a spoon. Flattered that his lies were being believed, Tony's mouth did what it so often did, it disengaged from his brain to the extent that he accidently let slip that Grace was *that* Grace Dobbs, Aussie heroine. And that was the moment when the reporter got all glowy-eyed excited, which pissed Tony off no end.

'That's the place,' Rob Douglas said, as they drove past the farm.

Tony screeched to a standstill just a little further along the road. 'What the fuck?' said the victim as he lurched forward so fast that his seatbelt bit painfully into his collarbone.

Flash of knife in left hand, right hand used to undo the seat belt plus unlock the door in a single swift move, one big shove and out of the car tumbled the corpse to be.

'Nosy fuck!' Tony said as he stepped over the sprawled body of the man gasping for the air that wouldn't come and bleeding profusely onto the narrow grass verge.

Once sure that the reporter was well and truly deceased, Tony wrapped him in bin sacks and shoved the body into the boot of the Pathfinder.

'Mother never told you not to take lifts from strange men, did she?' he said as he closed the boot. 'That'll learn ya.'

CHAPTER THIRTY-ONE

'You need to sleep, Frank,' Annie said.

'I'll sleep when I'm dead.' Frank kept pacing. 'Which might be any time soon once Vin finds out what happened to his crew.'

'We've been over this a thousand times.' Annie had watched Frank's back and forth performance since the early hours and she was weary of it. 'There was a fire, that doesn't mean anyone's dead.'

'Then where the fuck are they? Why can't you get Tony on his phone?' He halted for a moment and squinted at the computer screen across the room. 'Is there anything on the Internet about the fire?'

'Nothing yet, give it time.'

'Time? I thought all news was supposed to be instant these days.' And he resumed his compulsive walk.

'A house fire in Wales is hardly the kind to stop the presses, is it? It's not even bottom-of-the-telly stuff. Particularly if no one was home.'

'But what if someone was home? What about Grace? Was Grace in that house?' Frank looked distraught as he gave up his short march across the Persian carpet and slumped at his desk with his head in his hands. 'Jesus, Annie, this is a mess. I didn't mean for Grace to get hurt.' He looked up to Annie sitting in her chair in front of the computer screen 'She's my own flesh and blood.'

'I hate to sound harsh, Frank, but it was you who involved her in the first place.'

'I didn't realise ...'

'Realise what? That Grace is a real person and not just bait you can use to catch a bigger fish?'

Frank stared down at his desk and did not reply.

'Anyway,' Annie continued while searching for info on the web. 'Beats me why you've kept up this obsessive search for Celia for as long as you have.'

'Bitch did me over. Forty million ain't chicken feed.'

'You've made far more than that over the last quarter of a century. And legit … ish. Anyway, who says Celia's got much left after all this time? Laundering money and hiding away costs a bloody bomb. Every bugger wants their slice if only to keep quiet. The expression *silence is golden* might have been coined for these very circumstances.'

'Bitch did me over.' Frank's tone was petulant. 'Nobody gets away with that.'

'And you shot her husband. In the head. While he was speaking to her on the fucking phone. Wasn't that revenge enough?' Annie let out a gasp of annoyance. 'Not to mention stupid. A wall full of brains guaranteed that she'd go to ground. It's as though punishing Celia was more important to you than retrieving the money. Was that it?'

'I don't know,' Frank said. 'It was a long time ago. I was younger then and off my tits most of the time.'

'Well, whatever way you look at it, this is some sick shit, Frank.' Anne swivelled in her chair and gave him a hard look. 'And the question is: when will it end?'

'When I get to Celia.' Frank threw his next card into the game. 'I bet she killed Zoe, you know.'

'Who cares!' Annie spat out. 'That piece of filth was a fucking IRA hit man and bomber back in the day. Just because he changed his sex doesn't mean he changed his nature. A bastard never changes its spots. Just because he called himself Zoe means *nada* to me, Frank. He'd never be a real woman as long as he had a hole in his arse.'

'I never knew you felt that way, Annie.'

'You never fucking asked.'

'What about John? Another one gone before his time. Don't you care about him either? You two were pretty intimate.'

'I've been intimate with a lot of men.' She winked at him. 'Including you, Frankie boy. It's just sex, baby. The sating of basic instincts. It's just plumbing and, with me, there are no comebacks.' Annie leaned back on her chair until it was at tipping point. 'Unlike with Celia, of course. Your baby mother.'

'Watch your mouth!'

But Annie was not to be halted. She was just getting into her stride. 'It's easy for young men to deny their offspring, isn't it, Frank. But old men are different, aren't they? Old men need something more than just a bank full of money and a bed full of paid-for cooze. Old men need some meaning to their lives.' Annie laughed. 'And *you're* an old man now, Frank.' She eyed her boss sceptically. 'You sure this is all just about the money?'

Frank's face set into combat mode. 'I'm amazed to hear such insight into human nature from one who'll shag anything with a dick.'

But Annie was not to be baited either. 'And that's where you're dead wrong, Frank.'

'You are picky then? Never had it off with my young nephew, eh?'

Annie visibly shuddered. 'You *are* joking. The only way Tony would be able to get it up would be fantasising about his mother and baby sister sizzling in that fire he set.' She looked back at her computer screen and her vocal tone darkened. 'And if he was behind that blaze on Anglesey he's probably got an erection the size of the Menai Bridge right now.'

'What are you talking about?'

She indicated to her screen. 'Come and look at this.'

Frank got to his feet. 'What? What does it say?'

'The Welsh plod have just given a press conference. They've found six bodies in that building.'

'Six?' Frank slowly made his way across the room towards her.

'That's what it says here.' Annie looked up to see Frank stop dead in his tracks and his facial expression dissolve into grief.

'Oh dear God,' he said. 'Gracie, Gracie.' He crossed his arms over his chest and his hands gripped tight to his own shoulders, as though to keep himself from falling apart. 'What have I done? What have I done?'

And Frank began to cry.

***

At that moment, Grace was driving Celia's Land Rover towards Chester and hoping she could find her way back to Frank's house in the dark. Gwynn had cautioned that she should wait at the farm until morning, but Grace knew she had to get away before Celia returned from the police station. She also knew that Gwynn would never use strong-arm tactics to stop her from leaving. Celia, however, was another story altogether. She would probably hold a gun to her daughter's head to prevent her from doing what Grace was convinced that she had to.

Gwynn had insisted that Grace take his mobile phone with her, as well as his shotgun. She had agreed to the gun just to shut him up but had no intention of going into Frank's house armed to the teeth. Though she did have one secret weapon up her sleeve. She stopped the car just before she reached the bridge to the mainland and Googled the phone number of the TV company for whom she and Frank had been interviewed. Then she rang it.

'I'd like to speak to Aisha Hussein, please.' The memory of the encounter with the ambitious young reporter was still fresh in Grace's mind. A voice that Grace was not sure was a man or a woman, informed her that Miss Hussein was not available right now. Never expecting to get passed straight through, Grace said, 'Can I leave a message for her, please? Tell her that Grace Dobbs would like to talk about the shooting in Australia. And she has chosen to give Miss Hussein an honest and exclusive interview. Ask her to ring me straight away before I offer it elsewhere.' Grace left her number, turned the car engine back on and drove away.

Half an hour later, just as Grace was approaching the Chester turn-off, Aisha Hussein phoned back.

***

At six o'clock, Tony Boyle was at home in his flat above the greengrocers. His stolen Pathfinder was parked in a side road. Its roomy boot contained the arsenal of weaponry Tony had plucked from the dead hands of the men at the cottage. The other item being the gradually stiffening body of Rob Douglas.

Once he'd got home, Tony had started out by packing a suitcase. Then he had second thoughts. If everyone believed he was dead in that fire, then the disappearance of all his belongings would raise suspicion. He sat back down on his single bed beside his half-filled suitcase and pondered his situation. He needed to get the killing done, get the money from Celia and be out of the country before those bodies were identified. And he could never come back to this flat after today. He looked around at the place he had called home for five years. Was there anything he needed to take with him? There was nothing that had any significance in his life. All he needed was his counterfeit passport and driving licence. He emptied the contents of the suitcase onto the bed and packed a small holdall with essentials. Then he closed the door behind him without looking back and made his way down the stairs to the beckoning Pathfinder.

CHAPTER THIRTY-TWO

Celia was dropped off at the farm and waved goodbye to the driver of the police vehicle. She closed the gate behind her and walked towards Gwynn's house. She was pleased with her performance at the police station and chuffed that they had believed the explanation of her absence from her home at the time of the fire. Her story of the Irishman contacting her by telephone to book exclusive use of her cottage had gone down well, she thought.

'But why move out?' one policeman asked. 'Couldn't you put them up in one of the other cottages?'

'He specified my place.' Celia had even embellished the tale a little to add authenticity. 'Seems he'd seen a photo of it on TripAdvisor.' She shrugged theatrically. 'I'm a businesswoman. I wasn't about to turn down anyone paying over the odds in hard cash.'

'But the inconvenience to yourself.'

'Times are hard, it's winter and I'll usually have no clients at all until at least April. He paid summer rates as compensation. So, no. It was no inconvenience, whatsoever.'

'Your client was driving a black Nissan Pathfinder, you say?'

'Yes. I met them at the Irish boat to show them the way and settle them in.'

'Did this Mr O'Reardon say there would be two people coming over?'

'No, and I didn't ask. I charge a rate for renting the cottage, not for the number of people staying there.'

'And you say the two men did nothing to arouse your suspicions?'

'As far as I was concerned they were just two pleasant Irish guys who needed total privacy for a few days. Why they wanted that, is not for me to say. But I do sometimes get couples renting the other cottages for just a short stay out of season. They sometimes spend all of their time indoors with the curtains drawn. As I say, they were adults and it's none of my business.'

That final intimation that the two men may well have been secret lovers looking for a discreet hideaway did not fall on stony ground, so Celia felt that she had acquitted the interview and the statement that followed with quiet dignity and the odd tear shed, but mainly a message writ large in the minds of the constabulary. *Nothing to do with me, mate. I'm just another victim here. Now it's down to you to find out what went on.*

Right at that moment, the police were busy searching for the black Pathfinder the O'Reardon brothers had arrived in because it certainly wasn't the burnt-out wreck that had been found at the scene.

With that stage of the proceedings out of the way for the moment, Celia was mulling over her options and none of them looked too rosy. If two of those bodies found in the cottage did turn out to be the brothers O'Reardon she was in the deepest of deep shit with Dermot. The other four might possibly be Frank's crew. But who had set the fires and stolen the Irish lad's black car? It didn't make any sense to Celia unless to cover their tracks. One explanation could be that mad Tony Boyle was out there and loose, though. Celia resolved to talk to Gwynn about setting up some kind of armed watch on the farm, just in case it was Tony and he discovered their whereabouts. She took out her keys, entered the house and saw a worried-looking Gwynn waiting for her in the kitchen. He looked up from his place at the table and his face alone told her that all was not well, *Oh, Christ*, she thought. *What now?*

In the dark, when even roads one knows quite well can often assume a very different appearance, Grace found Frank's house more easily than she had expected. The two white pillars that stood at the entrance, the stables-garage to the right of the driveway and the strange sideways aspect of the building itself made it stand out from all the other more conventionally built, impressive homes in that area. She parked the Land Rover on the opposite side of the road to the gateposts and attempted to calm her nerves.

She was trying to convince herself that it was possible to appeal to whatever good there was in Frank Gilligan. Although however anxious she may have been about the outcome, she remained sure that confronting Frank was the only solution to ending the madness she had witnessed. She was hoping against hope that Gwynn would be able to persuade Celia to take herself out of harm's way. He had promised that he'd try but Grace couldn't afford to worry about that for the moment. She wanted her life back and was convinced that this was the only possible way to make that happen. It had to be either some kind of compromise on Frank's part or she feared it would become a case of last man standing.

She started the engine once more, turned the headlights back on, indicated right and aimed the Land Rover between the white gateposts. She felt as she had when facing down Benedetti, but this time she was going in unarmed and utterly vulnerable.

'And you just let her go?' Celia was incensed. 'After all that's happened, you let my daughter just waltz off back to Frank Gilligan?'

Gwynn sat impassively by the kitchen table. 'She's more like you than just looks, you know. She was determined to go, and I had no way to stop her.' He sat back in the chair and folded his arms. 'Anyway, maybe she's right about confronting him. She's his daughter, too.'

'And you think he cares about that?' Celia yelled at him. 'He used her to get to me. That's all she is to him. And he'll do the same again.' Celia recalled that final phone call from Eddie. The shout of 'Run!' and the shot that had killed the only man she had ever loved. She took a deep breath and, her initial anger swiftly turning to despair, sat down opposite Gwynn at the rustic table.

She was getting too old for this lark. It was too much. It was all too much. She'd come out of hiding just to save Grace and fallen straight into Frank's trap. 'My man, your dad, and so many more over the years. All dead in the pursuit of me and money that hardly exists anymore.'

'Forty million, though.' Gwynn shook his head in disbelief. 'You can't have spent it all.'

'More like thirty. Laundered down to twenty. Investments like the cottages, payoffs, back-handers, bent lawyers, and bank managers. And here's another example. I have ... I had ... at home, photographs and videotapes of Grace that Martha sent to me over the years. But to keep Martha safely in the dark, I got her to post them to a discreet accommodation address in the Canary Islands and they forwarded them to a similar type of address in Gibraltar who sent them to one in London, then on to Liverpool and I'd pick them up in person from there. Four addresses, three hundred-plus quid each per year, plus couriers, over twenty-five years and pop goes the weasel. It costs to stay lost.'

'But still ...' Gwynn remained unconvinced.

'Of course, there's quite a lot of money left. It's in a Swiss bank account. And it's for Grace.' Celia regained her composure. 'Frank took my husband off me and my life with my child, so he's not getting his sweaty paws on the only thing I can give her.'

Gwynn eyed her and said gently, 'You do care about her, don't you?'

'Of course, I do. She's my kid,' Celia snapped back. 'What do you think I am, heartless?'

'I've sometimes wondered.'

'Then don't. Not where Grace is concerned anyway.'

While Celia revealed a chink in her armour, Gwynn took the opportunity to make another attempt to persuade her to run. 'Then if you want to keep her safe just do as she asks. She wants you to leave the country.'

'Grace can want all she likes.' Celia leapt to her feet. 'Lend me a shotgun. I'm going after her.'

'How do you know where she's gone?'

'Know thine enemy, Gwynn. I've always kept tabs on Frank. He's still living in the house where Grace was conceived.'

'Bloody hell, Celia,' Gwynn said as he hooked his heavy jacket off the back of his chair. 'The more you tell me, the more twisted this whole thing sounds.'

She was headed for the door but stopped dead in her tracks. 'Where are you going?'

'With you.'

'I don't want you involved.'

Gwynn dangled the keys to his Range Rover in front of her face. 'Oh, piss off, Celia. I delivered a stolen car for you, and then I shot a man, dismembered his body, and fed it to my pigs. Erm, I think that counts as already involved, don't you?'

Grace parked the Land Rover at the front of the house next to Frank's Bentley, though she noted that the car didn't look as spruce as usual. No John, no wash, it seemed.

As she walked towards the house, the front door opened and it took Grace a moment to recognise the female figure standing there. Without her housekeeper get-up, Mrs John-who-wasn't looked very different indeed, quite a bit younger in fact and more casual.

'Hello, Mrs John,' Grace said breezily as she approached. 'Can Frank come out to play?'

'He's in his office. He'll be relieved to see you.'

'Really?' Grace said as she stepped into the house.

'Yes, really. And it's Annie, by the way.'

'Yeah, I know,' Grace said as she followed Annie towards Frank's home office. 'Celia told me all about you.'

'Nothing good, I take it.'

'How well you know her.'

'Damn right.'

Frank leapt up from behind his desk and came rushing over. 'Gracie, Gracie, thank God.'

Grace stopped dead in her tracks and raised her hands as though to push him away. 'Don't you touch me.'

Annie crossed the room, sat at her desk and swivelled her chair in their direction, all the better to view the spectacle unfolding before her. 'He's been worried about you,' she said to Grace.

'It's true, Grace.' Frank gave up any attempt to hug his daughter and retreated behind his desk.

'He hasn't had any sleep,' Annie said.

Grace stood in the middle of the room, arms folded across her chest. 'There are six people dead in a burnt-out cottage and I'm supposed to sympathise with Frank's lack of zeds. Jesus, what kind of people are you?'

'Set a killer to catch a killer.' Annie leaned forward in her seat. 'Where's John?'

'You mean the chauffeur, gofer, and random slaughterer?'

'That sounds like something Celia would say,' Frank said.

'How well you know her too,' Grace said. 'Yeah, she told me all about John, and Annie here and you too, Frank.'

'And Zoe?' Frank asked,

'Her too.' Grace had their attention now and she was not about to let that advantage slide. 'Except, Celia kept saying the name Jerry and for some reason Zoe was not best pleased.'

'So, Celia had her goons kill them both,' Annie said.

Frank was keeping very quiet and Grace could feel his eyes boring into her. *Does he have a gun in the drawer of his desk?* she wondered with an inwards shiver, but she stuck to her plan.

'Goons? What goons? Celia just has Celia … and me.'

'Celia took down Zoe and John?' Annie sounded astonished.

'No, Celia took down John. I shot Zoe.'

Frank let out what sounded to Grace like a long sigh.

'Look at her, Annie,' he said. 'Isn't she magnificent? Comes in here, unarmed, and tells me she's killed two of my oldest colleagues. The girl's got balls of brass.'

Or I'm fucking stupid, Grace thought but said, 'So how is this going to end, Frank?'

'When I find Celia.'

'The funny thing is she's been living virtually under your nose for the past fifteen years.' Grace let out a snort of derision in the direction of her father. 'And she'd made a nice quiet life for herself. But you burning her out has given her nothing left to stay around for.' Grace stood, hands on hips and felt a moment's triumph. 'You cocked up, Frank. Celia's gone.'

'Where?' Annie chipped in.

Grace shook her head. 'No idea. That was the deal. She gets on one plane, I get on another and neither of us knows the other's destination.'

'But you didn't hold up your end of the bargain,' Frank said. 'So why are you here?'

'Because you know where Martha lives. So what's to stop you doing exactly what you did with me and using her as bait to smoke us out?'

'You killed two of my closest colleagues; it might take me time to reassemble. You could move Martha anywhere in the world in that time,' Frank said calmly. 'So I'll ask you again. Why are you here?'

Grace spotted a chair, pulled it up at the other side of Frank's desk and sat down. 'I want to put an end to this, Frank.'

'I've told you how to do that. Lead me to Celia.'

'That's not going to happen.'

'Think you're that tough, girlie?'

'No, I'm not. But this has gone on for too long.' Grace took a breath and began the speech she had practised in her head all the way from Anglesey. 'All you've been deprived of is money that wasn't even yours in the first place. Half the proceeds from a robbery you and Celia took part in twenty-five years ago.' Grace looked purposefully around the room. 'And you don't exactly need it, do you? You're not exactly on your uppers.' She placed her elbows on her side of the desk, rested her head on the back of her cupped hands and looked Frank directly in the eye. 'Whereas Celia has lost a husband, she's been deprived of her child – and me of a mother, may I add – and now she's lost her livelihood. And you still want to hunt her down, send thugs to murder her, and me too.' She paused and stared him down. 'Are you really that evil, Frank? Should I feel *so* ashamed of having your blood flowing through my veins?'

Frank reached his hand across the desk to her. 'I never meant for you to get hurt ...'

'Stop!' Annie hissed across the room and held up her hand as though to halt traffic. 'I just heard a noise.' She turned her head towards the double doors that led to the hallway. 'There's someone in the house.'

CHAPTER THIRTY-THREE

Gwynn was driving, Celia was fidgeting, and some radio DJ was playing Steppenwolf's 'Born to Be Wild'. It was raining hard and the windshield wipers were slapping in time with the music.

'Turn that noise off,' Celia snarked.

'I need the company,' Gwynn said, 'Seeing as you're not talking.'

'What do you want me to say?'

'That this crazy shit has got to stop.'

She turned to him, her eyes ablaze. 'Don't you want to avenge your dad? After what they did to him? They tortured him, Gwynn, then threw his broken body off the cliffs.' She paused for a moment just to let the message sink in before she continued. 'And they walked away … laughing.'

But Gwynn was only too well aware of the facts and had come to terms with them long ago. 'Every war has casualties, Celia,' he said calmly. 'My dad was in a dangerous game, played with dangerous people. He was probably lucky to have survived for as long as he did.'

'That's an icy remark,' Celia sniped back. 'And *you* accuse *me* of being cold! He was your father.'

'And he was your friend, I get that,' Gwynn said, intent on gently soothing Celia's restless sprit. 'I also understand that you've lost a lot more than anyone in this war.' He took his left hand off the steering wheel to touch hers. 'But *every* war has to end. And it usually ends in a truce. That's what Grace wants to achieve by going to see her father.'

Celia slapped his hand away. 'She's a fool.'

'Have it your way.'

'I will.' Celia sulked for a moment and looked out of the side window. 'If that's how you feel, then why did you insist on coming with me?'

'To stop you from getting your stupid stubborn heads blown off.'

'And why should you care?' Celia snorted.

There was a long silence before Gwynn replied, 'Because I love you, Celia, I always have.'

This time Celia laughed out loud. 'Love me? What? Romantically?'

'Yes,' he said quietly.

'Give over,' she mocked. 'I'm old enough to be your mother.'

Gwynn gripped the steering wheel tightly with both hands and stared between the fast-sweeping wipers at the dark road ahead. 'What has that got to do with anything?' he half-whispered.

The moment Tony opened the double doors and strode into Frank's office Grace knew this was not going to end well, the sawn-off shotgun in his hands being a clue.

'Hey, Tone,' Frank said in a jovial manner. 'What you got there, my son?'

'I'm not your fucking son.'

Grace noted a frenzy in Tony's eyes that had only been hinted at before but was now being given full rein.

Tony squinted at her in the dimly lit room and she wondered if his eyesight was not all it should be.

'The bitch is back,' Tony said, slowly moving the gun in her direction. 'Come crawling now your heavies have been dealt with, eh?'

Grace noted the safety catch was engaged on the shotgun. 'Not my guys, or Celia's,' she said, inwardly calculating how long it would take him to disengage the safety and fire if she tried to jump out of the way. If he knew what he was doing, and she guessed that he probably did, then it would be milliseconds. *So,* she thought, *not a cat in hell's chance of escaping that way.*

'Let's all stay calm, shall we, Tony,' Frank interrupted.

Tony glared sideways at his uncle. 'Shut the fuck up, Frank.' His attention was back on Grace. 'So, who were they?'

'Celia didn't tell me.'

'Well, maybe I should just go back to that piece of shit pig farm she's hiding out in and ask her in person.'

'You know where she is?' Frank asked.

'That was my mission, wasn't it, Uncle Frank? To find Celia.' Tony smirked, and he remained still, his gaze crisscrossing Grace's body as he weighed up his target while pointing the shotgun at her midsection. 'And get this one back here.'

'But not to fucking torch the place.' Frank's eyes were firmly fixed on his nephew's face and though his words were confrontational, the tone of his voice was less so. Grace wondered if he was as antsy as she was about Tony's mental state.

'Me and the lads walked in there,' Tony said, moving his attention back to his uncle. 'And these two guys came out shooting. What the fuck was I supposed to do?'

'Five of you against two guys.' Frank was more brusque now. 'Who were they, the fucking SAS?' He sneered and stuck out his chin as though daring Tony to shoot him.

'And there's only you left to tell the tale,' Annie said dryly. 'How very convenient.'

'What are you saying, bitch?'

Tony started to turn away from Grace and swing the sawn-off in a half circle towards Annie. In those few seconds all the gun training Grace had done over the years in Australia came flooding back to her. She noted that Tony was right-handed, so Annie on his left was an easy target if he was going to shoot her. Grace calculated that he could disengage the safety in three to four seconds before firing. But with Grace being on his right-hand side, if he was forced to shoot at her instead, he'd have to turn back though 180 degrees. That meant he'd have to realign his aim, which would take eight to ten seconds she reckoned. And that, she prayed, gave her just enough time …

Grace took off from a standing start like a sprinter and charged at Tony across the few metres between them. She spotted Tony disengaging the safety on the shotgun as he started to turn back to her. One out-of-control gun in the hands of a madman meant anything could happen.

'Down!' she yelled and hoped that both Annie and Frank would take heed.

Grace made contact with Tony going full pelt, their heads connected with a sickening thud and they hit the deck together. The wild shots from the double barrel took out the floor-to-ceiling windows behind Frank's desk. The sound of the blast and breaking glass sent shockwaves through the room. The stronger of the two, Tony pushed Grace from on top of him and scrambled to his feet. Through the buzzing in her ears, Grace heard another shot ring out just before Tony hit her with the butt of the shotgun. Then the lights went out.

CHAPTER THIRTY-FOUR

Bone-breaking pain ricocheted through Tony's leg and he knew Frank had shot him. He guessed the old fuck was using that gun he kept in his desk drawer. Nobody keeps a full clip in a gun they use for protection, so Tony wondered if maybe that one bullet was it. Or maybe not. He glanced up at Frank who had the 9mm pointed directly at him. Tony could see concern cross Frank's usual poker face and knew that even if Frank did have another bullet in there, he wouldn't fire again for fear of hitting Grace. But with Grace unconscious on the floor, she was useless to use as a human shield to walk out of there. Unless.

'Step away from her, Tony,' Frank said.

No fucking way, Tony thought, as he withdrew his knife from the sheath beneath his shirt and squatted down behind the prone body of Grace.

'Pretty, isn't she, Uncle Frank?' he taunted, placing the blade of the knife against her throat. 'Wonder if she really is your daughter. Shall I do a blood test?' The tip of the knife nicked Grace's throat close to the jugular and a trickle of blood ran down her neck. 'Well it's certainly red, Frank.' Tony laughed. 'Should we try for some more?'

Frank stood, gun in hand, impotent.

'What do you want, Tony?' Annie said. 'You came here wanting something. What was it?'

'I came here to kill you cunts.'

Annie stood up and gestured for Frank to sit down. 'Then why not come in shooting from the hip? Nice big gun like that. Bang, bang, bang and it would have been a complete slaughterhouse.'

'Sit down or I'll slit her throat.'

'Then slice away, darling,' Annie said, languidly. 'Personally, I can't stand the woman. Too like her mother for my liking.'

Annie took two steps towards Tony.

'Get back or I'll gut her,' he warned and prodded the tip of the knife into the other side of Grace's exposed throat.

'You're bleeding yourself there, Tony.' Annie took another casual step closer and peered at his leg. 'Looks like it went straight through the muscle.'

'Get back!'

'You see, you're not in a very good bargaining position here, are you?' Annie mused. 'I don't care if you kill her but if you do, then your good old uncle Frank over there will shoot you right between the eyes.'

Annie stepped even closer. Tony, just two feet away from her, sprang at her from his crouched position, almost knocking her over. He grabbed her hair and positioned himself behind her, knife to her throat.

Grace opened her eyes. She'd been brought back to consciousness by the first nick of the blade to her neck but realising her predicament had decided to lie doggo.

What she saw was Tony edging towards the blasted-out windows. He held Annie around her waist with his left arm and his right hand held a deadly looking hunting knife to her throat. He seemed to be dragging his left leg and he was leaving a snail-like trail of blood behind him.

Frank stood silently with a pistol in his hand.

'Stay in the house, Frank,' Tony hissed as he dragged Annie out between the shattered glass. 'Follow me and I'll gut her.' And they were gone.

Grace got to her feet and made her groggy way over to Frank, using all her will to clear her pounding head and pull herself together. There was no telling what that crazy bastard might do to Annie.

'Give me that gun.' She reached out her hand to Frank, whose face had taken suddenly taken on a death-mask pallor.

He shook his head. 'Empty,' he gasped, breathing erratically, his tight fist held hard against his chest. 'Shotgun,' he said.

Grace crossed the room to where it had fallen and picked it up. 'Useless,' she said. 'Two shots only.'

And at that moment Frank's legs appeared to fold from under him and he collapsed on the floor. Grace rushed to him as he lay there plucking at his chest.

'Looks like you're having a heart attack,' she said. 'I'll call an ambulance.' She took Gwynn's mobile from her pocket.

Frank's face was a picture of agony, but he reached up towards her with one feebly shaking hand. 'You're bleeding,' he said.

'Don't worry about me.'

'I didn't mean for you to get hurt, Gracie,' Frank said just before he passed out.

Tony had parked the Pathfinder by the servants' entrance to the house. When he reached there, using Annie as his shield and with a knife to her throat, he sliced upwards from the side of her head and let loose of her momentarily. She screamed and clutched at her half-severed ear. He grabbed her by the hair and beat her head, face first into the brick wall of the house until she collapsed onto the ground. He kicked her. 'Stay there, bitch! Move and I'll cut your fucking head off.'

Annie slumped on the ground, stunned and sobbing. Tony opened the boot of the car, took out the canvas gun bags and dumped them on the ground. Annie was on her hands and knees, attempting to crawl away. He kicked her viciously in the behind, grabbed her by the hair and dragged her to her feet. He was well pleased to see that the blows to the head against the wall had smashed her previously aristocratic nose.

'Get in the boot,' he ordered.

She resisted. He sliced her arm and she screamed. 'Don't worry,' he sneered as Annie climbed in beside the plastic-wrapped corpse of the former Rob Douglas. 'You've got a companion in there. He doesn't say much so you'll get on just fine.' And he slammed the boot shut on her.

The Range Rover was parked up a hundred yards down from the house with Gwynn and Celia going at it hammer and tongs.

'That's a stupid idea,' she was saying.

'So is you marching in there with my shotgun. It's asking for trouble. I'll go in there on foot, scout around and if I'm not back out in five minutes you come in doing your Annie Oakley impression.'

Celia reluctantly agreed, and watched Gwynn walk up to the white gateposts and disappear from sight. She got out of the car, opened the back and took out the shotgun. She walked back to the driver's seat, climbed in and placed the loaded shotgun on the passenger seat she had just vacated.

***

Celia had given Gwynn a rough verbal layout of the property as she recalled it, so he knew he had to walk the few hundred yards to the building, pass the stables/garage on his right, then left at the top of the drive and around the corner to the front of the house. He was impressed by the converted stable, intrigued by the odd layout of the place and wondered if he should take a look around the back first, maybe find a way in that way. There were no lights in the drive itself and the first he knew about the vehicle that almost ran him down was the sound of screeching tyres on gravel and full-beam headlights bearing down on him as the black SUV missed him by inches.

***

Celia spotted the Pathfinder just as it turned out from between the white gateposts. Making one of those instant decisions that she almost always regretted, she hit the gas and gave chase.

What she didn't notice was Gwynn exiting the gates and an ambulance loudly declaring blues and twos hurtling down the road towards the house.

***

Frank was lying on the Persian rug with two paramedics working on him when Gwynn's phone rang. It was on the desk where Grace had placed it after she'd made the call to emergency services. She picked it up and listened.

'Gwynn, I've gone after the Pathfinder. Go in and see what's happened. Phone the cops if you have to. Just make sure Grace is safe.'

'It's me, Celia,' Grace said. 'Tony's driving that car and he may have Annie with him, if he hasn't killed her already.'

'Are you alright?'

'As can be expected. But Frank's had a heart attack.'

'I think I may cry.'

'Save the sarcasm.'

'Save your pity.' Celia ended the call.

The paramedics were manoeuvring Frank onto a stretcher when Gwynn walking in through the blasted-out window.

'What the hell happened here?'

Grace opened the desk drawer where she'd secreted the pistol, and grabbed a loaded clip from the same place.

'Did you just walk up the drive?' Grace asked Gwynn.

'Almost got knocked over by a black car,' he said.

'Did you see a woman anywhere?'

'No, just the car and then the ambulance.'

Grace headed out the way Gwynn had entered. 'Call the police, will you,' she shouted back to Gwynn. 'Tell them that an armed and dangerous man broke into the house; that he's kidnapped a woman and he's driving the black Pathfinder car the Welsh police are looking for.'

She ran down the steps in time to see Frank being loaded into the ambulance. 'Hang in there, Frank,' she called to him, though she wasn't sure he could hear her.

'Where are you going?' Gwynn shouted after her as she climbed into the Land Rover.

'I'm going to get the bad guy and to save Celia's arse.'

Grace sounded cockier than she actually felt. She had an inkling where Tony might be headed but also knew she could be totally wrong. All she could do was put her trust in her instincts until she could raise Celia on the phone, so Grace started the Land Rover and headed off into the night.

CHAPTER THIRTY-FIVE

Driving through rain that was turning to sleet and swiftly limiting visibility, Celia attempted to stay not so close behind her quarry. Eddie had taught her a few tricks of the trade way back when, so she was quite confident that, apart from something unforeseen happening, she'd be able keep up with the Pathfinder while keeping a reasonable distance such as two cars behind. Her mood was less buoyant about facing the driver down at a destination unknown to her, so she was a bit twitchy about where the driver was headed. She'd never met Tony Boyle, so found it impossible to second-guess him. Who did he know, what backup might he have access to? All unknown quantities in the dangerous waters she'd plunged into purely on impulse. All she could be sure of about him was his gruesome, youthful reputation, although she had seen what she assumed to be his handiwork at her cottage and also knew that he was a suspect in the murder of Dermot's grandson. Her mind retreated from the very thought of Dermot. He'd be expecting to hear back from his sons in the next day or so and if he didn't then he'd quickly be on her case. And if two of those bodies taken from the burnt-out cottage turned out to be the brothers O'Reardon, then there'd be hell to pay.

The cars ahead of her were just at the turn-off where Celia had dumped Grace's phone just a few days ago, when the Pathfinder indicated right. Was he going back to Anglesey? Celia smiled. Well, if that was the case then it was 'Advantage Ms Williams', because that was her home turf. She knew the island like the back of her proverbial mitt. 'Come to Momma,' she cooed at the black vehicle as it headed towards the Menai Bridge.

***

Grace had found Celia's number on Gwynn's phone just after leaving the house. She had rung it several times only to have it go to voicemail over and over again. The phone was fast running out of juice and her resolve was faltering. What if she was headed in totally the wrong direction, how hollow would be her promise to Gwynn to save Celia's arse? With a mere ten per cent left on the battery, she tried Celia's number one more time with crossed fingers. After a few heart-stopping moments when Grace feared it might go to voicemail one more time, Celia answered.

'Gwynn? Where are you?'

'I was going to ask you the same thing,' Grace said.

'Stay out of this.'

'No fucking way, Mother! That piece of garbage was threatening to slit my throat back there. And he's got your old mate Annie as a hostage. I'm in this whether you like it or not.'

Hearing a younger echo of her own grim determination coming back at her, Celia conceded with not a little relief. Much as she wanted to keep her daughter safe, she would be great at riding shotgun. 'I don't know where this bastard's going but I'm on his tail.'

'I think he may be heading back to what he described as 'that piece of shit pig farm' in search of you.'

'That makes sense.'

'Why?'

'Because he's just crossed the bridge.'

'See you there,' Grace said with some relief that her instincts had been as trustworthy as usual.

'If he goes somewhere else, I'll let you know.'

'Do that,' Grace said. 'I've got a nice 9mm in my pocket that will be pleased to see him.'

'That's my girl,' Celia said just before she ended the call.

Through the sleety rain, Grace saw Celia standing in the middle of one of those unlit windy roads that were typical of this island. Celia was pointing torchlight in Grace's direction and flagging her down. Grace pulled the Land Rover in behind Celia's vehicle and wound down the window.

'I didn't want you driving past the farm in the dark,' Celia said. 'This road isn't much used by anyone other than Gwynn and lost tourists, so headlights coming along here at this time of night might warn him that someone's around.'

'He's in there?'

Celia shone the torch into the car and squinted at Grace. 'You're hurt. There's blood on your neck and your jumper.' She sounded concerned and, despite herself, Grace felt emotionally warmed.

'He's got a hunting knife. He cut me. It's okay, it's stopped bleeding.'

Unexpected motherly concern for Grace out of the way, Celia was back to business. 'He's been in there for a good fifteen minutes. The car's outside the front door but as I parked here, I had to go around there on foot so was too late to observe much. But I did see him dragging Annie out of the boot.'

'How is she?' Grace couldn't help but feel that Annie had deliberately put herself in danger, but for what reason?

'She looks in a bad way, but she was able to stand up on her own, though she did throw up against the back wheel.'

'You've got good eyesight.' Grace recalled both the fairish distance between the farm gate and the farmhouse as well as the lack of any lighting other than that on the outside of the barn.

Celia indicated to the pair of binoculars hanging around her neck. 'We be country folk, we be,' she said in a cod-Cornish accent. 'We have stout shoes and spades and everything in us 'orses and carts.'

'Very funny,' Grace said. 'But we've got to get Annie out of there. From what I could tell he's totally off his nut, so Christ knows what he'll do to her.'

***

Knocking her unconscious was the easy bit. The tricky part was finding a long and strong rope that was thin and flexible enough to tie her hands and to push the other end through the narrow gap between the crossed wooden beams above his head and the ceiling itself. He'd left Annie lying in a crumpled heap on the floor. Her face was a mess, her hair matted from the head wound he'd just provided her with, and her clothes covered with blood from that half-severed earlobe. And vomit! Tony was appalled. The dirty bitch had been sick all over herself. He resolved to deal with all that once he had her hoisted. He searched all the kitchen cupboards but came up empty, until he found the perfect thing and almost whooped for joy. It was a blue climber's rope and Tony wondered if maybe the farmer was one of those volunteers who rescued walkers off the Snowdonia mountain range during winter blizzards. *Bloody fools*, he thought, putting your own life at risk to save idiots too thick to take the right gear with them.

He stood on the big wooden traditional farm table to thread the rope over the beam but, due to the stiffness in his right leg, he had to give it three goes before he finally got it right, which annoyed him so much he considered slicing through Annie's other ear as retribution, but restrained himself.

He lugged Annie onto the table, tied her hands to the other end of the rope and began to hoist her up. When the rope tightened enough, he tied the other end to the table leg then pushed the heavy table out of the way. It took most of his strength to shift the thing, and the feet made a loud scraping sound on the tiled floor as though it were reluctant to move. Sweating with the effort, Tony finally stood back to view his handiwork. Sweet!

Satisfied that this part of his hastily cobbled together plan was working, he set about sorting himself out, found a large pair of scissors, cut up the side of his trousers and patched up what was really only a flesh wound. Frank was a stupid incompetent old bastard, he sneered, couldn't hit the side of a fucking barn with a howitzer. Tony took a long glug from a bottle of whisky he'd found in the cupboard, downed five Ibuprofen he discovered in a drawer and turned back to the main event suspended from the ceiling beams.

There she was, the bitch who thought she was smarter than him, the loser ex-junkie who'd fuck anything that moved, the posh cunt who constantly belittled him in front of Frank. *Who* had *who* now, eh? Tony had *her*, hanging by the wrists, her toes three feet off the ground.

Ecstatic with his work and aware that when she finally came round the pain in her arms and shoulders would be excruciating, Tony took another drink from the whisky bottle and began to cut off all of Annie's clothes.

CHAPTER THIRTY-SIX

Celia hadn't been kidding about having all kinds of gear in her Land Rover. Walking boots were produced, both pairs a size six, waterproof jackets, and watch caps. 'Tuck all your hair under that,' Celia said. 'Blonde hair shines like a beacon in the moonlight.'

Not much chance of that, Grace thought, glancing up at the bleak, dark sky with its half-visible clouds hanging like bloated, pregnant ghosts above their tiny corner of the globe. Even so, she did as she was told. When they were both suitably dressed, Celia tossed a torch to Grace. 'Keep the light on the ground in front of you, and don't lift it any higher. We don't want him to spot it.'

Grace was reminded of her first night in Frank's house and the ominous sight of three figures picking their way along the catspaw pathway guided only by torchlight. The scene remained vivid in her memory: the unknown shackled man shuffling along behind the limping Frank while being urged forward at gunpoint by the out-of-control thug they were now hoping to sneak up on. Despite her heavy waterproof jacket, Grace shivered and tried to convince herself it was because the sleet was stinging her face but deep down she knew the truth. If she'd been out of her depth before, she was now going under for the third time and trying to stop herself from legging it back to her vehicle before it was too late. *This is Celia's fight, not yours*, said her inner voice of self-preservation. That was when Celia turned and smiled at her. 'I'm glad you're here with me, Grace.'

And that was that. Game on.

Instead of entering the farm though the large gate they had previously driven through, Celia was leading Grace to a smaller gate, down a muddy pathway that exited on the other side of the barn. 'It's a public pathway,' Celia said quietly, 'Gwynn keeps it open for the walkers. Some farmers get shirty about right-of-way ramblers but Gwynn thinks it a good thing.'

'He's a decent man,' Grace said.

'Of course, you have to know the path is there in the first place, and everyone keeps mighty quiet about it.'

'What are you saying?'

'That the Welsh are a wily bunch. They stick to the rules but there's always a strong element of silent subversion about them.'

The gate creaked loudly, through lack of use, Grace presumed, and both women stood still for a moment to see if there was any movement coming from the house that might indicate Tony having heard anything. However, as the front door remained firmly shut and there was no light in the front room of the building, they carried on along the way until they reached the barn. Celia nudged Grace to indicate that they should leave the muddy path and move slowly towards the house.

The sleet was gradually thickening, and flurries of snow flitted before Grace's eyes. As a child, she had watched festive American films on TV during the middle of the sweltering Australian summer. *White Christmas* had been Ma's favourite with its highly romanticised sleigh rides and jolly scenes of people skating on frozen ponds. But Grace had never seen actual snow before and recalled fantasising about experiencing it, rather as a virgin would about her first sexual encounter. Creeping around a pig farm in Wales in pursuit of a madman was the last thing on earth she would have envisaged as her 'first time' and she had to repress the fit of the giggles she felt about to erupt, so instead she stuck out her tongue to taste the snow.

As they moved closer to the house, Celia turned to see Grace 'experiencing' snow. Her face showed her disappointment in her daughter's childish delight and her voice echoed it. 'Jesus-fucking-Christ,' she hissed. 'Grow up, girl.'

And at that moment a piercing scream emanating from the house brought Grace back down to the reality of the here and now.

***

The bloodied line he'd drawn with the blade of the hunting knife stretched from beneath Annie's right breast to her left hip. Not much deeper than a paper cut but immensely painful. Annie, her face a mask of controlled horror, was staring at him from beneath bruised and swollen eyelids.

'You nose looks broken.' He reached forward and tweaked it; the sickening cracking noise it made was drowned out by Annie's screech. She tried to kick out at him but managed only to set herself swinging to and fro. He laughed and pushed her as though she were a child on a swing, and searing pain coursed through her as the motion almost tore her arms from their sockets.

'Come on, bitch, fight back! The more you struggle the more I'll enjoy hurting you.' He held his knife in front of his chest, the curved tip pointing outwards as though her next swing forward was intended to skewer her.

Annie's eyes widened with fear as she stared at the knife, but Tony stopped her forward swing with his hand just before the blade pierced her body. Steadying her shaking frame, he carved another line from beneath her left breast to her right hip. 'X marks the spot,' he taunted and slowly drew another bloody line from the middle of the X, down to just above her pubic hair.

He stood back, hearing her sobbing and smiled, 'I could peel you like a grape, you know. Shall I do that, Annie, leave you hanging there like a side of skinned beef?'

Tony walked over to where his jacket lay on the back of a kitchen chair. 'Let's see what Frank says, shall we?' He removed his phone from his pocket and turned back to face her. 'Come on, Annie,' he jeered. 'Smile for the camera.'

He took her photo and emailed it to Frank.

Wind was blowing sleety rain through the gaping hole in the wall of Frank's office when Gwynn opened the door to the hallway for a look-see. He turned back to the plain-clothes cop he'd just let into the house.

'Everything in that room will be ruined,' he said.

The man, who had not yet introduced himself, looked in and nodded his head. 'I'll get my officers to put plastic sheeting up,' he said. 'So, can you tell me how come you happen to be in Frank Gilligan's house, Mr, erm…?'

'Hughes,' said Gwynn. 'And it's a bit of a long story.'

***

Two miles down the road, in the intensive care unit, Frank Gilligan held out one hand to the young nurse by his bedside and struggled to remove the oxygen mask covering his mouth and nose with the other.

'No!' The nurse reached across him in an attempt to put it back in place.

Frank resisted, and he held the mask a couple of inches away from his face. 'Please, please,' he begged. 'Please tell Gracie.' He gasped for air that refused to come. 'Tell my daughter … Tell her … I'm sorry.'

'You can tell her yourself once the surgeons fix you up,' she said, firmly returning the mask to where it should be.

'Promise me,' Frank said but could not be sure that she heard him.

The machine he was wired-up to wailed out its shrill warnings, hospital staff sprang into action and the curtains were swiftly drawn once more around Frank Gilligan's bed.

With no lights visible at the front of the house, Celia had decided to use her key to enter the building and indicated that Grace should go around the back. Grace picked her way around the side of the house wondering just where Tony might have dumped Annie. When she got there, the lights in the kitchen were full on and projecting their harsh light onto the cobbled yard. The curtains were open and what confronted Grace when she crouched down to look inside was so sickening she wanted to kick the door down and drop Tony where he stood. Annie was strung up like an animal after slaughter, her head lolling to one side, her face a pulpy mess with marks carved into the pale flash of her body. Tony, with his back to the window, had a bucket in his hand and appeared about to douse his victim with liquid as though to bring her around from a dead faint.

Grace was so incensed that she no longer cared about Celia's plan of action, which was for Grace to check out the back while Celia snuck in the front way. Instead, Grace slid past the window and tried the handle of the door. It was locked.

'Who's out there?' she heard Tony shout.

Shit! She guessed he'd heard the movement of the door handle. *What the hell*, she thought and gave the old door an almighty kick. It didn't budge.

From inside the room, Grace heard Celia's voice. 'Cut her down, you sick fuck!' One glance in the window showed Celia standing in the doorway at the other side of the room with her shotgun. Tony had taken cover behind Annie.

'The elusive Celia, I presume,' he called to her. 'Put the gun down or I gut her.'

Standing outside, Grace swiftly considered her options. Tony had his back to her. He'd have been an easy target out in the open but right now he was too close to Annie, and Grace was worried that the bullet might go straight through him and hit his victim too. Then there was the clear obstacle that stood between them – the glass. As a purely competitive shooter, Grace had never fired a bullet through glass, but she was sure that any deflection would limit the accuracy of her aim, again endangering Annie. Her third option was trying to kick the door down again but as he'd just threatened to kill Annie if Celia didn't drop the shotgun, she was sure he'd do exactly that by the time she finally kicked her way through the door. Her only sane option was to act as back-up for Celia by heading around the side of the house and entering through the front door.

***

How, wondered Gwynn, do you explain to this Inspector French just what happened in this house without landing Celia and Grace in a whole pile of excrement? But he gave it a go.

'So,' said the cop. 'After the fire at her mother's cottage, your lady friend's daughter came here to see her father, Frank Gilligan.'

'That's right,' Gwynn agreed.

'And you and the young lady's mother followed on when Mrs Williams returned from giving her statement to the Anglesey police.'

'Correct again.' Gwynn was relieved that what he was hearing sounded more plausible when repeated back to him than when he'd actually told the tale.

'As for this ...' Inspector French indicated in the direction of the now-plastic-covered blown-out windows and said, without a hint of mirth, but drenched in sarcasm, 'It was like this when you got here.'

At which point a young SOCO officer drew the inspector's attention to the phone he was carrying in his latex-gloved hand. 'Guv! This photo was just discovered on Mr Gilligan's phone.'

Gwynn noticed a slight nervous tick appear at the edge of French's eye as he looked at the mobile proffered by the gloved hand.

'I wondered, Mr Hughes, if you'd tell us if you know this woman?' He looked up at the SOCO team officer. 'Don't be shy. Show him.'

Gwynn stared open-mouthed at the blurred but explicit picture of a woman who had clearly been subjected to torture. He swallowed hard. 'No,' he said. 'I don't know her ... but I can tell you where she is. That's my house.'

Despite the overhead lighting, Tony found himself squinting at the woman who looked like an older version of Grace. And he gloried in the fact that here she was, the key to his envisaged pot of gold. So, he had to suppress the blood lust he'd conjured up for Annie. She was no fun anymore anyway, passing out like that. Right now, he had to concentrate on getting to this new bitch before whoever had been trying to knock down the door came along to give her any back-up. But with a shotgun pointed at him it was not going to be easy. All his firepower was in the Pathfinder. *How stupid you are leaving those guns there,* he chastised himself. Still, he had in his hand the very thing that he was most expert at using. He took a moment to judge exactly where Celia was standing, while keeping Annie's body still in Celia's sightline; took a quick 45-degree step back and, keeping the knife horizontal to his target, threw it as hard as he could. The blade appeared to Tony to be cutting its way through the air in slow motion, although it hit the woman in mere seconds after it left his hand. Celia screamed as the knife penetrated her left shoulder and she dropped the gun.

Tony leapt across the room, got Celia in a neck lock and jiggled the knife, the blade of which was embedded two inches into her upper arm.

Celia screamed again.

CHAPTER THIRTY-SEVEN

Halfway around the building, Grace heard a scream that did not sound like Annie. She took off at a run, weighed down by the heavy jacket and clumsy boots, lost her footing on the snow-slippery ground, fell hard against the wall banging her head, and stood for a moment literally seeing stars.

A door slammed and the din of a car engine burst the silence. Grace finally regained enough equilibrium to be able to move once more but as she rounded the corner she saw the Pathfinder hurtling away towards the closed farm gate. She released the safety on her pistol and took aim at the back tyres; one, two, three shots. She'd seen tyres shot out in films but wasn't convinced it was possible on a moving vehicle in real life. She thought the bullets were more likely to bounce off rather than penetrate the rubber, but she gave it a go. After firing, she took off after the car, presuming that Tony would have to get out of the vehicle to open the gate and, if she could get closer, she'd have a good shot at him.

But the Pathfinder drove straight through the wooden barrier, skidded right to avoid the flying debris, regained control and was gone.

***

Gwynn was in the back seat of a police car heading over the bridge. The driver had them hurtling along at a speed that Gwynn found both comforting yet disconcerting, and Inspector French was talking to someone with the Anglesey force on the radio.

'You know the farm? Good. Get there ASAP. This man is armed and dangerous. He has at least one female hostage who may come to harm if he spots any sign of a police presence so keep it discreet. I have firearms officers with me. Do not approach until we get there.'

Gwynn turned to look out of the back window at the two cars following behind. He'd seen three officers getting in there, all armed to the teeth, and he hoped that poor woman, whoever she was, could be rescued. But where the hell were Celia and Grace? Hopefully nowhere near the farm.

***

Tony was winging it because he'd had no idea where he was going once he left the farmhouse. He knew a couple of derelict buildings just off the dock road in Liverpool that he could get to in about an hour and a half. He'd used one place before about six months previously. It was too far away from houses for anyone to be able to hear him as he softened up one of his dealers. The bastard had been smoking product instead of selling it on. Fucking crack addicts, you couldn't trust 'em. Breaking the scabby scrote's kneecap with a hammer did the trick after pulling what was left of his rotten teeth out with pliers. 'A little chastisement is good for the soul,' Tony had informed him. 'But do it again and next time it's your bollocks.'

Tony chuckled at the memory and glanced over his shoulder to Celia, all nicely trussed up on the back seat. He'd tied her hands behind her back, gagged her with a tea towel and taped it into place, so she could breathe just enough without panicking and throwing up. Drowning on vomit was not what he envisaged for this bitch. She was going to tell him where the money was stashed so didn't want her croaking before he could get to work on her. He'd told her that if she didn't move too much she probably wouldn't bleed to death. Unless he pulled the knife out and then she'd definitely be a goner. That had set the bitch straight.

So, Liverpool it was, he decided, but first he had to get off this shithole of an island.

***

Grace banged on the front door of the house. 'Celia?' she shouted but got no response. She kicked the door, but years ago they built these things to last and it didn't budge an inch. Her only alternative was to get around the back again and see what had happened to Celia. Looking through the window into the kitchen, she saw the only sign of life was Annie, who was at least still breathing. But there was no sign of Celia. Cold fear gripped Grace. Had Tony taken Celia with him? She had to get into the house to cut Annie down, find Celia and get help. But with the phone in her pocket as dead as a coffin nail and both the front and rear doors to the farmhouse closed, she had to improvise. The barn! Inside she found a spade and ran back to the house. There was a lower window at the front of the house she knew she could climb through if she could break it. Two shots from the 9mm shattered the glass, then she used the spade to knock out what remained, took off her waterproof jacket, laid it across the jagged edges remaining in the frame and climbed in.

'Celia,' she called once more but as she entered the kitchen and spotted the shotgun lying on the floor, her heart sank. Tony had Celia.

'Annie,' she said to the naked women hanging by her wrists from the ceiling beam. 'He's gone. You're safe.'

Annie made a grunting sound.

Grace went to the large farmhouse table to untie the rope that suspended Annie, took the weight and gently lowered her to the floor, untied her hands and went to look for a blanket to cover her shivering body. Annie opened her swollen eyes for a moment. 'Thank you.'

'Where's the phone?' Grace said out loud to herself and looked around to see one in a stand on the kitchen top. '999, right?' she said.

She looked back to see Annie's body stiffen and shudder into a seizure.

***

'Shots fired about five minutes ago,' the sergeant from Holyhead police told Inspector French on the phone.

'Any armed units with you?'

'They're on their way.'

'Then for Christ's sake, stay where you are. We're just a few minutes from you now.'

'Whoever he is, he's a brazen one,' the sergeant said. 'He's not hiding away at all. Every single light appears to be on in the downstairs rooms.'

'Just stay where you are, sergeant.'

Standing behind the vehicles parked a hundred yards from the turn-off to the Hughes farm, the sergeant was not best pleased. The rain had turned torrential and this was not how he had envisaged spending his evening. He was just a few months off retirement and that fire yesterday had been enough excitement to last him. He had joined the Welsh police to protect his community, not to go racing about like the bloody Sweeney. Things had changed a lot on the island since he'd joined the force and he didn't like it one little bit. He stood there, getting wetter and watching the house closely. That was when he heard the distinct sound of rotor blades. He saw the green and red taillights at first followed by the blinding head and ground lights as the pilot set down in front of the farmhouse.

'An air ambulance has just arrived, sir,' he told French.

'Get over there and stop them from going in.'

By the time the sergeant and his team reached the farm gate, the medics were already through the open front door.

And Grace was out the back way.

CHAPTER THIRTY-EIGHT

The Pathfinder had started pulling to the right. Tony cursed it then wondered if breaking through the gate had thrown the steering off-balance, though he doubted that. Then it occurred to him that one of the bullets fired by Grace as he retreated from the farmhouse might well be embedded in a rear tyre. Which meant a slow puncture. Not that he was in any position to have anything done about it, what with a back seat full of a bound and bleeding woman with a knife protruding from her arm, a bag of illegal lethal weapons on the floor of the car, and a slowly decomposing corpse in the boot. Given all that and the fact that he was not sure he'd get even halfway to Liverpool with a gradually deflating tyre, he had to think of some other plan.

He was just about to turn right at one of the numerous T-junctions he kept encountering when the solution to his dilemma loomed at him from beyond his headlights. He switched them on to full beam and there, illuminated against the black starless sky, halfway up an incline and isolated in the middle of a sloping field, surrounded by an ironwork fence and overgrown greenery, stood a church with its small bell tower pointing heavenwards. He stopped the car, grabbed a torch and stepped into the driving rain. He crossed the otherwise deserted road and examined the rusting chain that held the rotting double gates closed.

He noted the *For Sale* sign and boarded-up entrance. He shone the torchlight around the small graveyard that stood to one side of the building; the unkempt gravestones proclaiming the faded names of the long dead was a sure sign that nobody gave a toss about the place anymore. This was perfect. Not only was it isolated enough for him to be able to get down to business with the woman unheard, but he could also dispose of the bodies in one of those old graves. However, the real icing on this cake was that no one would ever think of looking for him in this place.

Abandon hope all ye who enter here, he laughed and headed back to the car to fetch the bolt cutters he'd spotted in the boot.

***

Grace crept along the pathway beside the barn, out of the creaky gate and headed towards where she'd parked the Land Rover. Too many questions awaited her with the police, but she had given the description of the car to the emergency services operator. When she was almost there, she spotted two police cars with local insignia blocking the lane in front of her car, but there was no sign of any human presence. She presumed they had all gone to the house. She opened up and climbed into the Land Rover. 'Good luck, Annie,' she said out loud as the air ambulance whisked its way into the air. Under the cover of the noise she started the engine. Unable to go forward, she did a five-point turn in the narrow road to head in the direction she'd seen the Pathfinder take. She guessed he'd be going back to the main drag and probably off the island. She knew she wasn't thinking clearly, that the chances of catching up with him were less than zero, but felt duty-bound to try. He had Celia as a hostage now and, if what he did to Annie was any guide, then he was capable of anything.

Lost in thought, she didn't see the unmarked car come hurtling towards her, closely followed by two police cars. Jolted by self-preservation, she swerved to avoid the oncoming traffic and ended up hitting the dry stone wall on the other side of the road. For a moment, and for the second time that day, she momentarily fell out of existence.

The next thing Grace was aware of was the flash of a police uniform in her peripheral vision and a voice saying, 'Out of the vehicle please, madam.'

The polite formality of his manner belied the reality of his pointing a 9mm carbine straight at her.

'I'm sorry,' she said, 'I feel a little dizzy.' She closed her eyes and leaned forward, which delayed her exit just long enough for her to slide the gun out of her coat pocket and quickly secrete it under the driver's seat.

'Grace!'

She heard Gwynn call to her as her feet hit the wet tarmac.

'Stay back, sir,' said the cop.

'It's fine,' French told the armed-response officer, 'This young lady is a witness.'

Gwynn was let through the uniforms surrounding Grace and he hugged her. 'Where's Celia?'

'He took her.' She turned to the police. 'Don't just stand here; go after him. He's driving a black Pathfinder. Put up some roadblocks or something. Keep him off the bridges.' Her head was buzzing; she felt unreal, detached and gripped Gwynn's arms as she swayed on her feet. 'His name is Tony Boyle and he's crazy. He's got my mother …'

***

It was pitch-dark inside and to his surprise, Tony's torchlight picked out the simple wooden pews that were still *in situ* when he had expected the church to have been stripped bare. His light fell on the unadorned altar and the lectern that stood beneath a stained-glass window, and he idly took them in. There were three panels depicting the crucifixion in the centre and a female figure to either side of the suffering Christ. Above that was a flower-shaped window with another figure in the centre and five glass petals with verses from the Bible. Tony hated the holy rollers who had visited him when he was inside, trying to persuade him to allow Jesus into his heart. He'd viewed them as a bunch of evangelicals, paying penance by visiting the most dangerous of lunatics.

So here he was in the house of their god, gleefully envisaging the scene: the early morning light would come streaming through those bits of painted glass to fall on the naked frame of Celia, sacrificed on the altar of cold greed. He shivered and reined in his imagination. Nice idea but it was freezing in there, and black as the devil's arse. If he brought her in right now, with the loss of blood she'd already suffered, the cold might send her into shock and she could die before she told him about the money.

What a fucking cock-up this was. Still, he could make the best of it. He would leave the bitch in the car until first light. The car was cold, but not like it was inside the church. When he'd shoved that reporter's body inside, he'd spotted a couple of travel blankets in the boot, along with a spade. It was as though the fates were on his side: the blankets to keep the bitch more or less alive until she coughed, the spade to bury the stiff. Sorted!

CHAPTER THIRTY-NINE

Grace woke up in a room she didn't recognise with the morning light filtering in through flower-patterned curtains. The single bed she was in was hard up against a wall beneath the window and she moved the curtain out of the way to look out but could see only a slate-grey sky above. She sat up, still feeling woozy and noted she was wearing a pink nightdress that she would normally never have been seen dead in. Lifting the duvet out of the way, she turned around, swung her legs out of the bed and felt instantly sick as the pink-patterned carpet appeared to judder beneath her feet.

At that moment, a woman entered the room. She was short and rotund with white hair. She reminded Grace of one of the fairy godmothers from Disney's *Sleeping Beauty*. That, however, was where the similarity ended. 'I'm Dr Dilys,' the woman said and added in a manner that brooked no argument, 'Back in bed, now.'

Grace obeyed and rested her head on the wall behind her to stop the room from swirling.

'What do you recall about last night?' Dr Dilys plonked her ample behind on the bed and took Grace's wrist with a firm hand.

'The last thing I remember is standing in the rain and yelling at the police to set up roadblocks.'

'And do you remember why you were doing that?'

'Of course I do.'

'That's good and none of my business. Can you tell me your name?'

'Grace Dobbs, but how did I get here?'

'The police brought you here after you collapsed. Suspected concussion from a couple of knocks on the head.'

'Where am I?'

'My house. You were quite lucid when you arrived, but a little memory loss is to be expected.'

'Where are my clothes?'

Dr Dilys pointed to a small wardrobe. 'In there. But it would be better if you stay in bed and rest until Gwynn Hughes comes to take you to the hospital in Bangor where I've organised a CT scan for you. I think you'll be fine after a few days' rest but better safe than sorry, eh?'

'Where is Gwynn?'

'Gone to see to his pigs, my dear. His house may be a crime scene but farm animals can't feed themselves, you know.'

'Have you heard whether they've caught anyone?'

'I don't know anything about any of this, I'm afraid. But I'm sure the police are doing their best. You leave everything to them.'

A bell rang somewhere in the house and the woman got up to answer it. 'That may be Gwynn Hughes now.' She turned back to Grace and smiled kindly. 'We always wondered whether he and your mother would get together, you know. There is the big age difference, of course, but that's nothing these days, is it?'

Here, gossip spreads quicker than a dose of the pox, Celia had said, and she wasn't wrong. In Grace's small corner of WA, gossip was the lifeblood of the community, for better or for worse. People often seemed to know that a divorce was brewing before the people themselves had made the final decision and whispers of some young girl getting knocked up swept around before the first pregnancy test was confirmed. Jungle drums, Ma called them. But they clearly hadn't picked up on this latest hot news on Anglesey.

Grace tried to stand and had to lean against the wall to steady herself as she got dressed.

A tap on the door heralded the arrival of Gwynn. 'Are you decent?'

'Come and help me with this sweater, will you?' It was one that had been loaned to Grace by Celia from her quite extensive wardrobe. All ash and cinders now, of course.

Gwynn averted his eyes as he helped Grace. 'You look so like your mam in that,' he said.

'Any news?'

Gwynn shook his head.

'You love her, don't you?'

He looked puzzled.

'Celia.'

'Of course I do, she's my friend.'

'The good Dr Dilys thinks the relationship should be more romantic.'

'I've known Dilys since I was a little lad. She's a good doctor but she also fancies herself as something of a matchmaker. Never managed to nab a man for herself though.' He laughed. 'Come on, let's get you to Bangor. We can talk in the car.'

***

Tony was pleased with the way things were going so far. The Pathfinder was well hidden at the back of the church where he was convinced it couldn't be spotted from the road. The body of Rob Douglas was now facing eternity in a shallow grave on top of a lady named Gwynneth whose gravestone declared her to have died a spinster in 1900, at the age of fifty. Tony had chosen her specifically just for a laugh. *First time she's had a man on top of her*, he'd chuckled as he dug the hole. He had also chosen another grave for when he finally did away with Celia. This was an elderly gent named Arthur, who had departed this life in 1899 and might well appreciate some female company,

He was pissed off that he'd missed his self-imposed deadline of Celia being laid on the altar at sun-up, but as there was little chance of seeing the sun itself today, then he'd just have to make do. At least it had stopped raining and right now he was more concerned about having to carry the semi-comatose Celia into the church. Being a dead weight would make her heavier than she looked, and he didn't want to dislodge the knife and have her bleed to death. With the wound to his own leg playing up a bit, the last thing he needed was to drop her.

He got in the back of the car with her and tried to slap her awake. She roused but stared at him with confused and frightened eyes before her lids drooped once more. Her face was cold and her lips a nasty shade of blue. *Damn it,* he thought, *she's gone into shock.* He grabbed her hair, held her head and propped her up on the seat, reached behind her carefully so as not to move the knife and untied her hands.

'Come on, Celia,' he whispered in her ear. 'I'll help you walk and we'll get you all safe and warm inside.'

Celia murmured something that Tony took to be consent and gingerly shuffled towards the open door. He lifted her down, put one arm around her waist, and helped her to walk the few yards from the car into the body of the church. Once inside, he closed the door behind them.

CHAPTER FORTY

'So … what *are* the police doing?' Grace asked Gwynn as he drove the Land Rover towards the main road that would take them across the bridge and onward to the hospital on the mainland. 'Did they block off the bridges, search the ferry port, go house to house?'

'They seem to think he's still somewhere on Anglesey but there are lots of places to hide here, isolated houses only used in the summer for example. I'm sure they're doing their best.'

'I'm sure that's very comforting for Celia to know the police are *doing their best* while she's being …' Grace choked up, which was not like her at all. She wondered if this was a side effect of the concussion that was making her feel so emotionally raw.

'Don't think like that,' Gwynn said calmly.

'You didn't see what he did to Annie … it was brutal, it was … sick.' She turned in her seat to face Gwynn and the motion of turning her head made her feel queasy. 'They have to find him before …' Grace held back the alien combination of seething anger and burning regret that was surging through her veins. The what-ifs that Celia had insisted could get you killed in her world. The what-ifs that would haunt Grace forever if the mother she had searched for was badly harmed as a result of her own selfish need to know; of her having fallen into Frank Gilligan's trap. *That's old news*, she told herself. *You chose your side in this battle but just how effective were you when push came to shove? For all your expertise on the competition circuit, what good was that in real life? What if you hadn't gone around the back of the house and had followed Celia through the front door instead? You could have backed her up. What if you hadn't been so shocked by seeing Annie strung up like a side of meat that you'd kept your cool? What if you hadn't tried the door – an act of rank stupidity that alerted Tony to your presence? What if, instead of spending time rescuing a relative stranger you had set off after Tony in the Land Rover right away?*

'I was told they'll be putting a helicopter up at sunrise,' Gwynn said.

Distracted by her own sense of powerlessness, Grace had lost track of the conversation. 'What?'

'Police helicopter. At sunrise, we might see it at any minute.'

With her sense of balance suddenly off-kilter and the scenery appearing to whiz by too quickly, Grace felt as though she was having some kind of panic attack as her heart thundered in her chest. 'Please stop the car, Gwynn, I'm going to spew.'

'You're going to what?'

'Be sick.'

Gwynn stopped the Land Rover by the side of the road. Grace opened the door, leaned out and dry heaved onto the narrow grass verge. With her head spinning she found herself looking down at a set of clearly visible car tracks in the muddy ground. Her eyes followed the marks that led to a set of half-rotting wooden gates just ahead of the car, and a memory surged back. She recalled having passed this way before, of being in this same car on the day she and Celia first met. Celia had been driving far too fast around these serpentine roads for Grace's liking. A little unnerved at the time, Grace had sought to relax by taking in the scenery and recalled seeing this sad, boarded-up place of worship with its unkempt graveyard and padlocked gates. But today, right now, all she saw was a rusting chain hanging loose from the splintered and cracked wood. Despite her befuddled head, Grace glanced around for any sign of the padlock and finally spotted it a few yards up ahead. It was almost as though someone had cut it loose and discarded it contemptuously.

'I think we need to take a look inside this church,' she told Gwynn.

'You've got a hospital appointment,' he said.

'Fuck that. Is your phone recharged?'

'Yes, but …'

'No buts, get on to the local police and tell them to get that helicopter over here. Now!'

'What the hell is this? Have you gone mad?'

'No, Celia's here, I know it. I can feel it.' She swivelled around and reached under the driver's seat. 'Where's the gun, Gwynn?'

He didn't reply.

'I pushed it under the seat when the police turned up. Where is it?'

'I got rid of it,' he said.

'Jesus!' Grace took a deep breath, 'Well, I'm going in anyway. You just get those cops here. Understand?' And before he could argue or try to restrain her, Grace opened the passenger door and jumped down.

Unarmed and with the ground shifting and swirling beneath her feet, she opened the gate and began to make her way along the pathway towards the church.

***

The chill in Celia's bones seemed to reach down into her very soul. She was in and out of consciousness, aware that she was in strange surroundings but confused as to how she came to be there. She was conscious of something sticking out of her shoulder, it was uncomfortable but her whole left arm was numb and she felt only a dull throb from it. She knew she was almost naked and lying on her back. She felt as though she was elevated above the ground and that whatever she was lying on was hard and unyielding, like wood perhaps. The strangest thing was, she could see glittery colours dancing before her half-open eyes. She felt exhausted and afraid. Then he came to her, like the devil, running his hand over her body. His palms felt warm against her cold alabaster skin. 'Where is the money, Celia?'

Was she enmeshed in some kind of a dream or was this a nightmare? Either would have been preferable to the instinctive knowledge that this really was happening, though she found it hard to recall how. Had she been captured by Frank? The very thought kicked in whatever adrenalin she had left in her depleted system.

'Swiss bank account,' she said woozily.

'Number?' the voice of the devil whispered.

'With my papers, in my office, in the cottage.'

Even in her dehydrated and weakened state she still expected the retribution that came painfully and swiftly, the knife in her shoulder, withdrawn an inch, the searing pain as the surge of blood from the wound scorched her cold flesh.

'I pull this all the way out and you die, slowly, shedding your lifeblood all over this altar,' said Diablo.

And at that moment she realised just who this was. 'You torched my home,' she said. 'You did it. You destroyed the papers. Can't get the money now.' And she drifted into semi-oblivion once more.

'Then there's no need to keep you alive, is there?' he hissed.

In one of the few moments of lucidity she had experienced in the past ten hours, Celia said, 'Fuck you. That money was for my child. Do your worst, sonny boy.'

When Tony withdrew the knife from her shoulder with a deliberate sawing action that was intended to do the maximum damage, Celia was jolted back into the real world and could not help but scream.

***

Creeping up the path, feeling disorientated and not in control of all her faculties, Grace swayed on her feet and rested her hand on one of the gravestones that stuck out at an angle onto the pathway. Almost overcome with nausea and in an attempt to regain her focus, she stared at the message etched into the aged granite. As the blurred words on the memorial cleared, she wondered why, in such a forgotten and abandoned burial ground, there should be a spade resting against the headstone of a woman who had died in the year 1900. Odd though it was, Grace saw this as some sort of godsend as she reached across, grabbed the handle and withdrew the head of the implement from the ground. With some effort she hoisted it over her shoulder and carried it with her towards the church. With each step she took, she was assaulted by anxious doubts. Was the concussion forcing her to think and behave irrationally? If Gwynn had done as she asked and called for the police helicopter to come here, and this was just her befuddled mind playing tricks on her and she was about to walk into the church and be confronted by genuine workmen, there on behalf of the vendor or buyer, then not only would she feel a fool but valuable time searching would have been wasted, putting Celia in even more danger. Perhaps she should go back to Gwynn and get to the hospital. She stopped in her tracks, on the verge of returning to the car.

The scream that came from within the church was her answer. Celia.

CHAPTER FORTY-ONE

With her heart pumping and adrenalin surging through her veins, Grace tried to run uphill towards the church, but dizziness forced her to slow down. Riding to the rescue but fainting dead on the floor when she got there was not going to be of any help to Celia, her practical mind informed her. When Grace did get to the church, she saw that where the boarded-up doors had been just days ago, there was now a gaping hole. She crept through and peered in, almost gagging on the musty, neglected smell emanating from the building. The sun had momentarily emerged from behind the grey clouds to cast its intermittent watery light through the stained-glass windows at the far end of the old parish church. Illuminated specks of dust flew about like tiny snowflakes falling on the figure standing in front of the altar with his back to Grace. He held his hands aloft, clasped together as though in prayer. Something that might be taken for an act of worship had not the multi-coloured light from the window hit the hunting knife he held in those clasped hands, its sharp and bloodied blade pointing downward, as though about to make a sacrifice.

'Tell Frank to go fuck himself,' Celia's weary voice echoed through the chapel.

'I'll take your severed head to him, so you can tell him yourself, bitch!'

Grace was halfway up the aisle, moving slowly, carefully, quietly, the stave of the spade gripped in both hands. 'He's dead, Tony,' she called out to him. 'Frank had a heart attack. He's dead.'

Tony turned towards her brandishing the knife like a street fighter.

'How's the leg?' Grace asked walking towards him.

'Stupid old bastard only grazed me. Fucking rubbish shot.'

'Not like me.'

Tony laughed, 'Yeah, but how are you with a shovel?' He took off at a run in her direction and lunged at her. It was all Grace could do to keep her balance, but she used the head of the spade as a shield. The knife sparked off the metal. Tony gripped the spade with one hand. They tussled for control. He struck out at Grace with his other hand and she dodged the blade but her balance gave way and she went down, Tony stood above her, a manic grin on his face.

'Fucking useless women,' he sneered.

'Don't hurt her!' Celia gasped, trying to raise herself up on one elbow. 'I'll tell you how to get at the money.'

'You said it was impossible.'

'I lied,' she said. All of her energy spent, she sank back down again.

'How do I know you're not lying now?' he called back to her while still staring down at Grace, his face a mask of gargoyle malevolence.

'What have you got to lose?' Celia's voice was losing its power – as though she was about to fall asleep and never wake up.

'I'd lose the pleasure of killing this bitch.' He kicked Grace as she lay winded with the chapel roof whirling around her.

Tony turned away from the floored Grace and walked the few paces back to Celia.

'My solicitor, Ivor Rossi, has instructions for Grace.'

Using all the strength she possessed, Grace got to her feet and grabbed the spade. She rushed towards Tony, wielding the spade like a cricket bat. He realised too late. Grace heard the satisfying clang and felt the thud from the blow shudder up her arms as the spade hit him in full swing at the side of the head. Tony slumped sideways onto the tiled floor.

The loud chop, chop, chop of rotor blades from a police helicopter hovering above, and Gwynn's voice calling to her from the door of the chapel, drew Grace's attention. Gwynn thundered up the aisle, phone in hand yelling 'Ambulance to St Mark's Church. Now!'

Seemingly unaware of anything other than the plight of the woman he loved, Gwynn took off his coat to cover the now semi-conscious Celia, ripped off his shirt and attempted to stop the bleeding. 'Stay with me, Celia. For God's sake, stay with me.'

Grace swayed on her feet and gripped hard onto one of the dusty pews. Men in uniforms burst into the house of the god Gwynn was invoking.

Grace thought she saw a gun.

'Where is he?' the armed cop yelled.

She looked down to where Tony Boyle had been lying. He was no longer there.

***

Tony crawled, snakelike, out of the small back door to what had once been a vestry. Despite his bombast to Grace, his leg was giving him hell and his left foot felt numb. Once in the doorway that led out to the back of the church, he knew that he had just seconds to plan his escape. He judged that the police helicopter would have spotted the Pathfinder parked behind the church but because the church was built on a steep slope, they would either radio in their findings and go or set down somewhere less hazardous. All of which gave him time. Although, jumping in the car and driving off with a helicopter in hot pursuit was a mug's game. He needed to brazen it out; collect the canvas bag from the Pathfinder, and sidle down the other side of the church while the local plod were dealing with Celia, before finally deciding to search the grounds. Which meant that he could just walk casually away. Hiding in plain sight.

Tony stayed and crept towards the Pathfinder until he was able to open the door enough to climb inside. Just as he closed the car door, an armed cop came out of the church entrance that Tony had just exited. Tony ducked down in the car, calmly withdrew a semi-automatic pistol from the canvas bag hidden underneath the middle seat, loaded the cartridge from the box of bullets and waited. The cop cautiously approached the vehicle as Tony lay in the footwell. Seconds ticked by before the cop cautiously opened the door and Tony let him have it full in the face.

Grabbing the canvas bag, he jumped out and over the dead body sprawled half in and half out of the door and fled down the pathway. Just outside the rotting wooden gate was a Land Rover. He glanced in as he passed by. The keys were in the ignition; he climbed in, dumped his bag of lethal weapons in the well of the seat beside him and drove away.

CHAPTER FORTY-TWO

Grace awoke in a hospital bed just as a middle-aged nurse walked by. 'When can I get out of here?' Grace called out to her.

The woman gazed at her with sympathetic eyes. 'You've got a nasty concussion. Better ask the doctor when he comes to see you later.'

'Do you know how my mother is?'

'I'm sorry, I don't know ...'

'Her name is Celia Williams; she came in an hour or so before me. She was brought here by air ambulance ... they took her to intensive care.'

'I'll ask for you. Celia Williams, you say?'

'She was admitted with a stab wound.'

'Dear, oh dear.' The woman shook her head. 'What a dreadful world we live in.'

'There's another woman too, her first name is Annie, she was brought here yesterday evening?'

'A lot of people were admitted then, dear,' the nurse said, obviously anxious to be getting on.

'How many by air ambulances, though?'

'I really can't say. You just rest, dear,' she said kindly. 'I'll see what I can find out for you.' And she bustled away.

With the fog gradually clearing from her mind and her memory of the events of the past days coming into focus, Grace began viewing Celia in a different light. Hard as nails, yes, but brave and resilient. A no-nonsense, get-on-with-it type but there had been moments when Grace had sensed real affection coming though, despite Celia's well-guarded carapace. *And at crunch time, Celia was willing to give up all the money she has clung on to for all these years, just to save me,* Grace thought, remembering the look on Tony's face when he stood over her, bloody knife in hand as she lay helpless on the cold hard floor of the church. She had really thought her time had come until she heard Celia's weakened voice call out to him, 'Don't hurt her.' Grace remembered that moment, the look of unadulterated loathing in his expression and how she had held her breath, uncertain how he would respond to Celia's siren call. And she recalled the deep sense of relief when Tony finally turned away, lured by the pull of money. Grace tried to recall what Celia had told him, but the details escaped her.

Suddenly Gwynn was at her bedside.

'Celia?' she said when she saw his concerned face.

'She's in a bad way,' he said, 'Lost a lot of blood. Hooked up to machines and heavily sedated.'

'What did they tell you? Will she recover?'

'The knife didn't hit the large artery in the shoulder, and the wound wasn't infected but there may be some permanent tendon damage.'

'But she'll survive?'

'She was also suffering from hypothermia when she came in and it was touch and go for a while.'

'Have you been here all night?'

He nodded his head. 'I got my farm manager to look after the pigs this morning; I'll have to pay the greedy bastard time and a half for that.'

'Where did the police take Tony Boyle?'

'They didn't catch him,' Gwynn said. 'He stole the Land Rover. They think he's on the mainland by now.'

Clang! The details of what Celia had said to Tony came flooding back and Grace made a move to get out of bed. 'Find out where my clothes are.'

'What the hell are you up to now?'

'Do you know someone called Ivor Rossi?'

'He's my solicitor.'

'And Celia's?'

'I think so, yes.'

'Then I've got a feeling that I know where Tony may have gone.'

***

Tony was amazed at just how easy it had been to break in. When he was driving away from the church, he'd Googled the address he wanted and headed in that direction. He was aware that, once anyone realised he'd nicked the Land Rover, the local cops would be on the lookout for him on the roads, so he'd parked in the long-term car park at the ferry terminal, convinced that would be one of the last places they'd look for a stolen vehicle. Then he'd hoofed it to the town's market square, with the canvas holdall casually slung over his shoulder. The office of Ivor Rossi was above an estate agent that wasn't one of your flash chains but very much a one-person local business that appeared to deal more in rentals, holiday lets, and the sale of ex-council houses. He looked at the photos stuck haphazardly in the window with sticky tape, the houses whose origins were all too clear and sold for a song to the tenants, only to be tackily tarted up and sold on a few years later at a tidy profit – a tawdry sniff at the capitalist trough for the masses. He recognised a picture of a holiday-let cottage as being one he'd torched along with Celia's home and he had to stop himself from laughing out loud.

The location of the solicitor's office was awkward in that it lacked the privacy Tony would have preferred, being as the building was squeezed between a tatty pub and a Chinese takeaway. But, looking on the bright side, it was also convenient at the same time because any noise he made would not be noticed above the din of what was clearly a karaoke night in the pub, and because he was starving hungry and vegetarian dishes were not entirely unheard of in Chinese chippies.

So, he'd checked out the back of the estate agent's place and found an easily breakable window that gave him access to the back door. And when some tipsy tart singing that karaoke fave 'Black Velvet' – out of key and at the top of her lungs – hit a top note he smashed the glass. The key had been left in the door lock, he turned it and was in as easy as that. Who the hell breaks into an estate agent's office? Well, not in this burg anyway because there was no alarm to be seen anywhere. After that, it was an easy thing to buy his takeaway and a can of warm Coke and dine in the comfort of the manager's office with his feet up on the desk and his arse plonked in a leather chair.

Once fed and watered he headed upstairs. The lock on the solicitor's office was a doddle to break, the metal cabinets less so. So why bother? Just have a night's kip and wait for the fucker to turn up in the morning.

Eight-thirty arrived and Tony heard a sound at the door. He took a handgun out of canvas holdall, loaded it sitting at the desk with the window view of the street behind him, pointed the gun in the direction of the doorway and waited.

CHAPTER FORTY-THREE

Discharging herself from hospital took longer than Grace had anticipated. Yes, she was aware that her leaving was against medical advice. Yes, she took full responsibility for her decision. Yes, she was quite prepared to sign any waiver needed that exonerated the hospital completely from any consequences that might occur. 'Where do I sign?'

Gwynn was dead set against the whole plan but reluctantly agreed to drive her to Holyhead. 'Why not just tell the police what you heard?' he asked. 'No need to go rushing there yourself.'

'And why would they believe me?'

'You know what you heard, and you were right last time. You found Celia before they did.'

Okay, she thought, *guess I'll have to spell it out.* 'Think about it, Gwynn. This money in the Swiss account that Celia has hidden away so carefully, would the police not want to know where it came from? Get them involved and you chance someone, somewhere, opening a twenty-five-year-old, very dented can of worms. It might be a movie cliché but there may well be some old, retired copper obsessed with this unsolved robbery. It is quite famous, you know. I looked it up on the Internet after Celia told me about it. It's textbook stuff. Millions gone, nobody hurt and never solved.'

'No need to sound so proud of it,' Gwynn said.

And no need to sound so fucking prissy about it, she thought but said, 'I'm just saying there could still be interest that could put Celia in danger of prosecution.'

'I take your point,' he finally admitted. 'And how do you intend to get round that?'

'If we catch Tony before he goes any further, or even in the act, that's all the cops will be interested in. They'll have him in custody and what with the *Garda* after him for the murder of that boy in Ireland, as well as arson here, plus a double kidnap involving attempted murder, they'll have their hands full.'

'And if he tells them why he went after Ivor Rossi?'

'Are they going to believe anything a nut job like him has to say? I doubt it, so Celia's Swiss bank account won't be given a second thought.'

'Aye,' he said, sourly. 'When it comes down to it, it's always about money. You're more like her than you know.'

'I bloody resent that!' Grace felt aggrieved by his comment. Wasn't the stupid bugger listening to a word she said? 'I'm not interested in Celia's dirty money. I don't want it. I wish I'd never heard of it. She can bloody keep it. I just want my life back and I want Tony Boyle back in the loony bin where he belongs, or preferably six feet under. What I do not want is for Celia to end up in prison for that heist she, *your* dad, and Frank pulled a quarter of a century ago. Particularly since insurance companies will have paid out for any losses long ago and any villains whose dodgy gear was filched are probably dead by now.'

'All right, I understand,' he said. 'But morally …'

'Says the man who chopped someone up and fed him to the pigs.'

'I did what I had to. To protect Celia.'

'And we have to do this for the same reason. Like you were happy to inform me at the time – this is war.'

'You're beginning to think like a villain,' Gwynn said.

'You and me both, sunshine. It's in the blood, you know.'

For an old guy with a foreign name, he was a cool one, was Ivor Rossi. Short, dapper and well into his sixties, he had walked into his office and eyed Tony and his gun with wry contempt before he said in a refined but distinctly Welsh accent, 'Conveyancing report not go well for you, then?'

'This is no joke,' Tony said.

'I'm sure it's not,' Rossi said. 'Any time a stranger breaks into my office brandishing a gun, I do consider him to be deadly serious in intent. Mind if I sit down?' He pulled up a chair at the client side of his own desk and said, 'So what can I do for you, Mr …?'

'My name doesn't matter.'

'Oh, I'm sure it does to someone.'

'I'm interested in Celia Williams.'

'Ah, poor Celia,' Rossi said with a shake of the head. 'She lost everything in that fire; you know, her home, her livelihood. Such a shame.'

'Not everything,' Tony sneered. 'She was telling me about that Swiss bank account of hers.'

'I know nothing about that.'

Tony cocked the pistol. 'Well you see, Mr Rossi, old chap, Celia told me a totally different tale. She said you have all the details here, in this office.'

'I know nothing of any bank account but on Mrs Williams' death, I have a letter to give to her daughter, Grace Dobbs.'

'Well, let's play a game of pretend shall we, Mr Rossi? You pretend Celia Williams has gone to her just reward and I will pretend to be Grace.'

'I can't do that, Mr …?'

'Well that's your problem because my little friend here insists that you can.' With a slight movement of the hand, Tony emphasised the presence of the gun just in case the gabby Rossi had forgotten about it. He closed one eye and aimed it directly at Rossi's head. 'In three minutes either that letter will be on this desk, or your brains will.'

Rossi slowly rose from his seat and indicated that he was going to move towards the locked metal cabinets. 'That's a line from *The Godfather*, isn't it?'

***

'What is Ivor Rossi like?' Grace asked Gwynn as he drove his Range Rover towards Anglesey.

'He's in his late sixties,' Gwynn said. 'Despite his surname, he's as Welsh as I am. His dad was in one of those Italian POW camps in Wales, his mam a local girl. Dad never went back to Italy after the war.'

'Let's hope either I'm wrong, or we get there before Tony does. I don't fancy an old man's chances against him.'

'Rossi was in the British army before training as a solicitor. He teaches karate to local kids in his spare time. Not a bad guy to have on our side.'

****

Rossi had Celia's file in his hand when he moved casually away from the filing cabinet and back to the side of his desk. He waited impassively for Tony to be distracted by the thud as the folder was dumped on the desk. In that instant, Rossi's hand went for the gun while his other hand jabbed Tony in the throat. A bullet exploded from the gun, shattering the glass behind Tony, and with another single blow from Rossi the weapon was ejected into the street below. Rossi, concentrating on the immediate danger of the gun, didn't spot the knife in Tony's hand.

CHAPTER FORTY-FOUR

The gunshot Grace heard had her yelling for Gwynn to stop the car. She opened the door, jumped out before the Range Rover had come to a complete halt and felt the jarring sensation as her feet hit the ground. She looked to her right and could see the place Gwynn had described as being 'sandwiched between the Chinks and the drinks'. She raced towards the place and saw a middle-aged woman standing by the door of the estate agent staring up at the shattered window on the floor above.

'Is this your place?' Grace demanded.

'Who are you?' the ashen-faced woman asked, key in hand.

Grace saw the key in her hand. 'Never mind that, just open up.'

'I'm not sure ...'

Grace took the shaken and suspicious woman by the arm. 'That was a gunshot you just heard.' She reached down to the pavement and retrieved the handgun. 'And that is what made that noise and broke the window up there.'

The woman shrank back at the sight of the weapon in Grace's hand.

'Someone may well be hurt or even dead up there, so stop dithering and open the fucking door.'

The woman's hand was shaking so hard Grace had to take the key from her. Once inside she headed up the stairs of the entrance shared by the estate agent and the solicitor. The stairs creaked beneath the worn carpet and she hoped not to have been heard. The door was unlocked and she tentatively pushed it open.

'Call for an ambulance,' she shouted down to the woman, just as Gwynn bounded up the stairs behind her.

***

Tony walked as casually as he could across the futuristic stainless-steel pedestrian Celtic Gateway Bridge that would take him back to the ferry terminal and the car park. He patted the pocket where he'd secreted the letter he'd taken from the Celia Williams file. In there was all the info he'd need to get the millions he suspected were hidden away in that Swiss account. He knew a prostitute who might pass for Grace and who'd do anything for money. A little jaunt to Switzerland would be a break from sucking dicks and when he had to bump her off, no one would miss her. He also knew how to get fake ID for her. But that was a way down the line yet. His current problem was how to get off this fucking island. The Irish ferry was one option but as he had only the fake driving licence he'd used for the car hire in Dublin he was loath to use that, just in case. No, a getaway on land it would have to be. Problem two was that the cops would have flagged up the Land Rover by now, so he couldn't use that. All he had left was just one of two solutions. He had to get another car or take the train. A car meant a carjacking, which would also have the cops on his arse. He needed to end the chase as anonymously as possible. The train it was.

***

Grace tucked the gun into her inside pocket and headed for the door, pushing past Gwynn. 'I'm going after him,' she said. 'You stay here and deal with the police. Tell them this was Tony Boyle's handiwork.'

'You've done enough,' he called after her, 'Leave this to the police.'

But she was gone.

Think like a gangster, Grace advised herself. *His car is on the police radar, so how would he get out of here?* It had to be on foot, either by the ferry to Ireland or the train.

She raced across the bridge and into the ferry port. There were queues of foot passengers waiting, but she didn't spot him. She was tempted to scratch that as one of his choices for escape. He was wanted by police in Ireland, although he may not know that, she reasoned. Either way, as she couldn't see him, she moved swiftly through the terminal towards the train station.

Down the long, open platform she spied the yellow livery of a train and there he was. Tony Boyle was boarding a train with a canvas bag in his hand that she recognised as having belonged to the brothers O'Reardon. Grace waited until he was out of sight and got on the final carriage of the same train.

***

Tony sat in a carriage close to the front of the train, looking out at the scenery. He placed the canvas bag on the seat opposite him, using it as a barrier should anyone wish to sit there if they got on at any of the six stops between Holyhead and Chester. He'd kept his head down at Chester station to avoid bumping into anyone he knew. From there, he could hop on a train to Liverpool. He had a few contacts there who'd put him up until he got everything sorted. But right now, he could sit back and relax for an hour and a half, buy a ticket from the Asian guy who was now moving down the train toting his little machine, get a bottle of water when the trolley came along and watch the countryside go by. He smiled to himself; yes, things were looking good and everything was falling into place.

***

There were four carriages on the train. The last one had a dozen people in it, men in suits working on laptops, mothers with toddlers in pushchairs, and a couple of youngish women texting. Grace cursed that she didn't have a phone with her to call Gwynn and the police. Maybe she could borrow one? An Asian ticket collector was coming towards Grace as she went from the final carriage to the third and noted that the passengers were the same in this carriage, too. 'Ticket please, madam,' he said as Grace almost bumped into him.

'I haven't got one,' she said.

'Where are you going?

'Wherever this train is going,' she said.

He eyed her suspiciously.

'Chester,' he said. 'And that will be twenty-seven pounds.'

Grace searched her pockets and came up empty. 'I have no money.'

'Then I'll have to ask you to leave the train at the next stop.'

'Which is?'

'Bangor.'

'I'm afraid you don't understand,' Grace informed him. 'There is a man on this train who is armed and dangerous.'

'Are you a policewoman, by any chance, madam?'

'No, but …'

'Then I suggest you leave it to them.'

'I can't call them because I don't have a phone with me.'

'Then I suggest you accompany me to the driver and he will radio through to the police for you.'

'I can't do that.'

'And why is that?'

'Because if he's not in the next carriage along, then he's in the front one and if I walk past him, he'll recognise me.'

'Ahh,' was all the ticket collector said and Grace finally realised that this man thought he had a madwoman on his hands.

'He's dark-haired and wearing a black jacket and blue jeans. He has a large canvas bag with him.'

'I have seen such a gentleman,' he said.

'Did he buy a ticket?'

'I'm afraid that is privileged information …' The guy stopped dead mid-sentence when he felt the muzzle of the gun press against his well-padded ribs.

'I haven't got time for this, mate,' Grace said. 'So just you turn around and take me to where he's sitting, and nobody gets hurt.'

CHAPTER FORTY-FIVE

Tony gazed out at the grey, choppy Irish Sea that kept popping into view while the train made its journey east. Pleasant though the view was considering the time of year, it was blue sea that he craved, and he was daydreaming it into his future. Maybe Thailand or Vietnam would be the place for him. Or Goa maybe. Though it depended how much money Celia had salted away. He'd been told that a man could live like a king in those countries without any hassle at all. He could reinvent himself and have anything he wanted, girls, boys, whatever he fancied for a song. A house, a boat, and an easy life with nothing to trigger the urges he was aware he possessed. Just so long as everyone did as he told them to, they'd all get along fine. Whoever said that money couldn't buy you happiness had never had any.

'Excuse me, sir,' said the voice on Tony's right-hand side. 'But this lady says ...'

'Shut the fuck up.' Grace gave the man a little shove forward while moving the gun swiftly from the ticket collector's spine to Tony's temple.

Tony stayed stock still.

'Go and tell the driver to radio through to the police to meet us at Bangor station.' She indicated to the canvas bag on the opposite seat. 'And take that up there with you. Look inside, you'll find guns in there and possibly a knife.'

The man hesitated, and Grace cocked the gun. 'Do it!'

A woman further down the carriage screamed.

'Police!' Grace announced with as much gravity in her voice as she could muster. 'Please move into the next carriage, madam.'

252

The woman rounded up her small child and dragged him with her. The door between the carriages made a hissy, swishing sound.

'What's going on?' A man's voice from further back.

'Terrorist incident, sir. Please follow the lady.'

There was a scuffle as he collected his laptop and fled.

The ticket collector grabbed the bag off the seat with an apologetic glance in Tony's direction and scurried off.

'You've got me, Grace,' Tony said, 'Why not sit down, take the weight off.'

Grace remained standing. 'Where's the knife?'

'In the bag, like you told that poor, terrified immigrant.'

'Keep your hands where I can see them.'

'It was very good, that. The way you dealt with the public. Very professional, should have been an actress, maybe.'

'Just shut up, Tony.'

'You've come a long way since I first saw you,' he continued.

'Yeah, around fourteen thousand kilometres.'

'From the Aussie avenging angel saving the little kiddies from the nasty man to a cold-blooded killer. You have found your true self, Grace.'

'Don't push it, Tony. I'm only doing what I have to do.'

'That's what we all say.'

An announcement came through from the driver. 'Ladies and gentlemen, for your safety, please move towards the last carriage on the train. This train will terminate at Bangor.'

The train slowed and was cast into darkness for mere seconds when it entered a tunnel; Tony made a grab for the gun in the dark. Grace felt as though someone had punched her just above her right hip. Tony grappled the gun from her grasp and headed for the door that led to the driver's compartment.

When the train emerged from the tunnel, Grace saw the blood on her shirt and realised that she'd been stabbed.

***

Tony held a gun to the head of the ticket collector. The driver, a man in his thirties, overweight and suffering from early-onset male-pattern baldness, stared at the tracks ahead of him. 'Anything you say, boss.'

'No stopping at the station, understand.'

'Sure thing.'

'When we get to the next tunnel, stop the train and open the doors. Do not turn the lights on. Wait two minutes, close the doors and go on your way. Got it?'

'No problem.'

'Any funny business and I'll paint your cab with this fucker's brains.'

'Good as gold,' the driver said. 'You'll get no trouble from me, boss.'

***

Bangor station rushed by, and Grace heard shouts and screams from far behind her in the other compartment as the people on board realised that this was not just one of those delays seemingly designed just to piss them all off. This was different, something was badly wrong. Grace attempted to stem the bleeding from her side without much success and the pain had started to kick in. The train was slowing, entering a tunnel on the other side of Bangor. The lights dimmed and suddenly the train was in total darkness. This time the lights did not come back on. Grace dragged herself to her feet and moved towards the door between the first carriage, the front exits and the driver's cabin. As she reached the exit, the train doors opened. Tony ran out of the driver's cabin straight into Grace, winding her. He hit her with the canvas bag but in his hurry to escape he dropped the handgun. Grace heard it thud and bounce as it skittered across on the floor. Tony jumped off the train into the blackness and Grace heard him begin to run away towards the tunnel entrance.

She scrabbled around in the pitch-dark for the gun on the floor. It took a moment before she found it as it had wedged itself against the inside of the opposite door. Relieved, she picked it up in hands sticky with her own blood and with great effort managed to lean out of the train door. She could see Tony silhouetted against the light from the mouth of the tunnel. She cocked the gun, aimed and fired. One, two, three. The train doors closed, the light came back on and the ticket collector emerged from the driver's cabin. He took one look at Grace and rushed back inside.

CHAPTER FORTY-SIX

'The March winds will blow and we shall have snow,' Ma said. 'It's strange being back in Chester after all these years, not that I ever lived anywhere posh like this.'

'Not exactly living, is it?' Grace looked at all the gravestones. 'Anyway, who gets buried these days?'

'Some people don't like the idea of being burned.'

'I don't like the idea of rotting in a box.'

'Same here. I hope you remember that when the time comes.'

They walked together in silence for a while along the ranks of the dead and gone. They were moving slowly towards the small chapel in the centre of the cemetery when Ma piped up, 'I'm selling the shop. I've decided it's time to move on.'

Grace was taken aback. 'But you always refused to do that before.'

'I wanted a secure base for you and for Celia to be able to know exactly where you were at any time.' She sighed, 'No need for that now is there?'

'Move on to where? Are you coming back to England?'

'We're a bit early, I think.' Ma spotted a bench. 'Can we sit down for a while? I worry about you with that wound.'

'I'm okay. Right now, I just move a little slower than I did, but I'll be fine.'

'Let's stop for a minute anyway. I have something to tell you and I hope you'll understand.'

They sat together and Ma took Grace's hand in hers. 'Remember Len? You liked him, didn't you? He's a really nice man. I know he's a few years older than me and a widower, but we get on really well. He has a son and two grandchildren in

Adelaide.' Ma smiled and Grace thought she hadn't seen her so relaxed – ever.

'He was very nice to me when I left,' Grace said, and Ma beamed.

'He's moving to Adelaide to be closer to his grandchildren, and he's asked me to go with him. And if all works out well, we may even get married.'

Grace hugged her. 'I'm so pleased for you, Ma.'

'Oh, I'm so relieved you said that.'

Grace swallowed the lump that had risen unbidden into her throat, hiding her feelings, unwilling to share the sudden rush of anguish. She was pleased that Ma was happy but couldn't help thinking of everything she'd been through just in order to get her old life back. Her mind was filled with how much she had been looking forward to going home, to regaining normality only to have it slip through her fingers.

'I love you, Grace,' Ma said. 'But I think I've already given you all that I can give.' She patted Grace's hand in reassurance. 'And you've changed in this short time, I can see it in your face.' She sighed. 'I can let go of you at long last.' Then she brightened. 'Half of the money I get for the business will be yours, of course.'

'You keep it, Ma,' Grace said, 'You need it more than I do.'

Ma smiled fondly at Grace, before her attention was caught by a figure walking along the same pathway. 'That woman is waving to you,' she said.

Grace looked round to see Annie making her brisk way towards them. Grace stood up. 'I'll just go and say hello to her,' she said, 'I'll be back in a minute.'

Annie's face was still bruised after having her nose reset but otherwise she looked just the same.

'How are you?' Grace asked.

Annie half-smiled. 'Scars heal,' she said. 'Both physical and emotional. In the end.'

'Where are you staying?'

'I'm at the house supervising the repairs to the place. Once it's all completed, you could sell it. There's a lot of people looking to buy in that area, you could get a very good price for it.'

Grace laughed. 'What do you mean? Sell it? I can't sell something that doesn't belong to me.'

Annie surveyed Grace with cold detachment. 'Didn't you know? Frank left everything to you. The house, the building business … everything.'

***

The inside of the chapel wasn't exactly packed. Grace saw a few faces she remembered from the dreadful party Frank had thrown and in a pew, alone, she spotted the TV reporter, Aisha Hussein. She was there to pay her non-respects no doubt and to make sure Grace made good on her promise to give her an exclusive, now, not only about Australia but also the gen on how she brought down the psychopath Anthony Boyle. *That can wait*, Grace thought, looking around and spotting several sombre men in dark suits taking up another three pews.

Grace sat with Ma on one side of her and Annie on the other. Ma was there purely for moral support having just flown in from Australia that morning. Grace was staying in a house on Anglesey, organised for her by a very grateful Ivor Rossi. 'I'd have died had it not been for you, Miss Dobbs,' he'd said. 'Anything I can do to help, just let me know.'

That morning had been spent at Liverpool airport. Ma had arrived at nine to be met by a tearful Celia and proud new husband, Gwynn. Grace and Gwynn left the sisters to talk for the three hours before the newly-weds' own flight to their Caribbean honeymoon. After that, it had been one mad rush to attend Frank's funeral.

In the chapel, Annie leaned over to Grace and whispered. 'Pity your mother isn't here,' she said sardonically. 'Just to make sure the old bastard's dead.'

'You don't mean that.' She recalled Annie's grief-stricken face when Grace visited her in hospital to tell her of Frank's second massive heart attack. The one that killed him.

'I rarely mean what I say,' Annie said.

A man walked into the chapel at that moment and Annie let out a noise that sounded contemptuous. 'That's Martin Evans,' she whispered to Grace. 'Frank's biggest rival in the new build business. He'll be here to make you an offer.'

'I don't know anything about the building trade.'

'Well, I do. If he suggests a meet, I'd be happy to come with you.'

***

Grace was back on Eastgate Street in Chester. The clock was in its tower and all was well with the world, although only on the surface. The ads she had seen dotted around this now bustling tourist town declaring 'the most haunted' pub or house had nothing on the imagination of Grace Dobbs. A shop now occupied by a children's clothing chain, had once borne the name Morgana's and belonged to Zoe Silver. The mysterious disappearance of this transgender woman was being decried by her 'community' as being the result of a hate crime. But no trace of Zoe or her car had ever been found. As Grace strode by the shop, the memory of Zoe's vermillion nails tapping on the window of the cottage that also no longer existed, sent a shiver down her spine.

Further towards her destination, John's tall, imposing ghost loomed from a doorway and she almost felt Tony's hand grasp her elbow. *Fuck off*, she warned them from inside her head. *Leave me alone. You're dead.*

By the bridge walkway she imagined she could smell the vile stench of the coat Celia had worn as a disguise, and pictured her slumped beside the pavement, hand out, saying, 'Got any change, mister?' and Grace managed a smile. She ambled through the pedestrian access and came out the other side looking for the five-star hotel where she was to meet up with Martin Evans.

***

Annie was already waiting for Grace in the hotel's coffee shop. They had agreed to meet up an hour before to discuss any offer that Martin Evans might make that would be both acceptable to Grace and a fair price.

'There was a lot of bad blood between Frank and Martin Evans,' Annie said. 'Often made worse by Tony, if you want my opinion.'

'Neither are relevant now, though,' Grace said.

'True, but if Evans can get away with it, he'll have everything you have undervalued. Watch him, he's a crook.'

Grace couldn't help but smile; *pot kettle*, she thought.

Annie caught the implication in look and lobbed it back. 'Frank was a bad 'un in many ways but he always treated his workers fairly, paid them decent wages, kept them on through dry periods. There were a lot of those guys at the funeral who would sing your dad's praises as a boss. Evans, on the other hand, hires the cheapest dodgiest foreign labour he can find and lays them off without a second thought.'

'What about the restoration work?'

'He bids down on those contracts to get the job and then Frank's guys often have to go in later to clear up the damage. Evans is the epitome of the word 'cowboy'.'

Grace thought back to the conversation she'd had with Frank on the day she first arrived in England. She recalled how proud he'd been of the work his company had done to restore old houses. It seemed to be his passion, she'd remarked, and he'd grinned from ear to ear, 'How well you know me already.'

Annie was anxious to prove her point. 'Frank has one guy, Alun, working for him who is an absolute genius when it comes to those jobs. Frank used to say that if Alun had had a decent education he'd have been an architect rather than a builder.'

'What about you?' Grace asked. 'What are your plans?'

Annie shrugged. 'I don't know, I'll think of something.'

***

Martin Evans swaggered into the conference room he'd booked for the meeting. He was smarmy, cocky, and appeared sure he was about to put one over on this Australian bint. Grace took an instant dislike to him.

Evans made an offer. Grace refused. He upped it. She refused again. Grace Dobbs sat forward, placed her elbows on the polished wooden surface of the long conference table that separated her from Evans, rested her chin on her cupped hands and looked him straight in the eye. It was a gesture that instantly reminded Annie of Frank.

'I'm not selling anything to you, Mr Evans,' Grace said.

Annie sat bolt upright on her seat. What the hell was this?

Evans, also taken unawares, opened his mouth to speak but Grace held up her hand to stop him.

'But I tell you what I will do,' she said. 'My company will stay out of the new builds and you stop arsing around with restoration. How's that for a deal?' She held out her hand to be shaken.

Evans, a grin spreading all over his face, took it.

'You'll be out of business in six months, girlie,' he said.

'Oh, I doubt that,' Grace responded, 'Annie and I will be in partnership.' She glanced over at Annie whose mouth had fallen open in surprise. 'She knows the business inside out.' Grace smiled at her and then turned back to the dumbstruck Evans. 'And I'm informed that we have some of the best tradesmen in the country on the payroll.'

'You don't know a thing about the building trade,' Evans blustered.

'No, but I'm a quick study. I am Frank Gilligan's daughter, after all. It's in the blood, you know.'